Bell Bottom
Blue

Adventure, Romance, and

Magic on the High Seas!

JASON A CAPLAN

To Mary Beth,
Enjoy the saltwater
life!

Jah

Copyright © 2024 Jason A Caplan

All rights reserved.

ISBN: 979-8-876-38396-9 (paperback)

This is a work of fiction. Unless otherwise indicated, all the names, characters, businesses, places, events, and incidents in this book are either the product of the author's imagination or used in a fictitious manner. Any resemblance to actual persons, living or dead, or actual events is purely coincidental.

DEDICATION

To my OBX Boys of Summer fishing buddies: Clay, Steve, Kim, Kevin, Greg, Cole, Gordo, Jake, Jim, Malcolm, Terry, Chip, and George.

ACKNOWLEDGMENTS

Many people provided invaluable support for this book. I'd like to first thank my wife, Stephanie Caplan; daughter, Hope Caplan; and friend, Jed Fahey, for providing critical editorial insights. Hope also wrote the song "Pamlico" sung by the brother/sister duo Holly and Colt in the book and she also provided the author photo. Ellen Sullivan created the original art and Lauren Byles prepared graphic design for the book cover. I would like to thank Jim Burchette (aka, "Pipes") for supplying firsthand details on hooking and boating blue marlin on a fly rod. I would like to thank Austin Felix and Kyle Welcher, professional bass fishermen on the B.A.S.S. circuit. Austin and Kyle supplied valuable information about competing and winning on the B.A.S.S. circuit. I would also like to thank Madison Struyk, Executive Director of the Big Rock Tournament in 2023, for providing clarity on the rules and regulations for the Big Rock Tournament as well as some important historical information about the tournament. And finally, I would like to thank Dale Britt, a charter boat captain in the Morehead City area who successfully competed in several Big Rock Tournaments from 1990 to 2023. Dale supplied critical firsthand knowledge of what it takes to successfully compete in the Big Rock.

Belhaven Blue

I. Twenty Years Ago

The storm came out of nowhere. Just an hour earlier, 12-year-old Sonny Blue and his dad, Jacob, were fishing Willow Point on the Pamlico Sound. The sky was blue and the bite was on. They boated and released some impressive puppy drum in the 20- to 26-inch range. Sonny had only been fly fishing for about two years but was a quick learner and wielded the long rod like a symphony conductor does a baton. Even Jacob was impressed with how effortlessly his son gracefully moved the rod back and forth before expertly laying the line near the target. It had taken Jacob many more years to acquire the casting skills that Sonny bore now.

It was as if the storm originated above their boat. Without warning, lightning flashed and thunder exploded. Jacob quickly grabbed Sonny's rod and his own, then laid them flat on the deck to avoid lightning strikes. The rain and wind came next, pelting them as they donned their rain suits and life jackets. Jacob started the motor of their 20-foot fishing boat and steered the boat toward the Pungo River and their ultimate destination of Belhaven, North Carolina. Normally this would have been a 30-minute boat ride but, given the conditions today, it would take longer. A lot longer.

By the time the boat reached Wades Point, the intersection of the Pungo and Pamlico Rivers, the storm was in its full glory. Rain pelted both anglers as their center console boat provided little protection from the elements. Waves were churning from both rivers, creating an unpredictable mixing bowl of pure chaos. Despite the purgatory around them, Jacob somehow kept his cool and loudly gave instructions to Sonny in the event the previously unthinkable occurred. Now that possibility was staring at Sonny smack in the face.

As if on cue, an enormous wave and gust of wind lifted and flipped the boat upside down. The force of the wave catapulted Sonny away from the boat. His father, however, was not as fortunate.

II. Early March (Present Day)

Sonny peered across the lake horizon and noticed a light mist dancing on the March morning water. He changed fly rods to one rigged with a surface popper to take advantage of a possible top water bite. The lake was so still that small shad could be seen rippling the shallows. Sonny false casted his fly rod a couple of times before laying the popper just beside a fallen tree. He let the popper rest for 30 seconds before twitching the popper ever so slightly. Nothing. Sonny needed a large fish badly. He was Number 11 on the leader board of the Professional Bass Fishing Organization (PBFO) tournament at Falls Lake in Raleigh, North Carolina, and was trying to make the Top 10 to finish in the money. It was the last day of the tournament and Sonny estimated he would have to bag 12 pounds of fish to make this goal. He was three months behind on his mortgage and his bass boat loan. Plus, his girlfriend, Louise, tended to spend more than she saved…of his money.

He stripped a bit more line and stopped. Nothing. On the third pull of the line, the explosion from the water stunned Sonny so much that he almost forgot to set the hook. Fortunately, the bass took care of this problem and just about jerked the rod from Sonny's hand. As a precaution, Sonny set the hook again and the fight was on. At first, he wasn't sure exactly how large a fish it was but then it went airborne.

"Good Lord," exclaimed Sonny to his amateur partner, Brad West, "That fish has to be eight or nine pounds!" The tournament rules allow one amateur to be paired up with each professional angler so long as he does not aid the professional in any manner. Amateurs pay for this right to learn the trade as well as qualify for future professional tournaments themselves.

"Try ten pounds, partner," replied Brad in excitement. "Don't horse her, Sonny." Sonny winced when he heard that warning.

As he was fighting the bass, Sonny's thoughts turned to the payoff with a fish of this size. First, he would receive $5,000 for the largest fish of the tournament. The typical tournament size bass is only three or four pounds. If he could catch another 10 or 12 pounds of fish after this monster, he might even break the top three or even win the tournament. His take could be up to $50,000 plus about $250,000 in endorsements if he won! Finally, after seven years of struggling on the circuit making just enough money to squeak by, his time had come. No more fast food, cheap hotel rooms, or off-brand sodas.

Sonny had the rod tip in the water to prevent the bass from surfacing again. Most anglers lose their target when it leaves the water. After being hooked, a bass typically takes flight to shake the lure from its mouth. Sonny did not want to risk this. His fly rod was bent like a willow branch, but the fish was getting closer to the boat. Finally, when the fish was only about 10 feet from the boat, it appeared to be worn down. Sonny was smiling now. The worst part was over. The bass made a valiant effort, but modern technology and skillful anglers are just too much for a lessor creature. After Sonny retrieved the last few feet of line toward the boat, he grabbed the line attached to the fly to yank the fish into the boat.

"Sonny, don't grab the line!" yelled Brad, but it was too late. In the instant that Sonny held the line, the bass gave one last thrash of his massive head, snapped the line, and swam off to the depths. At first Sonny didn't move. He simply could not believe it happened. He violated the number one rule of fishing: Never grab the leader until the fish is in the boat. He flashed back to a scene from the movie, *Midnight Cowboy*. Ratso Rizzo, played by Dustin Hoffman, was a New York City street bum who was sick and out of money. His goal in life was to go to Florida and become a big success. In the last scene of the movie, his friend, Joe Buck (played by Jon Voight), stole some money to take Ritzo to Florida. On the bus ride south, Ritzo had fantasies of beautiful women, being healthy, and drinking by a pool. Then his dreams became nightmares as he became sicker and sicker when he realized those dreams would never be reached. Ritzo died just before reaching the Florida state line.

Sonny did not recover from this lost fish, nabbing only one small bass the rest of the day. He finished well out of the money, dropping to Number 19. The most humiliating part of the day was that his amateur partner, Brad West, placed six spots ahead of him and won the top amateur spot and a new $75,000 bass boat. He won the amateur event by observing the areas where Sonny was fishing and successfully boating the fish that eluded Sonny. He also recounted to reporters and fellow anglers the story of the big one that got away from Sonny Blue. Brad guessed that Sonny may have lost the fish due to equipment issues rather than angler incompetence. It was well known in the circuit that Sonny was the only professional bass angler who used a fly rod rather than a conventional rod-and-reel to catch fish. In Brad's opinion, a view shared by many of his peers, using a fly rod is a distinct handicap.

Brad was now qualified as a professional PBFO angler at the next tournament on Lake Wylie near Charlotte. He was well on his way at the tender age of 23. On the other hand, Sonny at 32, was heading in the opposite direction. The irony of this fact was not lost on Sonny as he headed home in his pickup. Sonny lost track of the number of times he had let tournaments slip away from him. Two years ago, he boated a 7-pound bass that would have won the tournament. After a TV camera operator in a nearby boat asked Sonny to display the fish for the camera, Sonny proudly pulled the bass from the livewell, holding it by the mouth. At that moment, the fish jerked out of Sonny's hand and flipped over the boat. Sonny lost over $30,000 responding to that request. But it did make the highlights of the evening news. Just last year, he lost a tournament by a mere ounce when one of his bass coughed up a bait fish at the weighing table. And the list goes on.

It was about a three-hour drive from Raleigh to Sonny's cottage in Belhaven, a small coastal town in North Carolina's 'Inner Banks'. The rolling Piedmont hills of Raleigh were flattening out to the coastal plains as Sonny approached his hometown. After Sonny pulled into his driveway, he gazed at his reflection in the rear-view mirror. He saw a rugged man with some early gray creeping into his wavy black hair. Some lightly creased crow's feet fanned out from his blue eyes and his square jaw gave an appearance of a determined man. He picked up the mail and thumbed through the late notices for the mortgage, utilities, and boat and truck payments. He did not look forward to facing Louise tonight. When he opened the door to their two-bedroom house, Louise was waiting for him in the living room.

"Well, I saw the debacle on the local news tonight," she began in a high-pitched Eastern North Carolina drawl. She had a different look on her face tonight than most nights. Her eyes were red and puffy and her nose was running. Then Sonny looked down and saw the suitcases. "I'm sorry, Sonny, but I just can't take it anymore. I know it's not your fault, but we've been waiting four years for you to make it on the circuit. Honestly, I just don't think you can do it. Your heart is good and I care for you, but I need to move on with my life."

"But Lou, I was so close today. I had the winning fish on my line. That damn Brad West stole my fishing spots and ended up winning the amateur portion."

"Sonny, it's the same old thing. You're just a fish-scale away from winning but it never happens. It never will. As soon as you realize this, you too can move on with your life."

"Do you mean the family farm?"

"You can do what you want. I'm leaving. Goodbye, Sonny." Louise grabbed her suitcases and rushed out the door.

Sonny thought about running after her but stopped just short of the door. He had to keep some pride. That was all he had left. Plus, the look of determination on Louise's face told him it was pointless to ask her back. He leaned back on the easy chair with his eyes focused on the ceiling. Sonny Blue was not having a good day. *"Maybe she's right,"* he thought. *"I've been struggling for seven years now with nothing to show for it."* But as soon as this thought came into his head, he quickly shoved it aside when he remembered working on the farm.

Growing up on a 1,000-acre cotton farm, Sonny knew hard work and wasn't afraid of it. However, he also remembered his first big fish caught on one of three large ponds on the farm. He was 10-years-old and was using an old bamboo fly rod given to him by his father, Jacob. Sonny had just learned to cast the rod a few months earlier as his father patiently taught him some elementary lessons on fly casting. On that particular spring morning, Sonny was using a small popper which typically catches bream and small bass. Sonny's 8-year-old brother, Dill, was fishing on the other side of the pond. Dill was catching a bucketful of bream using a tried-and-true setup of a bobber, hook, and worm tethered to a Zebco rod and reel combo. Every time Dill hooked a fish, he let Sonny know with a taunting "Got 'em!" followed by a laugh. Sonny was tempted to move over to Dill's side of the pond, but something told him to stay put. Just then, a large wake appeared just behind the popper. Sonny took the slack out of the line preparing for the strike. Then the popper went under water and out of sight.

Sonny instinctively set the hook and the line immediately went taut. The rod bent over with the tip almost touching the surface of the pond. Fortunately, Jacob previously showed Sonny how to set the drag on the fly reel so that a large fish can be caught on light fishing line. The fish broke water and Sonny could tell this was the biggest fish he'd ever hooked. Dill saw the commotion from across the pond and galloped over to join his brother.

"He's huge! Don't fuck it up," yelled Dill. Normally, 8-year-old Dill would not use such profanity, but the excitement of the moment got the better of him.

The bass was taking a lot of line before allowing Sonny to finally gain some ground. Sonny had never felt anything like this in his life. Through the rod he could almost touch the bass. He sensed its struggle for freedom with every run and jump it could muster. He almost felt sorry for the fish with the possibility of its demise. Finally, Sonny prevailed and dragged the bass up the bank. Sonny was shaking from the experience. The boys convinced their father to haul the fish into the local tackle shop to determine its weight. The fish weighed 9.7 pounds. Sonny's picture was taken by the *Belhaven Times* and a small article was written in the next week's edition. Sonny was hooked on fly fishing.

For the next several years, Sonny's passion for fishing grew. He entered several junior tournaments in the state during his teen years and fared reasonably well. He then took a hiatus from fishing during his college years to complete his B.S. degree in Biology at the University of North Carolina at Chapel Hill

(UNC) and an M.S. degree in Marine Biology at North Carolina State University in Raleigh. After earning his degrees, he realized that there was only one thing he wanted to do for a living, and that was to fish. He started up a guide service and built up a reasonable clientele over the next few years. His territory covered the eastern part of the state and included many rivers, lakes, and some estuaries such as the Albemarle and Pamlico Sounds. He stayed in Belhaven while his brother Dill completed law school at UNC and moved to Chicago to join a large law firm specializing in corporate acquisitions.

Even though Sonny enjoyed the fishing part of his job, he barely eked out a living. After travel costs, boat maintenance, insurance and tackle, there wasn't much left for savings. Then one rainy Sunday morning when his bookings were cancelled, he was watching fishing shows on cable television. He noticed that anglers could earn big bucks by winning PBFO tournaments. The usual format was to keep a maximum of five bass per day over a 3-day period. The angler with the largest poundage over this period won. Sonny was so excited at the thought that he could make a living catching fish, he immediately took the necessary steps to get on the professional PBFO circuit. After three years of qualifying in amateur tournaments and placing in the Top 20, Sonny finally made the professional circuit at age 28.

During his first year on the professional circuit, he met Louise at a tournament held in Greensboro, North Carolina. Louise was a groupie who was waiting to latch onto a professional fisherman who was on the way up. Only 20-years-old, she couldn't wait to leave her mother in their low rent rural home in nearby Benton. Her dad had left home when she was only 5-years-old. During the past two weigh-ins she saw that Sonny was single, good looking, and in the Top 20. That combination made him a good catch. She was tending a refreshment booth and caught Sonny's eye when he ordered a Pepsi during a weigh-in. She wore skimpy denim shorts with a low-cut blouse that revealed her ample cleavage. The bait was out. Her perfumed red hair was tied in a French braid that she waved in front of Sonny when she waltzed back and forth. The scent was on. She smiled her perfect teeth. Sonny nibbled. As they conversed, Louise leaned over the counter, revealing one of her assets. The hook was set. Sonny then asked her to dinner that night. The game was on.

After grabbing dinner at a nearby Italian restaurant, they went to Sonny's hotel room. Sonny was not a one-night-stand kind of guy, but he was in lust with Louise. After the tease at the refreshment booth, he longed to see more. Louise sat on the bed and patted the space next to her. Sonny eagerly sat down and peered down her top. She unfastened the top three buttons of her blouse. She slowly licked her full lips. Sonny moved closer and pressed his lips to hers. The kiss became bolder. Sonny unfastened the remaining buttons. Now she wanted his lips. Sonny was boated. He never stood a chance.

Over the next four years, they slipped into a comfortable pattern except for one thing. Whatever Sonny did for Louise, it didn't seem adequate. She felt Sonny should be earning the big money the top anglers make. They traveled together for the most part and returned to his house in Belhaven for breaks between tournaments. She hated Belhaven. There was nothing to do in town and it reminded her too much of Benton. She figured if she stuck with Sonny for a few years, he might make it big on the circuit and she'd finally get what's coming to her. But it never panned out. Her spending habits exhausted what little was saved and when Sonny came home empty handed from Raleigh tonight, that was the final straw. After all, she was

24-years-old and not getting any younger. Fortunately for both, they never got married.

Sonny was still staring at the ceiling when a call on his cellphone jolted him from his reflections.

"Hello?"

"Hey Sonny!" It was Dan Jones, a close friend from college as well as a fellow Belhaven resident. Dan earned his MBA at NC State University and could have worked for any number of large corporations in the Raleigh area with significant compensation. And yet, he returned home to the small town of Belhaven to start his own financial consulting business. Belhaven, by itself, could not support his practice so he reached out to people from surrounding small towns and communities. He helped fledgling entrepreneurs with paperwork and accounting services as well as some small- to medium-sized companies that could not support a full-time financial employee. Dan also functioned as a quasi-agent for Sonny by arranging some tournaments and trying to sell Sonny's name to sponsors.

"Not so good, Dan. Lou just walked out on me and I lost another close one today."

"You call nineteenth place close? I'm sorry to hear about Louise leaving though. I know how much she meant to you. I hate to say this, but I think you're better off without her. She was awfully restless." Dan never beat around the bush. He would make a lousy politician but if you wanted the truth, you could count on Dan.

"Thanks for your sensitivity, Bud." In North Carolina, it's a prerequisite that all boys and men have the second name, "Bud". If you ever forget a male North Carolinian's first name, simply call him Bud and no one will even know that you forgot his actual birth name.

"If you want sensitivity, call a therapist. I'll tell you what Dr. Dan thinks you need right now -- a visit to Tommy's Tavern."

Sonny did not feel like socializing tonight, but maybe a few cold ones might shake his depression. Just talking with Dan was already lifting his spirits.

"Alright, I'll let you drive tonight since I may need a few more brews than you. Give me a half hour to shower up."

Tommy's Tavern was Belhaven's main drinking hole. It was its only drinking hole. With a population of less than 2,500, very few people were strangers in the place tonight. As Sonny and Dan entered the bar, several heads nodded toward the pair as they plodded over peanut shells on their way to an empty table near the back. There was no consistent theme to the bar. There was a splash of Texas with a longhorn head over the bar, a bit of sports with (formerly) Washington Redskins paraphernalia on the ceiling (even with the Carolina Panthers football team, most Eastern North Carolinians remained loyal to the Washington Skins), and a hint of North Carolina appeared on the menu as evidenced by the trademark vinegar-based barbecue that many Northerners might compare to cat food. But the strangest motif in the tavern was the huge jar of fortune cookies placed smack in the center of the dining area. For a quarter, patrons received some of the most unexpected, often spot-on fortunes ever written.

The legend of the fortune cookie jar grew with the retelling of local lore. It was rumored that about 10 years ago an engaged couple went to Tommy's Tavern with some mutual friends. The girl to be wed placed her quarter in the cookie jar and received a fortune that read, "Kiss the boy that you want to kiss, not the one that you're supposed to kiss." Not exactly Confucius, but the message was clear. To the surprise of everyone, she did not kiss her fiancé, but turned to the boy from the other couple that joined them and gave him a deep, enthusiastic kiss that he joyfully returned. Instead of marrying her original intended, she eventually married the boy she kissed at Tommy's Tavern.

And about five years ago a group of workers from a nearby plastics manufacturing plant were dining at Tommy's for lunch. They capped off the lunch with a fortune from the cookie jar. They agreed that each one would read their fortune aloud. When the plant's accountant read his fortune to himself, he was visibly shaken. The co-worker next to him noticed the reaction and playfully grabbed the fortune from him. He then read the fortune to the group, "Do not line your pockets with other peoples' fortunes". About six months later, the accountant was found guilty of embezzling over $250,000 from the plant.

After a couple of Yuenglings, Dan cleared his throat and ran his fingers through his thinning blond scalp.

"Sonny, this is probably the wrong time to ask, but how long do you think you can continue on the circuit?"

"Et tu, Daniel?" Sonny was having a very bad day.

Dan lowered his voice and continued with an understanding tone, "Look, Sonny, I'm not only your best friend but I'm also your business consultant, unpaid I might add. In your five years on the circuit, you've never made more than $20,000 in any one year. I can't get you sponsors because you never finish in the Top Five in any event. You're an excellent overall fisherman. My God, I've never seen anybody catch more fish on different bodies of water than you. But you're a generalist losing to specialists. And the money is gone."

Sonny glanced over at Dan and noticed the pain on his face. It probably hurt Dan more to say these things than for

Sonny to hear them. Sonny then bolted upright and shot a grin across the table.

"Let's get a cookie, Dan. My treat." It was not what Dan expected to hear.

Sonny walked over to the jar and plunked down two quarters.

"Alright, Dan. What does yours say?"

Dan smashed the cookie with his hand, plucked the fortune from the table and brushed the crumbs off to join the peanut shells on the pine floor. "Let's see, 'Patience is only a virtue for the virtuous'. Very deep. What the hell does that mean?"

"What the hell do any of these fortunes mean? Alright, here's mine. 'Your lure to people is within---not out'. Well, I sure didn't lure Lou to stay, did I?"

Dan paused before answering, "Maybe you should look at Louise's departure as a chance to start over again. Get into a new line of work."

"You mean like selling shoes?"

Dan chuckled at this remark. Dan's father used to sell shoes when the Jones kids were growing up. The family would often sit around the television at night and watch movies or TV programs. They would always get a kick out of the numerous references to financial solutions for destitute families. After the family's fortunes were washed away, someone would invariably say, "We could always sell shoes," like it was the most heinous job imaginable. The Jones family would burst out laughing when the punch line finally dropped. Mr. Jones had the last laugh. He eventually opened his own shop and realized some moderate financial success just prior to his passing a year ago. He died a proud man having put three children through college and leaving his business to his oldest son, Mark.

"Well, you have a degree in marine biology. Why don't you work in research?" Dan suggested.

"Dan, I'm thirty two-years-old. No one is going to hire an entry level scientist at my age with no experience. Besides, I'm not ready to give up the circuit yet. I don't know why, but I just have a strange feeling that things are going to get better. They can't get much worse," he chuckled sardonically.

But Sonny knew he would be lonely tonight. He already missed Louise and it would take some fortitude to get through the next several weeks. His urge for Louise was mainly physical but it was strong, nonetheless.

"Alright, Sonny, let's talk about Lake Wylie next week." Sonny was grateful the conversation switched to the more comfortable topic of fishing. The two spent the next half hour plotting strategies for the next tournament.

At about midnight, they left Tommy's and walked toward Dan's SUV. All the shops were closed now so the town was virtually dark and there wasn't a soul in sight. They were about to step into Dan's vehicle when Sonny noticed a bright light emanating from a shop window a block away.

"That's strange. I've never seen Benny's open this late at night. How about you sit tight and I'll check it out?" Dan nodded and hopped in the driver's seat while Sonny began his walk.

The bright light pulled Sonny toward the shop and the cool spring air injected new life into his veins. Gazing up at the moonless sky, the stars were winking down at him. He noticed one...two...now three shooting stars. A large planet, maybe Jupiter, was proudly taking over the sky in place of the moon. Sonny had never seen the night so alive.

Benny's Bait & Tackle was owned by Benny McVie, sole proprietor for over 30 years. Benny helped spawn Sonny's interest in fishing from the time he and Dill brought in the 9.7-pound bass from the Blue Farm Pond 20 years before. A faded picture of the brothers hoisting the lunker still hung proudly on the wall behind the register. Dill did not want to be in the picture since he felt he was a spectator rather than participant in the event, but Sonny insisted that he be included since his wise advice, "Don't fuck it up," was so critical in landing the fish. Benny encouraged Sonny to experiment with new flies rather than traditional baits. He even gave Sonny several new flies to try out in exchange for feedback about their effectiveness in getting strikes.

The countertops were arranged in a horseshoe formation near three walls of the shop. For a modest sized tackle store, Benny's was packed with choice artificial baits. Sonny always got a tingle when he browsed in tackle shops, but Benny's was special. One of the most unusual aspects of the store was the round table and five chairs placed in the center of the floor. Every afternoon, Benny's retired friends would sit around the wooden-planked table, stained with years of use, and play cards, drink sodas, and smoke cigarettes until closing. It was a tradition that began many years ago. Even though Sonny never played cards with the group, it was comforting to him that Benny's was still in business. Most fishing tackle today is sold online or in huge retail stores with carpeted floors and perfectly aligned, well-lit rows of merchandise. Sonny liked the fact that Benny's Bait and Tackle was different from the rest.

Sonny cautiously walked up to the door of the rustic shop while Dan let Allison Krauss seduce him with her angelic voice from the SUV radio. The padlock was off the door so visitors were welcome. Sonny pushed open the door and the familiar bells above announced his arrival.

At first glance, the shop appeared empty. After closer inspection, however, he noticed a small, bearded man sitting on a chair at the end of the center counter. His head was just above the counter and he quietly stared back at Sonny with jet black eyes. Sonny almost jumped when he finally connected with his eyes. Sonny gathered himself and began a conversation.

"Hey. I just came out of Tommy's and noticed your light was on. Is Benny around?"

"No. Benny is off for the evening." The man stood up and revealed his slender 5 foot 2 inch frame.

Sonny walked over to the man. "Hello, I'm Sonny Blue. I don't believe we've met." The man shook Sonny's outstretched hand.

"It's a pleasure to meet you, Sonny." The man did not offer his name, so Sonny did not press.

"If you don't mind, I'll just browse a bit." The elfin man slowly nodded.

It had been a couple of weeks since Sonny visited Benny's so he took a quick stock of the racks. There were the usual styles and colors of artificial baits typically used in nearby waters. But the item that caught Sonny's eye was a solitary artificial fly dangling from a rack near the side window. He picked it up for closer inspection. It was the most peculiar fly he had ever seen. The eyes appeared to follow Sonny when he moved the fly back and forth. The fly's body was medium length and translucent with just a hint of pink and chartreuse. The body gave way to the tail, which was long, thin, and tapered to a point. The hook that exited the belly was razor sharp and even drew a dab of blood from Sonny's index finger after he tested the point. But the most unusual thing was that it appeared to glow and flicker in a random pattern. There were no batteries or lights that Sonny could spot.

"What do you call this one?" Sonny inquired.

"It's called *Percival*."

"Interesting name," Sonny said thoughtfully. Searching his memory, he added, "Isn't *Percival* the knight from the King Arthur legend?" The bearded man nodded.

Since there was no packaging around the lure, Sonny then asked, "Who made it?"

The man replied, "I did."

"Well how much is it?" Sonny was growing a bit annoyed at this mystery man's curt answers.

"I would like you to have this fly, Sonny," the man smiled.

"No, really, mister, I would like to pay you for the fly. Please name your price."

"I'm sorry, Sonny, but I will not sell you the fly. It is a gift with no strings attached."

Even though Sonny did not like to accept gifts from strangers, he did not want to offend the man. After all, maybe Benny had hired this guy to help drum up more business with special promotions, free samples, and longer business hours. Sonny made a mental note to call Benny in the next couple of weeks to find out more about this strange man. Sonny politely thanked the man and walked out of the shop, glancing up just in time to see one more shooting star before climbing into Dan's SUV. Sonny's luck was about to change.

III. Mid-March

A week later, Sonny was having a terrible time. It was the third and last day of the Lake Wylie PBFO tournament near Charlotte and Sonny had only one barely legal sized bass in the livewell with less than an hour before the final weigh-in. His total weight for the first two days was just 20.2 pounds, which placed him at number sixteen, six places away from the money. Hardly anything was biting today. The combination of crystal-clear water with bright sun was spooking the bass. The little bit of shade that could be found was covered with other anglers. On the flip side, if Sonny could manage a decent size bass, he could move up significantly on the leader board given the difficult fishing conditions. He tried to shake the memories of the past two evenings but he couldn't. On Day One of the tournament, Brad West was already Number Five on the leader board. "A professional for just one week, for Pete's sake, and he makes the Top Five on opening day of his first tournament!" mumbled Sonny to himself.

Even though fishing popularity had grown significantly over the years, the audience for TV fishing shows is predominantly men. Cable TV producers have been trying in vain for years to expand the viewership to include women. The stereotypical image these producers were trying to fight was the overweight, tobacco chewing, twang-talking fisherman. The reality is that many of these professionals had former careers as varied as dentistry, law, teaching, engineering, and accounting.

One of the strategies these producers hoped to employ was to latch onto a rising star who was single and good looking. Sonny's former partner, Brad fit the bill. His slim build, youthful exuberance, blond hair, and blue eyes were a perfect match for television. The TV producers wasted no time in playing the angle of a youthful star struggling to make it in the big leagues. A camera operator was glued to Brad's boat on Day Two and Brad did not disappoint the viewers. He landed a 7.5-pound bass, the largest fish of the tournament thus far, and moved up to fourth place. The story was embellished with tidbits of Brad's one-year "struggle" on the amateur circuit. After watching the mini profile on the local news that evening, Sonny noted that the story failed to reveal that Brad's family was wealthy and an executive position was waiting for him if the circuit did not pan out. Nice safety net.

Sonny scoured his fly box for something different. He had tried a variety of different flies, including poppers, Deceivers, and Clousers, but nothing was working. He only had 30 minutes left before weigh-in. Searching for answers, Sonny spotted *Percival* from Benny's Tackle Shop in the bottom of his fly box. He'd almost forgotten that he'd slipped the fly in at the last moment before heading out to Charlotte on Thursday afternoon. The fly gave a somewhat dark pink hue today and Sonny could barely detect any of the chartreuse he noticed last Sunday night. Normally, he would never experiment with a new fly during a tournament. It's not only unfair to the fisherman but it's unfair to the fly as well. You never fish the same way in a tournament as you do on your own. Some people fish better, usually worse, but never the same. The conditions are too varied: significant fishing pressure by your peers, boat noise, adrenaline, released fish, and so on. To experiment with a new lure, or fly in this case, in the last hour of a tournament is suicide. Sonny at once tied it on.

Sonny flipped down his polarized sunglasses to get a read of the water. Immediately ahead, he noticed a fallen, submerged tree just beyond the bank. He false cast his fly rod two times before accurately laying the fly right next to the tree. As he started stripping the fly line, he felt a strange sensation, as if the line were vibrating. Because the water was so clear, he could see the fly from the moment it landed. It took on a brighter pink color as it crossed a branch. It then seemed to darken after it passed. It then grew brighter at the next branch…and what was that? Sonny noticed a large olive flash at the second branch. It must have been the sun reflecting off the water, he thought. But after the fly passed the third branch, the olive flash returned and engulfed the fly. Sonny was ready. He jammed the rod up and drove the hook into the upper lip of the fish. The fish's first move was to head down to the tree for cover. Many an angler has lost it quarry when a hooked fish wraps the line around submerged tree branches. Without the ability to give line, the fish immediately breaks the line.

Sonny knew this and at once pulled the bass away from the tree. With its initial escape route gone, the fish then went airborne. Sonny saw the entire fish. He was at least nine, maybe ten pounds which is a giant for any bass tournament. Sonny was running out of time. He only had 20 minutes left before weigh-in and that included a 10-minute boat ride back to the dock. He applied pressure to the rod again, ensuring the hook would not shake loose. It didn't. Sonny did not have time to finesse the bass. Instead, he horsed the fish in like a rookie. Amazingly, the line did not break and Sonny had the bass beside the boat in another minute. After one last desperate leap, Sonny reached down and grabbed the bass by its mouth and pulled it into the boat. Sonny looked up and smiled. Not one TV camera was in sight. He didn't care because he knew he boated the largest fish of the tournament. It wouldn't win him the tournament, but it would be worth $5,000 and a Top Ten finish. And, just as importantly, it would draw a huge cheer from the crowd and give him one week of bragging rights.

He turned the engine over and took off for the ramp. On the ride back, Sonny glanced over at the fly dangling from the rod. Its color had dimmed from bright pink to an almost rusty hue. It did not look particularly remarkable but he could not deny the results. Sonny made a mental note to go back to Benny's Bait & Tackle to get a few more of these flies. He couldn't wait to try it this week at some of the local ponds. Professional anglers have maintained a well-kept secret for several years: There is no better place to test new lures than isolated farm ponds. It's like shooting ducks in a barrel. You can't miss if the lure is any good. If you don't get any hits from a lure in a farm pond, throw it out.

Sonny was about a half mile from the dock when his boat motor quit. He looked down at the gas gauge; the needle still read a quarter of a tank. He then tapped it a few times and watched the needle shake loose and plummet below the "Empty" reading. He glanced at his watch and saw that he had five minutes to cover a half mile with his electric trolling motor that was mounted on the bow of the boat. He'd never make it. Sonny leaped into the pedestal seat on the bow and engaged the electric motor at full speed which was painfully slow compared to the combustion outboard motor. At two minutes to 5 o'clock, Brad West came roaring by Sonny's boat and flashed him a huge smile. He raised both hands and shrugged as if to say, "Sorry, Sonny, but I don't have time to help you," and raced toward the dock. Sonny's boat finally limped into the loading dock at 15 minutes after five. Of course, his catch today was immediately disqualified.

Sonny left the fish in the livewell and strolled over to the weigh-in stage. He got there just in time to see Brad West grab the top spot on the leader board with four bass weighing over 17 pounds. The catch also included the largest bass of the tournament, weighing in at 8.3 pounds. The crowd went nuts when Brad hoisted the lunker over his head and slowly turned his torso so all could see it. The lead held and Brad won $50,0000 for the tournament plus $5,000 for the largest bass, the fishing equivalent of a daily double. Sonny was surprisingly calm over the sudden success story unfolding in front of him. However, he was taken aback when he noticed a beautiful young lady jump up beside Brad on the winner's podium. Her white cotton sundress revealed a slender yet fully developed figure. Her smile shot a pang in Sonny's heart. When Brad bent down to kiss Louise on the lips, Sonny had to turn away. He couldn't believe it. Just one week after breaking up with Sonny, she hooks up with a rookie who wins his first tournament. He looked up into the darkening twilight sky and mouthed, "Really?" and then shook his head.

With his head down, Sonny returned to the dock to clean up the boat and put it on the trailer. Just as he was finishing, Sonny glanced up to see Brad and Louise leaning into one another, bouncing down toward Brad's boat next to Sonny's. Brad let go of Louise's hand when he saw Sonny looking up.

"Sorry pal, I just got lucky today."

Sonny looked over at Louise and shot back at Brad, "In more ways than one, good buddy. By the way, thanks for the lift back to the dock."

Louise glanced up at Brad with a puzzled face. "Look Sonny, I only had five minutes to make the dock and if I had to tow your boat, there's no way I'd get back in time. Besides, would it have made any difference? What was your haul today, four or five pounds?" Brad couldn't resist this shot after witnessing Sonny's poor technique last week.

"I suppose you're right, Brad." Sonny then opened the livewell hatch and removed three bass that weighed about four pounds each. He looked up and noticed a smirk on both Brad's and Louise's faces as if they were thinking, "Just what we figured." Then Sonny reached down and, with both hands, hoisted the monster out of the livewell. The change in facial reactions from Brad and Louise was dramatic. It wasn't quite worth $50,000, but it was close. Brad's eyes grew wide and his mouth opened just a bit before he caught himself and quickly shut it. He tried to keep his cool but it was too late. Sonny drank in the moment. Louise was not as cool. Her mouth opened and remained so for a good bit before moving her gaze back up to Sonny's smiling face.

"My God, how big is it?" she inquired.

"We'll never know." And with that, Sonny gently moved the bass back and forth in the lake to allow oxygen to pass over its gills. After the bass was clearly revived, Sonny let go of its mouth. The fish gave one slap of its tail and was gone. In that moment, both Brad and Louise knew Sonny should have won this tournament. Sonny read this in their faces. Unfortunately, nobody else did, as shown by the flock of TV and newspaper reporters that suddenly descended in front of Brad's boat. Brad shook off the shock of the last few moments, smiled, and enthusiastically answered all their questions. As Sonny pulled his boat from the water, he glanced back at Louise. She recovered nicely as well. Her arm slipped around Brad's waist and she grinned her perfect teeth at the reporters as if to say, "He's mine."

Sonny half smiled to himself and took off for home. On the drive back, he slid the sunroof open to let the brilliant Carolina stars keep him company. Jimmy Buffet was twanging tunes on the radio and Sonny accompanied him. It was strange, but for some unknown reason, Sonny wasn't down tonight. As he sipped a cold Pepsi, his mind told him he lost his woman to a rising star. He suffered yet another heartbreaking loss at this tournament to the tune of $50,000 plus endorsements. Sonny's gut was telling him something entirely different. He had finally reached bottom. There was something comforting in this thought for he knew the only direction left was up. He now had something that had been missing for a long time: hope.

"What a sap," laughed Brad on the drive back. "Not only does Sonny show me where to catch bass at Falls Lake in Raleigh, but today he loses the tournament in Charlotte by not making the dock on time."

He shook his head and glanced at Louise perched next to him. Her citrus cologne sent a tingle down his waist. Brad simply could not believe his good fortune over the past few weeks. First, he won top amateur spot at Falls Lake and now, in his rookie debut, wins his first tournament as a pro. And the icing on the cake was sitting right next to him. When Brad found out that Louise left Sonny, he wasted no time in calling her for a dinner date earlier this week. They dined on succulent steaks at Angler's Inn in Raleigh, Brad's hometown. Afterwards, Brad took Louise back to her hotel room, where she was staying until she could find an apartment. She kissed him lightly and said goodnight. At first, Brad was a bit disappointed but when she agreed to go with him during the next tournament at Lake Wylie, he perked up considerably.

For the past two nights, Louise would not sleep with Brad even though they shared the same hotel room in Charlotte— she'd insisted on getting a room with two beds. Brad knew tonight would be different. Brad casually slipped his right arm across Louise's exposed shoulder. This was fun. They pulled into the hotel parking lot and walked into their room holding hands. Brad was right. Tonight was different.

IV. Late March

"Ava! Where the hell's my copy?" barked Ed Gray, popping his head over the wall of the reporter's cubicle. Gray was managing editor of Sports for the *D.C. Tribune*.

"It's coming, Chief. Just give me two minutes," replied Ava Tyson as she pounded out the last paragraph of her article on the upcoming training camp of the Washington 'Commanders' (or 'Skins' as the old timers still called them). Once again, they'd missed the playoffs, so it was a challenge to present the right blend of hope and reality. Ava had mixed feelings about this article because she had a love-hate relationship with the Skins. On the one hand, she grew up adoring the Skins, as her father was a die-hard Skins fan. Her dad was fortunate enough to see the glory days of that team in the 1980's and early 1990's before he died 6 months ago from lung cancer. So naturally, Ava continued the Tyson tradition of steadfastly rooting for the Skins. Unfortunately, Ava was too young, or not even alive, to have experienced those glory years. And yet, she somehow still clung to the hope that they could once again return to that magical period in the city. Thus far, her wishes have gone unfulfilled.

"It's in your in-box, Chief!" Ava screamed over her cubicle wall two minutes later.

"Stop calling me Chief, Lois! This is NOT the Daily Planet!" Ed screamed back from his office a few steps away. A slight smile crept across Ed's normally gruff face as he begrudgingly got a kick out of this Lois Lane-Perry White interchange that the two shared from time to time. He carefully read Ava's article and had to admit that it was a fine piece of writing. She captured the major elements of the story without letting her own feelings of loyalty toward the Skins seep in. He made a few minor edits and fired it off for publication.

A short while later, Ed walked by Ava's cubicle and poked his head inside and said, "Can you stop by my office before you leave?"

She replied with a slight smile, "Sure, Chief." Ed rolled his eyes and went back to work.

At the end of the workday, Ava stopped by Ed's office.

"Please sit," said Ed, as he motioned toward the dilapidated leather chair in front of his desk.

"Uh oh," sighed Ava, "Am I in trouble, Chief?"

"Not at all, Lois…I mean, Ava."

"So, what can I do for you, Chief?"

Ed ignored the nickname and continued. "Okay, here's your next assignment. There's this professional bass fisherman from North Carolina named Sonny Blue."

Ava tilted her head a bit wondering where this was going.

"The thing is…he's not your normal bass fisherman."

"What do you mean?"

"He's the only professional bass fisherman who uses a fly rod instead of conventional fishing equipment -- you know, spinning or bait casting rods and reels."

Ava had some rudimentary knowledge of fishing and understood the distinction between fly rods and conventional rods. "Is he any good?"

"Well, it's not that simple. His fellow anglers claim he has an uncanny knack of finding fish, but something seems to blow up during critical moments of his tournaments, causing him to literally snatch defeat from the jaws of victory."

Ava chuckled at that comment. "So, are you asking me to cover a perennial loser?"

"Get down to Buggs Island at Kerr Lake, Virginia tomorrow."

"Say what, Chief?"

"Yeah, there is another bass tournament coming up this weekend and Sonny has entered the tournament. I know you've worked a full week; I got the OK to pay you overtime…you're welcome!"

"That's what--four or five hours from D.C.?"

"Something like that" mumbled Ed.

"I don't get it. First, why is this a story? And second, why me?" pleaded Ava.

"I don't really know, but something's happening with this guy and I'd like us to be there when it breaks."

"Okay, Chief, what aren't you telling me?" He smiled at her knack of cutting to the quick.

"Sometimes you're too smart for your own good. Alright, you got me, Ava. Sonny is my nephew--my sister's kid. He lost his dad when he was only 12-years-old, so I try to keep tabs on him from time to time just to see how he's doing. My sister said he's run into some bad luck lately barely missing out on the money. The few sponsors he's got are walking away from him. I figured a little media attention might help him get back on his feet."

"Does he know that you're trying to help him?"

"Hell no! And you will not tell him either. Both he and his mom have too much pride to ask for help. But he's a good kid, Ava. He needs a break. Besides, how long has it been since you got to do a feature story? It'll be good for you to write about something besides football losses!"

Ava smiled slightly and said, "I knew you were an old softy at heart, Chief!"

He brushed the comment aside and said, "So you'll do it?"

"So, it would be for just this weekend?

"Yup."

"Then, yes, I will be happy to help."

With that, he handed her a sheet of paper with the tournament details and Sonny's contact information.

The next morning, Ava left her tiny Georgetown apartment wearing sweatpants, an old Skins T-shirt, and running shoes, her blonde hair pulled back in a ponytail. She turned right onto M Street and started jogging west along the Potomac River. A block into her run, she glanced to her right and grunted when she saw the infamous concrete stairs from *The Exorcist*, the 1973 movie about a young girl possessed by the devil. At the end of the movie, the priest convinces the devil to jump from the young girl to him, whereupon the priest hurls himself down the steep stairs simultaneously killing himself and exorcising the devil.

Even though the movie was made well before Ava was born, she vividly recalled a conversation with her dad about that movie during a family dinner. When she asked him what movie he considered the scariest movie of all time, he immediately answered, *The Exorcist*. The irony was not lost on either of them when, a year after that family dinner, she moved into her Georgetown apartment, a mere block from *The Exorcist* stairs.

When M Street turned into Canal Road, pink blossoms were just beginning to pop on the numerous cherry trees dotted along the banks of the Potomac River. Despite the chaos of D.C., Ava appreciated the beauty of these glorious trees each spring.

A mile into her run, she reflected on the past year. Like the movie, she had her own demons to exorcise, albeit not as frightening. She took the first step a year ago by dumping her boyfriend of two years, Hector Lockwood. A rising attorney at a big D.C. law firm, Hector had decided to expand his love life to include his personal secretary. When Ava came home early from an assignment, she found Hector and the secretary together in bed...her bed. Without a word, Ava packed her bags and never looked back.

But Ava was in a social rut. She didn't regret dumping Hector but missed some of their mutual friends. The D.C. social scene was anything but boring, but she didn't have the emotional energy to seek a new boyfriend. She couldn't put her finger on it, but she felt something important was missing from her life. She shook her head as if to cast off any more negative thoughts banging around her head. She kept running...

V. Late March

"Damn!" Sonny spat at his fly rod as he flung another carp over the side of his boat. It was late March and the water was surprisingly hot. The spa-like water temperature was due to an early heatwave and the shallow water nature of Lake Mattamuskeet, NC. One week had passed since the Lake Wylie tournament. Lake Mattamuskeet was producing fish, but not the kind that Sonny had hoped for. *Percival* attracted fish but, unfortunately, it did not discriminate by size or type. By mid-morning, Sonny had boated over 50 fish: bass, catfish, bream, crappie, and carp of all things! Sonny did not like carp, but he begrudgingly acknowledged they put up a great fight on the fly rod.

But he had to admit to himself that this fly was the most productive one he'd ever tested. Lake Mattamuskeet was heavily fished, so this feat was even more remarkable. One of the strangest things was how the fly's color seemed to change depending upon the species caught. The fly had a chartreuse hue for bream and bass, white for crappie, dark brown for catfish, and pale yellow for carp. Sonny suddenly broke out in a cold sweat when he realized he had only one fly of this pattern. For the second time, he made a mental note to stop by Benny's to get several more of these unusual flies in case it broke off the line. As a matter of fact, Sonny immediately put the fly away for fear of losing it to submerged structure. Sonny then switched to some other standard flies and it was like adding poison to the water. Not a single bite for the rest of the morning. He headed back to the boat ramp.

After loading up the boat on the trailer, Sonny took off for Benny's. Hardly any bass boats were on the water as temperatures soared into the high 80s. Water skiers and jet skiers now dominated the scene. Sonny noted with interest the human transitions that took place on a large body of water over the course of a year. In the late fall through early spring, anglers ruled the roost. Occasionally, he'd see a die-hard water skier with a wet suit, but for the most part it was fishermen who owned the lake. As the warmer months approached, water skiers and jet skiers took over the lake and were oblivious to anglers and the patterns they were trying to fish. Many a time, Sonny recalled to himself, these pleasure boaters spooked a previously successful bass honey hole. It wasn't intentional. It's just that many of these boaters don't have a clue how to fish and therefore don't recognize how disruptive their behavior is to anglers. Consequently, most anglers tend to resent both jet skiers and water skiers sharing the water.

Sonny pulled into an open parking spot in front of Benny's. Sonny fetched the fly from his fly box and walked through the door. The bells above the door drew attention to his arrival. The five old-timers around the table shot quick glances back at Sonny and immediately went back to their nickel/dime poker game. They all had gray or white hair, what was left of it.

"Hey fellas, how's everybody doin'?"

"Rough tournament last week, eh Sonny?" inquired a large tobacco chewing man named Earl. With that said, he spat his juice into the spittoon at his feet. About half of the thick, dark spittle made it. The rest was spread about the floor in an ever-growing stain under the table.

"What happened this time, did you forget your boat keys?" winked Carl to the rest of the group. Carl was the most annoying of the bunch because he had this high pitch squeal of a laugh which had an effect like fingernails on a chalkboard. He was a short, toothless wonder.

Benny looked up sympathetically and said, "Seriously, Sonny, we heard about Lake Wylie last week and all of us feel really bad about what happened. As a matter of fact, the boys chipped in and got you a present to make you feel better."

Sonny didn't know if Benny was referring to the lost tournament, his girl, or both. News in small towns travels fast, so it wouldn't have surprised him in the least if they knew about Louise. Regardless, he was touched that the guys thought enough of him to give him a gift. Benny handed over a medium sized rectangular box that was nicely gift-wrapped. Sonny quickly yanked the ribbon and opened the box. Nestled inside some tissue paper was a one-gallon sized gasoline tank with a label glued to it reading, 'For use in case you are dumb enough to run out of gas a mile from the dock.' Sonny slowly peered up just in time to hear a burst of laughter from the group. Several of them were slapping their knees and rocking back and forth in their rickety chairs.

"Very funny. I appreciate your sympathy, fellas." This set forth another series of guffaws that didn't subside for at least five minutes. Sonny let them have their fun since he was sure it was the highlight of their week, even if it was at his expense. Carl's squealy laughter made Sonny cringe.

"Benny, can I talk to you for a minute?"

"Sure, Sonny," Benny had tears in his eyes. "I'm sorry, Sonny, but me and the boys have been waitin' for almost a week for this moment and we just couldn't resist."

"That's alright Benny," Sonny said. "I suppose I deserve it. Listen, I bought a fly from one of your workers a couple of weeks ago when Dan and I were heading home from Tommy's Tavern. I was wondering if you had any more like it." Sonny then pulled *Percival* from his pocket and handed it over to Benny.

Benny gazed down at the fly with a puzzled look then back at Sonny. "One of my workers? Who was this fellow?"

"He didn't give me his name, but he was short and had a beard."

"Sonny, I don't have anybody working for me who looks like that. As a matter of fact, it's only me and my boy Ray that work here."

"That's what I thought, Benny, but what was that guy doing here that night if he wasn't working for you? Do you suppose he was a burglar or something?"

Benny scanned the store and shook his head. "We haven't lost any cash lately and nothing of value is missing. Who else saw this fellow?"

Sonny thought for a moment and realized that Dan was outside while Sonny was in the store. "Just me."

"And how many beers did you have that night at Tommy's?" Benny's pale blue eyes twinkled when he asked this question.

Sonny saw where this conversation was heading. "Alright, Benny, let me just buy some more of these flies."

Benny picked up the fly and inspected it carefully before replying, "Sonny, we have never sold a lure, or fly as you call 'em, like this. As a matter of fact, I've never seen a lure, I mean fly, like this in my life. Who makes it?"

Sonny slunk a bit. "I have no idea. I was hoping you could tell me."

Benny pulled out his lure and fly catalogs from beneath the counter and both men poured through them. Benny's catalog collection was legendary. If there was a lure or fly to be found it would be contained in this collection. But for 30 minutes, they drew blanks. Benny scratched his thick white hair.

"Sonny, I am clueless. That is the most peculiar fly I have laid my eyes on. Is it me or is this thing changin' colors?" With that said, Benny took off his wire rim glasses and wiped them with a cotton cloth hanging from a nearby hook.

The guys around the table were oblivious to Benny and Sonny as their poker game intensified. Earl was spitting tobacco juice more frequently now, a sure tell that he had a good hand. Everyone knew this except Earl. Carl was squealing up a storm, which meant he was bluffing. Everyone knew this except Carl. The other two men, George and Percy, immediately folded. Carl tried to make Earl run but he wouldn't budge. Carl's laughs were now reaching a fevered pitch, but were silenced abruptly when Earl showed him a full house against Carl's two pair. Now the other three men were laughing as Earl raked in the pot.

"You're right, Benny, it does change colors. As a matter of fact, it changes colors even more when I'm fishing."

"Now for the $64,000 question, Sonny. Does it catch fish?"

"That's the strange part. It catches fish like crazy, but not the way you might think." Sonny then explained his experience on Lake Mattamuskeet earlier that morning. Sonny knew he could confide in Benny without the risk of him revealing secrets to his competitors. They had a long history together beginning with that nine-plus pound bass caught on Sonny's farm when he was 12-years-old. Ever since then, Benny would not divulge any of Sonny's favorite flies to his competitors because he understood that this might someday take money away from Sonny's pocket.

"Tell me more about this fellow you saw in my shop." Benny listened intently as Sonny recounted that evening.

"Well, I suppose I'd better get the locks changed today," Benny mumbled aloud.

"I don't know Benny. For some reason I don't think you have to worry about that guy anymore. If he wanted something he probably would have taken it that night."

Benny shrugged in confirmation. Sonny smiled and waved goodbye to Benny and the other men. He also thanked them for the "gift" and told them he hoped he'd never need it. They chuckled and waved goodbye.

When Sonny arrived back at his house, he immediately took steps to ensure he would not lose *Percival*. He started by replacing his monofilament fishing line with a 30-pound, high strength nylon/fluorocarbon line. He then added a fly retriever to his tackle box. This coiled ringed gadget was tied to a spool of 200-pound test line and would slide down the fly line attached to a snagged fly. Once it wrapped around the fly, one pulled the 200-pound test line until, hopefully, the snagged fly was jerked free of the tree or rock from which it was attached. As a final precaution, Sonny created a hiding place on his boat that would keep curiosity seekers from viewing *Percival* during tournaments. He then rustled together a tuna salad sandwich, chips, and a Pepsi for lunch. Sonny was ready for tournament battle.

VI. Mid-April

Sonny had two weeks to recover from the Lake Wylie debacle. This week the bass fishing pros were competing on Kerr Lake, a mammoth 50,000-acre reservoir that straddled the North Carolina-Virginia border. For some reason, Dan decided to make the trip this weekend with Sonny and provide him moral support from the dock. Sonny appreciated this gesture and offered to pay his expenses. Dan scoffed at this offer and said he would take it out of Sonny's earnings. Sonny just laughed.

Because of its immense size, Kerr Lake presented several challenges for the angler. Figuring out a fish pattern early was paramount since there was so much water to cover. This was only a two-day tournament with a five-fish-per-day maximum. Therefore, fish quality was as important as fish quantity. The prize money was modest with $25,000 going to the winner and only the top five anglers receiving prize money. For this reason, many of the top anglers skipped this tournament for greener pastures down south. Sonny looked at this lack of competition as an opportunity to receive at least some prize money.

At 6 a.m. on Friday, the PBFO armada of anglers throttled out to various points on the reservoir. Sonny decided to start in the deep water first since high-water temperatures in the shallows often chase large bass into the lower depths. He was alone in this thinking, as all the other anglers immediately went to the points along the shoreline to entice an early morning surface bite. After an hour with no fish, Sonny was beginning to feel a bit embarrassed about being the lone angler in the middle of the lake. He had cast *Percival* several times with only small sunfish and crappies taking the fly. What fool would fish in the middle of the lake in the early morning? Many of these anglers were aware of Sonny's hard luck stories, so they ignored his solo presence there.

Using his GPS/Depth finder, he re-positioned the boat to a drop-off area where the depth changed rapidly from 10 feet to 30 feet. Sonny's first cast with *Percival* in this transition area was uneventful. On his second cast, Sonny let *Percival* drift to the bottom before beginning his retrieve. He immediately felt a tug. Sonny jammed the fly rod up to set the hook. The rod tip bent over and touched the water. Sonny had never felt a bass this large before. The rod began to move left to right. Sonny played the fish masterfully before it finally surfaced a full five minutes later. The fish turned sideways and rolled on the surface revealing a series of horizontal stripes along its side. Sonny's heart sank when he realized it was a striped bass, not a largemouth bass. Sonny was aware that striped bass, also referred to as stripers or rockfish, are not eligible keepers for PBFO tournaments. Stripers are typically anadromous fish, meaning they spend part of their life in saltwater and part of their life in freshwater. Their populations were almost wiped out along the East Coast back in the 1970s due to several factors including pollution, overfishing, and loss of habitat. However, strict conservation efforts over the past 20 years have led to a gradual increase in striper population all along the East Coast. The stripers in Kerr Reservoir are landlocked and can survive without migrating to salt water.

Just for grins, Sonny netted the striper and pulled him in the boat to get a weight reading on his scale. The fish weighed just over 20 pounds, a medium weight for a striper but would have been a state record for a largemouth. Sonny smiled and gently released the fish. Sonny was having fun even if he wasn't making any money. His next strategy was to position his boat in more shallow water closer to shore. He wasn't close enough to reach the shore on a cast, but his fish finder revealed some nice fish (hopefully largemouth bass) in this shallower water. The move paid off. Within an hour, Sonny landed four largemouth bass that ranged from three to four pounds in weight. He also caught three crappies, two stripers, and one catfish. The fly appeared to change colors for each species caught in a similar fashion to what had happened at Lake Mattamuskeet a week earlier. It was only 11 a.m. and Sonny almost had his limit. In this tournament, there was no culling, or exchanging newly caught bigger fish with smaller fish already in the livewell. Since amateur partners did not take part in this tournament, a lie detector test would be given to each angler who finishes in the money.

Sonny pulled his electric trolling motor out of the water and then fired up the outboard to seek a different spot. He headed toward the dam which is typically where stripers are caught. He found another transition zone near the dam and nabbed two more stripers in the 10- to 15-pound class. The wind picked up more on this open water and began to form a chop on the surface.

Sonny was about to move to a different area when he spotted some commotion in the water about 30 yards from the stern. He at once moved to the stern of the boat and cast *Percival* about six feet behind the disturbance. Within seconds, an explosion on the surface sent Sonny's fly reel humming. Fortunately, he kept his drag setting on the loose side to avoid a hard strike and subsequent breakoff. After losing about 40 yards of line from his reel, Sonny gently tightened his drag and slowly retrieved the lost line. Once it was about 10 yards from the boat, the fish caught sight of the boat and began a second run. This lasted another five minutes before the bass was finally within reach. With one hand on the leader, Sonny grabbed the mouth of the bass with his other hand and hoisted the lunker into the boat. Sonny couldn't believe it. The bass was at least eight pounds, he had a half tank of gas, and there was over an hour left before the deadline. Life was getting better.

On the boat ride back to the weigh-in station, Sonny relaxed enough to enjoy the surroundings. Kerr Lake was a project about which Virginia and North Carolina could truly be proud. Other than a few houses and hotels that were grandfathered in before the two-state agreement, no one was allowed to build within 200 feet of the water line due to flood control established by the U.S. Army Corps of Engineers. The net effect was a huge body of water that was mostly surrounded by trees with little evidence of human population.

The check-in dock was now in sight and Sonny's heart skipped a beat. He felt good about his catch but not overly confident. Too many heartbreaks in the past prevented him from being cocky about anything. The crowd turnout that day was modest in size. Fortunately, Brad was not there, so Sonny didn't have to endure seeing Louise and Brad together this weekend. After the official weigh-in, Sonny was in a very respectable third place position. For the first time in many years, Sonny was near the top of the leaderboard going into the final day.

"Well done, Sonny! Great first day!"

Sonny turned around and eagerly accepted Dan's outstretched hand.

"Thanks for being here, Dan."

"Of course," Dan replied smiling. "You look beat. How about we head back to the hotel, shower up, and strategize about tomorrow over dinner?" Sonny nodded.

That evening over beers and ribs at a restaurant within walking distance of their motel, Dan remarked, "Sonny, I can't explain this but you look different tonight. I don't know. You just seem like you've made peace with yourself or something."

"Yeah, it's weird. I feel like a burden has been lifted. I mean, I haven't won squat, I have no money, I lost my girl and yet..." Sonny trailed off.

"Well, whatever the reason," Dan continued, "you've got that sparkle in your eye that I haven't seen in years. But you've still got some work to do tomorrow so I think you'd better get some shut-eye."

Dan was right, of course. So, after clinking their mugs in a final toast for the evening, both men retired to their respective motel rooms.

A gentle rain greeted Sonny the next morning. After a light breakfast at 4:30 a.m., he trailered the boat over to the check-in ramp. Once in the water, the anglers revved their motors not unlike a NASCAR race just before the start. It was quite comical to watch the boats take off like bats out of hell trying to find their honey holes. Often the speed of the boat is as important as the actual fishing equipment used. The guy that gets to the best honey holes first often wins the tournament.

Sonny had scoped out another spot the previous day that most of the other anglers overlooked. It was an old, submerged roadbed about five miles northeast of the check-in dock. In fact, it was barely noticeable from the shore and the only reason Sonny came upon it was because he snagged his fly on one of the shoreline shrubs. As he trolled over to retrieve the fly, he saw the remnants of the road on the shore going into the lake. Sonny loved fishing submerged roadbeds because the asphalt and gravel supply cover for bass which makes it easy for them to attack prey from above.

Just then, the horn sounded and they were off! Almost simultaneously, the fifty plus boats flew off toward the cove opening. The sound was deafening. Sonny did not have the most powerful motor, but it got the job done. He found a gap between Hoss Powers's and Dukey Perkins's bass boats and shot through it with inches to spare. Sonny liked this part of the tournament. The wild sense of freedom as the wind ripped through his hair was a thrill which never grew old. After about 15 minutes, most of the boats split apart from the pack and glided toward the fishermen's honey holes. Sonny kept his northeast bearing until he spotted the roadbed hole from the evening before. It was partially covered with ground shrubs which is probably why it was overlooked. He glanced around to ensure no one else had a bead on it. No one was within a half a mile of Sonny.

He killed the outboard about 200 yards from the spot to avoid spooking any bass. Sonny quietly walked to the front of the boat and very gently lowered the electric trolling motor into the water and parked himself in the pedestal seat. Using a wireless remote control, Sonny silently guided the boat toward the submerged roadbed. Relaxing a bit from the stress of the start, Sonny calmly pulled his fly rod rigged with *Percival*. The rain had let up but left behind a cloud that hugged the water. The fly took on a green sparkly hue, different from any color he'd seen thus far.

"Well, here goes," mused Sonny. And with that, he cast *Percival* toward the bank and let it sink to the bottom. Within seconds of retrieving his line, it suddenly went taut. "Damn it," Sonny thought, "I hit a snag." Then slowly, the rod started pulling down.

"Holy Hell!" He was so shocked the rod was moving that he almost forgot to set the hook. Fortunately, the fish did most of the work. Not wanting to take any chances, Sonny jammed the hook home. Immediately, the bass took flight. Sonny's eyes bugged open when he gazed at the full view of the bass. It was a monster! "Now, don't choke," he muttered to himself.

Sonny's fly rod was now bent over like an archer's bow. He loosened the drag on his fly reel just a bit to let the fish run and minimize the risk of a line break. This was fun! Not wanting to jinx his catch, Sonny tried to hold back a smile, but it was impossible. The beast was moving back and forth and back and forth until the line started moving toward the surface. "Dang!" Sonny thought. "It's going airborne." Sure enough, the fish shot in the air like a scud missile and flipped head over tail before submerging back into the water. Fortunately, Sonny kept the tension on the fly line and didn't lose him.

Now the bass was close to the boat. Sonny raised the rod as high as he could and reached down for the fish. The first swipe was a miss but the second was pay dirt. He struggled to bring the fish onboard but finally managed it. It was huge! Sonny guessed nine to ten pounds. Sonny's hands were shaking and his heart was beating like a drum. He quickly but gently placed the "beast" in the livewell for preservation.

Sonny caught his limit of five bass, all at the roadbed area within the next four hours. Although none approached the size of the beast, Sonny estimated the range at four to six pounds, nice tournament size bass. With plenty of time to spare, he cranked the motor and cruised back toward the check-in dock.

As he pulled up to the dock, he noticed a considerable crowd surrounding the weigh-in station. Several anglers had already caught their limit and were anxiously awaiting the results. Sonny calmly tied up his boat for his turn to weigh-in. Dan was there to greet him. He opened his hands as if to say, "Well, how did you do?" Sonny just winked at him and nodded his head. Dan smiled back at him and knew that Sonny won the tournament.

The image of Sonny reminded Dan of their poker games at college more than a decade ago. Every Sunday night, the guys would gather in the dorm lounge for a friendly game of nickel, dime, quarter poker. When either Dan or Sonny would fold early, the folder would help squeeze a winner on the last card pulled for the guy remaining. Sometimes the squeezer would either wink or nod indicating the hand was a sure winner. It was uncanny how often the squeezer would pull a winner for his friend. The fellow with the hand would not even look at his last card and bet the maximum. It almost always won.

The target to beat so far was 29.8 pounds for the two-day total. Now the focus of the crowd was on Sonny and he couldn't wait to show his catch. To add melodrama he would, of course, save the "beast" for last. The crowd politely clapped when he pulled the first bass from the well, a nice five pounder. Each of the next fish was successively larger causing the crowd to bunch up a bit closer to the weigh-in dock. Sonny's two-day cumulative total was 25.3 pounds with only one fish to go. The tension was thick with anticipation. His next fish needed to exceed 4.5 pounds to win the tournament.

Now Sonny played with the crowd. He gazed into his livewell and held his hands up as if it were empty. The crowd let out a collective sigh. Many were aware of Sonny's woes. He was a virtual folk hero with the litany of disasters that followed him from tournament to tournament. The crowd pulled for him as a home crowd would root for an aging quarterback. Then he started scratching his head as if he'd lost something. He then gave an "Oh yeah" kind of look and reached in for the beast.

When Sonny wrestled the monster out of the livewell, the crowd paused in shock when they saw the size of it. Then they screamed in unison. When the fish hit the scales, it weighed a whopping 13.5 pounds. Sonny won the tournament by a country mile. No one else was even close. It was a surreal moment for Sunny because it had been so long since he won anything, not to mention a tournament that paid $25,000 to the winner. Dan looked up at Sonny on the podium and broke into a huge smile. *"It's about time,"* he thought. He had no idea of the excitement to follow.

Tribune reporter Ava soaked this in as well, watching the drama unfold from the rear of the crowd. Like the rest of the modest-size crowd, she smiled when Sonny hoisted the last bass from the livewell. She couldn't help but admire the easy balance that Sonny displayed between mischievousness, confidence, and humility. She also couldn't overlook his rugged good looks. She had the sense that he didn't have to work at achieving that look either. Although fit, he didn't seem like a gym rat. No, whatever he had going for him came from genes and hard work.

After the paperwork and checks were signed, Ava approached Sonny. Sonny was softly joking with a fellow pro when he felt her presence. Sonny glanced up and gazed right into her ocean green eyes. Both froze when their eyes locked. Something indefinable passed between the two at that moment. Neither could speak for a long pause. As if coming out of a trance, Ava shook her head and fumbled, "Ah, Mr. Blue? My name is Ava Tyson and I'm from the *DC Tribune*. I write an outdoor column for the paper. I wonder if I might have a word with you?"

Sonny recovered as well and said, "Hi, Ava. Please call me Sonny. If you continue to call me Mr. Blue, I'll mistake you for an attorney."

Ava laughed and replied, "Okay, Sonny it is."

"Where are my manners? I'm sorry, Ava. This is Dan Jones, my friend and business manager."

Dan couldn't help but notice what transpired between the two people. He smiled and offered his hand, "A pleasure to meet you ma'am."

"Would you mind if Dan joined us as well?" Sonny inquired.

"Of course not."

The three walked over to a nearby picnic table with Ava sitting across the table from Sonny and Dan. The crowd had dispersed by then so they had the park to themselves.

"First off, congratulations on your victory today, Sonny." Sonny smiled in thanks. "Even before your victory today, our paper has followed your story over the past couple of years. To be candid, I don't know much about fly fishing but it's my understanding that you are the only professional bass fishermen who uses a fly rod to catch your prey, correct?" Sonny nodded his head.

"Well, that is remarkable. Add that to your victory today, and this makes a compelling story."

"I should be upfront with you about something, Ava. The top pros weren't entered in this tournament. Most of them are competing down South in a much bigger tournament with double the prize money. So, it's quite possible that I would not have won this tournament if those pros were present." Dan looked at his friend in disbelief and almost kicked him under the table!

Ava glanced at Dan and said with a laugh, "You might want to work with Sonny on his marketing skills."

Dan shot back with a laugh, "I was thinking the very same thing, Ava! But that's who he is -- for good or bad".

"Hey, you all. I'm sitting right here!" Sonny quipped. But he was smiling, too.

"Anyway," Ava continued, "My editor wants me to write a story, maybe even a series of stories about you, Sonny. I'd like to follow you to each tournament over the next few months and interview you along the way. Today's victory would be a great kick-off that we can build on."

Sonny's smile faded. "Would that editor, perchance, be Ed Gray…my uncle?"

Ava was taken aback by Sonny's correct assessment but quickly recovered, "Well, in fact, yes. Is that a problem, Sonny?"

Rather than answer Ava's question, Sonny stood up, tipped his fishing cap, and said, "It's been a pleasure, ma'am," and then walked toward his pickup.

Shocked, Ava turned her gaze to Dan and said, "Did I say something offensive?"

Dan shook his head and said, "Not at all. Sonny has a lot of pride. Too much, if you ask me. He doesn't want any help from anyone. He gets along quite well with his uncle, your boss. So, it has nothing to do with Ed, per se. It's just Sonny's stupid pride."

Ava was relieved that she didn't offend Sonny, but disappointed that he rejected her offer to write a multi-part series on him. Of course, she still could, and would write about the Kerr Lake Bass Tournament, but the story would have been much more colorful if Sonny were a continuing voice in the series and not just a one-time subject.

"Dan, this could be a good opportunity to get some exposure for Sonny."

"I agree, Ava. Let me see what I can do, if anything, to change his mind. When do you need a commitment from him?"

"How about 24 hours?"

"Okay, I'll get to work."

"Thanks so much, Dan!"

They shook hands and departed.

A short while later, Dan rapped on Sonny's motel door. As soon as Sonny let him in, Dan turned to him and said, "Are you friggin' crazy? You're presented this terrific opportunity to gain some traction with sponsors and then you turn it down? What gives?"

"I don't know, Dan. I guess I got my back up when it became clear my uncle was behind all this. I mean, even if his motive is good, it still bothers me that I can't make it on my own."

Dan chuckled, "Welcome to the human race, pal. You've heard the expression 'It takes a village', right?"

Sonny nodded.

"Well even if it takes a village, city, and state for Criminy sakes…take it, Sonny!"

Sonny paused for a while and then laughed "I guess you're right. I'm not getting any younger, that's for sure. So how should I manage this, Dan?"

"Don't sweat it. I'll take care of it. Just meet Ava for breakfast tomorrow morning at 7 at the local diner. I've got to head back early tomorrow morning, so I won't be able to join you."

"Which diner?"

"You're kidding, right? The ONLY diner in town…Elmos."

The next morning, Sonny woke at 6 a.m. to the hydraulic screaming of a garbage truck hoisting a dumpster right next to his motel room. *"Nice room selection, Dan,"* Sonny thought to himself. He grunted, extracted himself from the bed and stumbled into the shower. After shaving and dressing, he arrived at Elmo's a few minutes past seven. He gazed down at a line of dilapidated faux leather booths and spotted Ava reading a newspaper. She glanced up and locked eyes with Sonny. His heart skipped a beat yet again. She smiled broadly and motioned for him to join her.

He eased into the bench seat across from her and said, "Good Morning, Ava."

"Good morning, Sonny."

"I apologize for walking out on you last night, Ava. It's just that…"

Before Sonny could continue, Ava waved him off and said, "Don't worry about it, Sonny. The important thing is that you're here now and, presumably, agreeing to let me write your story?"

He responded, "I think so, but, if you don't mind, I have a few more questions."

"Of course. Shoot."

At that moment, a server arrived at their booth and asked, "Coffee?"

"Yes, please," responded Sonny. "And you can just leave the pot."

Ava laughed and said, "A man after my own heart!"

After a breakfast of bacon, eggs, grits, and toast, plus three mugs of hot coffee (each), they finished ironing out the details of the coming months.

"So let me see if I've got this right, Ava. You're going hang with me for a couple of tournaments and write a story after each tournament?"

"Yes, that's the gist of it."

"Do I get a say in what you write."

"Nope."

Sonny chuckled, "Seems fair to me."

Ava extended her hand, "Do we have a deal, Sonny?"

He hesitated a bit but then shook her hand. "Deal. So, what's next?"

"Where do you live?"

"That's a bit forward, don't you think, Ava?" Sonny responded mischievously.

Ava's face reddened, "No, no. I mean, which city?"

"Belhaven," Sonny proudly said.

"Belhaven? Where is that?"

Sonny pointed at Ava's iPad. "If you open Google maps, I'll show you."

A minute later, Ava had the town on her screen. She then zoomed out. "Boy, it looks like a whole lot of nothing around there."

"Quite the contrary. There is lot more than meets the eye. You'll see…"

"I'll have to take your word on that. Okay, here's the plan. Dan mentioned that your next tournament is Lake Mattamuskeet in early October. I'll head back to D.C. today and then meet you in Belhaven a few days before that tournament. That's a few months away so I should have plenty of lead time to book a hotel or B&B right?"

Sonny laughed aloud. "No worries about that. We don't have any hotels in Belhaven but there are a few B&B's near the waterfront that I can recommend." He wrote the names on a paper napkin.

She glanced down at his near illegible handwriting and smiled sarcastically, "You weren't, perchance, studying to be a physician, were you?"

"Very funny. I'll see you in October!"

VII. October

A day before Ava was scheduled to meet Sonny in Belhaven, her cellphone chirped. Her pulse increased when she recognized the person from Caller ID.

"Hey, Sonny! I'm looking forward to seeing you tomorrow."

"Hey, Ava. I wish I had good news. A Nor'easter is forecasted to hit our area in the next five days. As a precautionary measure, the PBFO officials announced today that they are cancelling the Lake Mattamuskeet Tournament for the upcoming weekend."

Ava's heart sank. She was not sure if her disappointment was due to the loss of her story or not seeing Sonny again. Perhaps both. An idea struck her.

"What is the weather forecast for the next several days?" Ava inquired.

"Here's the crazy thing. It's forecasted to be beautiful with sunny skies and calm winds. Why do you ask?" Sonny asked.

"Well, we planned to meet ahead of the tournament anyway to get background on you and Belhaven. I believe you also promised me a boat ride. There is no reason we can't still do those things, right?" Ava asked hopefully.

Now Sonny's heart pumped a bit faster. "I see no reason at all. I'll see you tomorrow!"

On the five-hour drive south to Belhaven on Tuesday morning, Ava thought to herself how flat this part of North Carolina was. And deserted. Within 30 minutes of peeling off I-95, it was as if she entered a different country. The single lane country road weaved through huge cotton and corn fields that stretched miles on end. She felt a wave of relief to leave the snarling D.C. traffic in her rearview mirror. Country music was the only choice on the radio, so she immersed herself in the Southern genre, a pleasant change from her usual D.C. choices. It was a warm autumn day, so she opened her windows and let the season envelope her. Her thoughts then drifted to Sonny and his deep blue eyes.

A couple of hours later, she drove through the quaint town of Bath, NC. As she crossed the first bridge entering the coastal city, she glanced to her right and spotted several sailboats moored at a marina. The water sparkled in the noon sun. A sign proudly boasted that Bath was North Carolina's first city, incorporated in 1705. Ava decided to explore the town. It did not take long. She stopped at the Visitors Center and viewed a 20-minute movie on the history of the town. She was fascinated that the infamous pirate Blackbeard lived in Bath for a short stint before pillaging the waters again. His demise seemed inevitable, yet it was surprising that it took so long to capture and behead him. Before leaving the visitor center, she bought a couple of wine glasses engraved with the name "Bath" over a pirate ship at the gift shop.

A half hour later she arrived in Belhaven. She meandered through the streets to get a feel for the town. She was struck by the simplicity of this quiet coastal town. No malls, high rises, or hotels crowded the horizon. Water was everywhere including the "downtown" area. It was as if she were transported back in time, 50 or 60 years ago. She was reminded of the line from the Joni Mitchell song her dad used to play, "They paved Paradise and put up a parking lot." Growing up in D.C., Ava became almost numb to the massive development that never seemed to end in the surrounding area. In stark contrast, Belhaven seemed frozen in time. The adjoining buildings seemed untouched by major construction and included a hardware store, a diner, a gift shop, and even an ice cream parlor. Even though she just arrived, she already felt a bond with the town and hoped it wouldn't succumb to a similar fate as other coastal cities in the U.S.

A short while later, she checked into one of the B&B's Sonny recommended, a two-story Georgian house with an expansive view of the Pungo River. A middle-aged couple greeted Ava as soon as she walked in the door. The woman smiled warmly and said, "Hi. You must be Ava. My name is Rita and this is my husband, Robby. Hence the name of our home: R&R."

Ava smiled back and said, "Cute name. I love your home!"

That brought a smile to Robby's face as well. "Thank you," he said with obvious pride. "It was quite a project restoring it to her glory years, I can tell you that. After surviving decades of hurricanes and Nor'easters, the original house finally succumbed to Hurricane Irene in 2011. The house was in my family for three generations, so we didn't have the heart to tear it down completely. So, when the restoration project began two months after Irene hit…"

"Darlin', let's not bore our guest as soon as she walks in the door, okay?" Rita gently interrupted.

"Oh…of course" Robby stumbled. "I'm so sorry."

"Not at all," Ava replied. "I would love to hear all about the restoration project at another time if that's okay. But I must meet someone in a little while. So, if you don't mind, I think I'd like to check into my room, take a quick nap, and then head out."

"Absolutely," Rita replied. "What time would you like breakfast tomorrow?"

Ava forgot that breakfast was included. She paused before answering. "I'm an early riser. Is 6:15 a.m. too early?"

"Not a problem. We'll see you then," Rita said smiling. "Thank you!"

Rita then handed her a key and said, "If you follow me, I'll take you to your room upstairs."

It was only 5 p.m. so Ava had time to unpack, shower, and nap before meeting Sonny at 7 p.m. The soft evening sun cast comforting rays through slits of the bedroom blinds. She pulled the blinds up to reveal an expansive view of the river. Several live oak and pine trees dotted the landscape between the house and the river. Despite partially blocking the river view, the trees only added to the charm of the property. Something else was different about this town that she couldn't put her finger on. She thought for a minute or two and then it came to her. It was so quiet. There was no airplane or traffic noise of any kind. Growing up in the D.C. area, noise was a constant backdrop: traffic, planes, construction, police sirens, ambulances, and the like.

After her shower, she slept soundly until her phone alarm jolted her awake a few minutes before seven. Ava quickly slipped into some tight jeans and a white blouse that accentuated her lithe physique. She wasn't trying to come on to Sonny, but she saw no reason to be shy about her appearance either.

A few minutes later, Ava breezed into Tommy's Tavern, a mere three blocks from her B&B. She scanned the bar and was dumbfounded by the amount of Washington Skins paraphernalia mounted on the wall and shelf behind the counter. She grew up a Skins fan and was shocked to see autographed pictures, jerseys, and helmets by so many notable players, including John Riggins, Earnest Byner, Art Monk,

Darrell Green, and even Sonny Jurgenson. Her gaze then drifted to a corner booth where she saw a ruggedly handsome man glance up from his cold beer. His deep blue eyes locked onto hers. He smiled in recognition. Sonny. *"Damn, what is it with this guy,"* she thought to herself. She shook her head slightly to clear her head and glided over to his booth.

Sonny rose to greet her. She extended her hand and said, "Hi Sonny. Thanks for meeting me tonight." He grinned and shook her hand, "Of course. My pleasure, Ava." He waited for her to sit across from him before sitting down himself.

"I have to say, Sonny, this is a most interesting tavern."

"You don't say?" Sonny responded with a laugh. "You are probably wondering why a tavern in eastern North Carolina has so much Washington Skins stuff, huh?"

"Yes, the thought crossed my mind," Ava laughed back.

"Before I tell you the story, how about a cold drink?"

"Absolutely! What do you recommend?"

"How about a Belhaven Ale?"

This shocked Ava more than the Skins paraphernalia. "What? Belhaven has a brewery? How big is this town?"

"About 2,500 people," Sonny replied.

"Sure, I would love a Belhaven Ale."

Sonny caught the attention of a woman clearing the next table nearby and said, "Ellen, would you please bring a Belhaven Ale for Ava, here, and another one for me?"

"Sure thing, Sonny. Anything to eat?"

It was only a little after 7 p.m. and he wasn't quite hungry enough for dinner but didn't want to deprive Ava of a meal if she were hungry.

"How about we have drinks first and then order dinner?" he asked Ava.

"Perfect!"

A few minutes later, Ellen brought the beers and shot a sideways glance at Ava.

"Who's your cute friend, Sonny?"

Slightly embarrassed, Sonny replied, "Sorry for my manners. Ellen, this is Ava. Ava, please meet Ellen."

Ellen smiled and extended her hand. Ava warmly accepted it. "A pleasure to meet you, Ellen."

"Not to pry," although this is exactly what she was doing, Ellen asked, "So what brings you to this part of the country, Ava?"

Ava nodded toward Sonny, "Him."

"Really? Do tell more, Ava," Ellen shot an eyebrow up, eager for the juicy details. She said this with no jealousy as she was quite content with her husband and two boys.

"Okay, that's enough, Ellen. Don't you have some other tables to tend to?"

"Nope, the dinner crowd hasn't arrived yet, Sonny." She then scooted next to Sonny in the booth. "So, Ava, please continue…"

Ava smiled, "So, Sonny, can I tell her?"

Sonny rolled his eyes in defeat. He was concerned that Ellen would tell half the town by tomorrow morning, but realized they would eventually find out anyway. He threw his hands up in exasperation "Why not?"

"I'm a sports reporter for the *DC Tribune*. I'm planning to write a story about Sonny…"

"About Sonny?" Ellen inquired in shock. Ellen was well aware, along with the entire town, of Sonny's catastrophic tournament failures. "No offense, Sonny," she smiled sheepishly.

"None taken," Sonny replied with a half-smile.

"Please continue, Ava".

"Of course. Well, as you may know, Sonny is the only professional angler on the circuit that is a fly fisherman. That alone makes this an interesting angle for our readers. But his winning the bass tournament in Kerr Lake this past April…"

"Wait a minute," Ellen interrupted. "Sonny won a tournament? How come I didn't hear about that, Sonny?"

Sonny shrugged modestly.

Ellen then stood up, cupped her hands together, and shouted to the thin crowd, "Hey everyone. Believe it or not, Sonny actually won a tournament!" This announcement brought a few claps. But then she added, "Drinks are on him!" This addendum brought forth a rousing round of applause along with some screams of congrats.

"Thanks a lot, Ellen," but Sonny looked at Ava, not Ellen when he mumbled those words.

Ellen grinned from ear to ear and went about getting drinks for everyone…on Sonny's dime.

"Oops," Ava replied, "Sorry, Sonny."

"Ahh, no worries. It's all good. An hour later, Ellen's announcement would've cost me a lot more!"

Ava was relieved to see that Sonny seemed more bemused than perturbed by her disclosure to Ellen.

Ava took a sip of her cold ale and raised her eyebrows in appreciation, "This is really good! I still can't believe this little town has a brewery. Hey, wait a minute…" Ava looked closely at the label as her words trailed off. "This ale is from Belhaven, Scotland, not Belhaven, North Carolina!"

Now Sonny was laughing, "Fine investigative reporting, Ava! I think a Pulitzer is in order!"

Ava laughed back, "Okay, you got me there, Sonny. How about we order some food? I'm famished! What do you recommend?"

Before waiting for his response, Ava turned her gaze to a nearby makeshift stage where a couple in their 30s with a guitar and piano were playing and singing softy:

Down Pamlico Sound Road
The path you know by heart
Following the saltwater in your veins
Like a map- leading the way home
Take me where I want to go- back to Pamlico

Early sun warms the water- like hearts in love
Drop a line and wish on the waves
For a fin, a fight, a win
To retrieve all you can
Take me where I want to go- back to Pamlico

We make pictures from the pier
With the pinpricks through the backlit night
And reflect on today and tomorrow and yesterday
Take me where I want to go- back to Pamlico

After they finished the song, both smiled and waved at Sonny. Sonny waved back.

"Wow, they are good! Who are they?" Ava inquired.

"It's a local brother-sister duo, Holly and Colt Capwell. They're children of a good friend of mine. I sort of grew up with them."

Twenty minutes later, a dozen raw oysters were placed between them. They devoured them in no time. A short while later, they feasted on grilled Mahi, baked potatoes, and slaw.

"This place is a gem," Ava remarked after her last bite. "And the prices are ridiculously low! How does Tommy stay in business with prices this low?"

"Well, it's never been about money for Tommy. This is a lifestyle business for him. About 25 years ago, he lived in Annapolis with his wife Jane. They hated the rat race. On one of their vacations, they took their 30-foot sloop on a sailing adventure and worked their way down the East Coast via the Intercoastal Waterway. One of their stops was the Old River Manor in Belhaven, about three blocks from here. After walking through the town, they looked at each other and decided on the spot, this is where they would live. And they haven't looked back since. Their tavern only stays open Thursday through Saturday, so they can spend the rest of the week enjoying life. The tavern makes just enough money to support their modest lifestyle. And while they will never be rich, they are one of the happiest couples I know."

"Wow, I wish I had the guts to do that," Ava remarked in admiration.

"Yeah, me too. The only problem is that I hardly make any money at all, so even a modest lifestyle wouldn't work for this cowboy. That's why I, like many others in this area, work several jobs just to make a living."

"Well, how about your winnings from the Lake Kerr tournament? I'm sure that will help," Ava pointed out.

"True enough. But most of those proceeds will go toward past due loan payments for my boat, truck, and house, plus tournament expenses. It doesn't take long to burn through $25,000 less tonight's drink bill, of course."

Ignoring the slight dig, she plowed ahead, "So what other jobs do you do?"

"During the summer months, I work with a local crabber to collect crabs from the pots each morning and deliver them to a wholesaler on the Pamlico River. During the winter months, I help a local carpenter with light home repairs and the like."

"Do each of these employers give you any grief about the time you miss due to your fishing tournaments?"

"Not really. These guys are all good friends and understand and support my dream to eventually work full time as a professional angler."

Ava had pulled out her iPad and began taking notes. "How old are you, Sonny"

"Thirty two. How old are you, Ava?"

"None of your business," she laughed, paused, and then added, "Twenty seven. Continuing, so how many professional fishing tournaments have you won, including the one in April?"

Sonny scratched his chin and replied, "Hmm, let's see…. there was that tournament in Gaston. Oh, that's right, I lost that one by a hair. Okay, there was that tournament near Rock Hill…scratch that. My alarm clock didn't go off on the final day of the tournament, so I was disqualified even though I was the leader the prior two days. Okay, I've got the number figured out."

"Yes?" inquired Ava

"One," Sonny smiled.

"Including last April's tournament?" Ava asked incredulously.

"Yup" Sonny answered proudly.

"Excuse me, Sonny, but given your lack of tournament winnings, how and why have you remained in the game for this length of time?"

"What can I say? I'm a glutton for punishment," Sonny joked.

"Seriously, Sonny. How many years have you been a professional angler?"

"Seven years".

"Seven years?"

"Yup. Okay, do you want to know the real reason I've stuck it out this long?"

"Yes," Ava anxiously replied.

"Okay. Here goes. I was only 12-years-old when my dad died. Before he died…"

"How did he die, Sonny?" Ava gently interrupted.

Sonny casually waved her off, "I'm not ready to talk about that now." He continued, "Before he died, he told me if I were faced with a decision wherein I could make a lot of money in a career that I hated versus making a modest living in a career I was passionate about, take the passionate path. He said if I loved what I did and was good at it, I'd find a way to make a living in that field. I was passionate and skilled at fly fishing, so I chose that path."

"How's that working out for you?" inquired Ava.

"No so well," Sonny laughed. "But the glass is always half-full," he added with a smile.

"It seems like you are competing on an uneven playing field in the bass tournaments that you enter. Don't your competitors have a significant advantage using conventional fishing equipment versus the fly rods that you use?"

"That is a great question, Ava!" Sonny was impressed. Her questions went to the heart of the matter. "The truth is, there are indeed many challenges using a fly rod to catch bass compared with using conventional rigs. But there are also some advantages that help balance the equation."

"Such as?" Ava probed.

"Well, I tie all my own flies so I can tailor each fly for a given situation. For instance…"

"Do you mind if I record this?" Ava cut in. "It sounds like this is going to get technical, and I want to make sure I get this right for our readers."

"No problem," Sonny agreed.

Ava then placed her cellphone on the table and hit the 'record' function.

"Okay, Sonny, please continue."

"As I was saying, you can tie a huge variety of flies. There are so many different materials to choose from for the body, eyes, flash, hook, and so on. "

"So why is this an advantage compared with conventional tackle?" Ava probed.

"Good question! The variety and flexibility of making your own lures -- in this case flies -- allows you the opportunity to more closely 'match-the-hatch' than conventional, off-the-shelf lures. For instance, I'll sometimes throw a cast-net in unfamiliar waters to see what bait is present. I'll take pictures of the bait with my cellphone and then tie flies later using these pictures as guides to closely mimic the bait."

"Why don't you just take the bait back to your shop?" Ava asked.

"I don't really like to kill any critters unless I absolutely must. But please don't mention this in your article," he whispered, "because a lot of people in this area use live bait to catch their prey and I don't want them thinking I'm judging them for their choice. It's just a personal choice for me."

"Gotcha. Please go on, Sonny."

"I'll then take the flies I tied the night before, attach them to leaders of my fly lines, and then return to those same waters the next day and see if I can connect with some bass."

"Do you use this same approach for saltwater species?"

"Wow- another great question!" Sonny remarked. "Yes, I do."

"Okay, so are there any saltwater fishing tournaments in which you could compete using a fly rod?"

"Well, there are indeed some saltwater tournaments, but most of them don't pay much prize money except there is this one tournament..." Sonny trailed off.

"Yes? Which one?"

"It's called the Big Rock. It's held in Morehead City, North Carolina, only a couple of hours from Belhaven."

"Wait a minute..." Ava searched her memory. "Isn't that the blue marlin tournament with huge prize money?"

"Spot on! Blue marlin is the target species, but there are also prizes for the biggest Wahoo and dolphin, aka Mahi-Mahi, and tuna as well. The prize money this past year was more than $5 million. There are different prizes depending on the species caught, size, timing of the catch, and so on. But the biggest winner last year hauled in over $1.5 million because he won prize money for the first caught marlin over 500 pounds, plus it ended up being the largest marlin caught during the tournament week."

"Wow! Why don't you enter that tournament?"

Sonny laughed uproariously, "What? Are you crazy? The people who compete in that tournament have serious money, sponsors, boats, and gear for those types of fish. I mean, some blue marlin can tip the scales at a thousand pounds or more."

"So? Don't they make fly rods geared for large game fish?"

Sonny was continually impressed with Ava's questions. "True, but the biggest game fish I've ever caught on a fly rod was a 51-inch red drum that only weighed about 48 pounds and was on a ten weight fly rod. I have no idea what weight fly rod it would take to bag a blue marlin. To go from a 50-pound fish to a 500-pound fish would be like a single A minor league ball player skipping AA and AAA leagues and going straight to the majors. It just doesn't happen."

But the idea was gaining traction in Ava's head. She continued, "Let's say you get some tips from an offshore fishing guide. And you could get a fly rod manufacturer to sponsor your equipment and the entrance fee. Would you consider entering the tournament?"

"I don't know, Ava. As you now know, I've only won one tournament in my career and it was a freshwater bass tournament. I don't exactly have the credentials for the type of sponsor you're suggesting. Besides, even if I landed such a sponsor and got into the tournament, the odds of me boating an offshore fish of any kind are remote, at best. Most of my experience is freshwater or brackish water fishing, not ocean fishing."

"What are you afraid of, Sonny?" Ava softly inquired.

"Afraid?" Again, Ava went right for the jugular. "Well, failure for one thing. At least in freshwater tournaments, I have a reasonable chance of success. But for the Big Rock Tournament, the odds are probably a thousand to one to boat a saltwater fish of any kind that even qualifies for a paycheck. And a million to one to catch a qualifying blue marlin."

"What else?"

Sonny paused. "Loss of momentum. I just won my first bass tournament, so the logical career step would be to enter another bass tournament and build on my success of last spring. To suddenly change direction with such long odds doesn't make much business sense."

Ava couldn't argue with that logic. "True, but don't you think the publicity alone would warrant that risk?"

"Only if I do well in the Big Rock."

"Then do well, Sonny." Ava beamed a lovely smile that caught Sonny off guard a bit. Her green eyes sparkled mischievously. Gawd she's pretty, Sonny mused to himself. He took a moment to take her in more fully. Ava wore next to no makeup and was a stunningly beautiful woman. In addition to her silky blonde hair and dreamy green eyes, she had a button nose, full lips, brilliant white teeth, and a splash of freckles that accentuated her natural beauty. He guessed her height at 5 foot 6 inches.

"So, do you have a boyfriend, Ava?" Now Ava was caught off guard.

Ava quickly stopped recording their conversation.

"Where did that come from?"

"Just curious."

"How about we circle back to the Big Rock Tournament?" But Ava couldn't help but smile a bit.

"Sure. Sorry for being nosy."

Ava waved a hand as if it were nothing. "No worries, Sonny. It's all good. Okay, how about I contact Dan tomorrow to see if we can work together on finding out more information on the Big Rock Tournament including deadlines, entrance fees, sponsors, and so on?"

"Sure, but after our fishing trip in the morning, okay?"

"Of course. I'm looking forward to our adventure! Speaking of which, I'm kind of tired so I think I'll turn in for the night. Where would you like to meet me and at what time tomorrow?"

"There is a town dock just a couple of minutes' walk from here. Rita will give you directions. How about I meet you there at 7 a.m. tomorrow?"

"Sounds good, Sonny. I'll see you then." And with that, she smiled, packed up her iPad and phone, and breezed out of the bar.

VIII. October

Sonny pulled up to the town dock in his ancient 20-foot center console fishing boat at seven the next morning. He was pleasantly surprised to see Ava was standing there with a smile on her face and a small day bag draped over her shoulder. She was equally surprised to see a golden retriever wagging its tail from the bow of the boat. As soon as Sonny secured the boat to the dock, the dog leapt off the boat and proceeded to lick Ava's hand. She kneeled next to the dog and was instantly rewarded with a big lick on her face.

"And who might you be?" Ava laughed.

"Oh, that's Milly. Sorry about the slobbery greeting. She doesn't usually get so friendly when first meeting people. Very strange…"

"Oh, that's perfectly fine. I love dogs, so perhaps she can sense that."

"Maybe. Are you ready for our adventure?"

"Absolutely! What can I do?"

"Grab my hand, sit back, and relax." Sonny then helped Ava onto the boat and she sat in the seat next to Sonny's. Milly jumped aboard and proceeded to the bow.

"So, what is the name of your boat, Sonny?"

"*Whisker.*"

"I'm sure there's a story there," Ava probed.

"Yes, there is," Sonny responded but didn't elaborate any further.

Sonny untied the bow line and kicked the boat away from the dock. It was a cool, crisp autumn morning so Ava was glad that she'd donned a fleece that morning. As they motored down the Pungo River, Ava soaked in the scenery. She was amazed at how few boats were on the water as well as the scarcity of houses and commercial buildings along the shoreline. The amount of wildlife was another pleasant surprise. It had been just 10 minutes since they left the dock and, already, she'd spotted an osprey diving into the river and nabbing a fish with its talons. Pelicans skimmed inches above the water as only they could do. And then a bald eagle soaring high above took a sudden interest in the osprey. The eagle swooped down toward the osprey with the fish gripped tightly in its talons; drama was about to unfold between the birds of prey, but Ava lost sight of the battle as *Whisker* motored down the river.

Despite the engine noise, they carried on a conversation.

"Here's our plan for the day," Sonny began. "We'll cruise down the Pungo River, then turn right at the Pamlico River and explore a few creeks. After that, we'll grab an ice cream in Bath and then head back to Belhaven."

"It seems like we're covering a lot of water today," Ava remarked.

"It does but the water is relatively calm and this old bucket will cruise at 45- to 50-mph under these conditions."

"This thing will go that fast?" Ava exclaimed. She then paused and almost bit her tongue when she realized how offensive that sounded. "Ummm, no offense intended."

Sonny laughed, "No offense taken. Look at the engine."

Ava pivoted her head around and was surprised to see a large, relatively new 200-horsepower motor fastened to the stern.

"The motor is a bit oversized for this boat but the new motor design has more alloys than metal so it's a lot lighter than previous models. The net result is less weight and more speed."

"Is speed important?" Ava asked.

"Storms can appear almost instantly in these waters so if you're trying to stay ahead of them, yes, speed is very important."

"Gotcha."

On cue, Sonny pushed the throttle down and the boat lurched forward.

It was like a different gear and *Whisker* started skimming the surface effortlessly. Sonny glanced at Ava and was satisfied to see the surprised look in her eyes.

"Wow! *Whisker* can really move!" Sonny was pleased with her reaction and that she used the boat's name.

Milly had been sitting on the bow soaking in the autumn air but, once *Whisker* was kicked into high gear, she quickly walked behind the console and plunked down on all fours with her head on Sonny's feet. Sonny bent down and scratched her neck. Milly groaned with contentment. Ava smiled at the obvious love between Sonny and Milly.

They passed a few boats along the way and Sonny waved at each one.

"Do you know every boat out here?" Ava wondered aloud.

"Not all of them, but it's polite to wave nonetheless."

After about fifteen more minutes, they came to the intersection of two rivers. Sonny slowed the boat a tad. "Okay, we are about to turn right onto the Pamlico River. Straight ahead is the Pamlico Sound. As you can see, the Pungo and Pamlico Rivers run about 90 degrees from each other. The Pungo River runs north to south; and the Pamlico River runs west to east…more or less.

Ava just nodded.

Sonny then increased the throttle and *Whisker* leapt forward up the Pamlico River. Ava was impressed by the width of the river.

"How wide is the Pamlico River at the mouth?"

"About four or five miles," replied Sonny.

"Wow, I had no idea. So are the Pungo and Pamlico Rivers saltwater or freshwater?" Ava inquired.

"Both rivers are brackish meaning they have a blend of saltwater and freshwater usually in the range of 10 to 20 parts-per-thousand, depending on several factors including rain, wind velocity and direction, and the like. For a point of reference, ocean water is 35 parts per thousand."

Ava smiled to herself at Sonny's science knowledge. It was clear he knew his environment.

"So, what does that mean in terms of fish species that these rivers hold?"

"Well, each river can support several saltwater species -- red drum, flounder, and speckled trout to name a few. You'll even see dolphin on occasion."

"Dolphin, the mammal?"

"Yup."

Ava looked skeptical but didn't pursue this line of questioning.

As *Whisker* motored up the Pamlico River, Ava glanced at the riverbanks. "I don't see any hotels or mega mansions on this river. Why is that?"

"A lot of these cottages have been passed down from generation to generation. There are no major businesses in this area so most of the homes were originally built as weekend vacation cottages in the 1940's and 1950's for people who live in nearby cities like Greenville, Wilson, and more recently, Raleigh, Durham, and Chapel Hill."

A few miles up the Pamlico River, Sonny waved toward the right bank. Ava followed Sonny's gaze and caught sight of an older bearded man waving back.

"Let's make a quick detour, okay?" Sonny asked but didn't wait for a response as he steered *Whisker* toward the sixty-ish man.

Ava laughed and said, "Sure."

As they got closer to the pier, Ava said, "Hey, is that a fly rod in his hand?"

"Good observation, Ava!"

"I'm certainly no expert, but his casting looks a bit awkward."

"Ha! Another good observation! It's true that he is not the most fluid fly-caster in the world, but I give him credit for trying. Afterall, he didn't start fly fishing until he was about fifty."

When *Whisker* got within earshot, Sonny put the boat in neutral and smiled and said, "Hey Alan."

"Hey, Sonny. Who's your cute friend?"

"Boy, you don't waste any time do you, old man?" Sonny chuckled.

"Alan, this is Ava Tyson. Ava, this is Alan Capwell."

"It's a pleasure to meet you, Alan."

"Likewise, Ava." Alan beamed.

Ava searched her memory. "Wait a minute. Sonny said your last name was Capwell, right? Are you related to the sister-brother duo we heard playing at Tommy's Tavern last night? If so, they are wonderful!"

"I am indeed. They are my children," Alan answered with pride. "You just earned yourself a fresh cup of coffee!"

"I don't want to put you out, Alan."

"Nonsense. What do you like in your coffee, Ava?"

"Black is fine."

Milly was on the bow of the boat furiously wagging her tail.

"Well, hey Milly! How's my girl?" Milly barked hello.

Alan gently placed his fly rod in one of the rod holders attached to the side of the pier and then secured the boat from the line that Sonny threw him. Milly hopped off the boat onto the pier and bolted straight to Alan's open hand for a pat and a scratch. Given the ease of this operation, Ava could sense this process had been done many times before. Ava glanced back at the modest cottage where Alan and Milly were headed.

"Why is Milly following Alan?"

Sonny laughed, "Alan claims that he is a dog whisperer, but my guess is that he has doggie treats back at the cottage."

"That is a lot of open land around Alan's cottage."

"Yup. He's got about five acres of waterfront property. He started out with just an acre of land and, over the years, he kept buying adjacent lots. Don't get me wrong, Alan likes people, but he likes his privacy as well."

A few minutes later, Alan returned with three steaming mugs of coffee. Milly was close on his heels.

The humans eased into some Adirondack chairs on the pier and sipped their coffee while Milly plopped down by Alan's feet. Alan scratched her neck.

"So, Ava, how long have you and Sonny been dating?"

"Jeez, Alan, how about a few introductory remarks like 'nice weather' or 'how's the fishing' and the like?"

Alan waved him off, "What's the point? I'm going to eventually ask you the question, so why not just get it over with? You know I don't have any filters."

Ava instantly liked this guy…perhaps because he didn't have any filters.

"Actually, we are not dating. I'm a reporter for the *DC Tribune*. I'm working on a story about Sonny and this boat ride is part of my research."

"A story on Sonny? Darlin', you must be desperate for news!" Alan chuckled. Even Sonny laughed, mainly because Alan's laugh was contagious.

Defensively, Ava continued "I don't know if you heard the latest news, Alan, but Sonny won the Kerr Lake Bass tournament in April."

Alan's eyes opened wide, "What? How come you didn't tell me this, Sonny?"

Sonny shrugged, "Well, it wasn't that big of a tournament. Besides, I know you like your privacy here and I didn't want to bother you."

"Apple crap, Sonny. So how about some details?"

Ava filled in Alan with the highlights of the tournament.

Alan looked thoughtful and even proud. "My, my, my, Sonny. I knew you had it in you. You just need to believe in yourself."

Sonny smiled modestly, "I'm getting there, Alan. I'm getting there."

Ava said, "So, Alan. I noticed that you were fly fishing from your pier before we pulled up. Did you teach Sonny how to fly fish?"

This drew laughs from both men. "Hardly, Ava. But I appreciate the compliment. It's the other way around. Sonny taught ME how to fly fish. When Sonny lost his dad, I took him fishing on my boat several times a year and couldn't help but notice that he continually out-fished me. At the time, I was using conventional spinning gear and he was using a fly rod. I couldn't believe it! So, I asked Sonny if he would be willing to teach me how to fly fish. And to his credit, he did. He also taught me how to tie saltwater flies. Of course, I don't have the skill or youth that Sonny has, but I get by."

"You more that get by, old man. I've seen you pull some pretty good fish out of these waters," Sonny added. "Well, we've got some fishing to do ourselves so we'd better head out. Thanks for the coffee, Alan."

Ava smiled warmly, "Yes, thanks for the coffee. It was a pleasure meeting you, Alan."

A few minutes later, Sonny, Ava, and Milly were motoring back up the Pamlico River.

"I like Alan," Ava volunteered.

"I thought you might. That's one of the reasons I decided to stop by. Alan and my dad were good friends, so when my dad died, Alan took me under his wing. Nothing was said. He just pulled up to our pier in his boat about a month after my dad died and asked me and my brother Dill if we wanted to go fishing. Dill is not really into fishing, but I immediately accepted Alan's invitation. We've been fishing together ever since."

"Very nice," Ava nodded.

About 15 minutes later, Ava's mouth dropped open and she pointed her finger at a large manufacturing plant on the left bank of the river with smoke billowing out of several stacks. "What is that?"

"Oh, that's a phosphate mining operation," Sonny responded.

"It looks like a massive operation. That can't be good for the river…can it?" Ava inquired.

"It's complicated. From a monetary standpoint it's one of the largest employers East of I-95. In fact, this is one of the largest phosphate mining operations in the world. So, the plant supplies many well-paying jobs in an economically stressed area."

"And from an environmental standpoint?" Ava pressed.

"The verdict is still out on that…" Sonny trailed off.

"Do you care to expand?" Ava probed.

"Not really. Several of my friends work at that plant and I have no wish to bring attention to their employer."

"Understood." Ava dropped it. "So where are we heading now?"

Grateful that Ava changed the topic, Sonny replied, "Bath Creek…just ahead on the right."

A few minutes later, Sonny pulled up to a bank, turned off the combustion motor, and swung the electric trolling motor mounted on the bow into position.

"I like to quietly approach a target area with the trolling motor so as not to spook any predator fish. Hence the electric motor. We'll start fishing after we go another one hundred yards or so. Once we start fishing, we should whisper rather than talk. Even the sound of our voices might spook a predator. Here's a lightweight spinning rod I brought for you."

"Oh, I'm fishing too?" Ava asked.

"Of course you are. Do you know how to use that type of rod?"

"Yes. My dad took me fishing to ponds and even the Chesapeake Bay when I was a kid. We used similar types of rods."

"Very good. I tied a surface lure on your rod because it's still early enough in the day to draw a strike from a speckled trout or red drum. The odds are longer you'll get a strike on the surface than down below, but the thrill of a surface strike is worth the long odds. Here's how you work the lure. If I may?" Ava handed the rod back to Sonny.

He cast the lure in the open water and let it sit still for about thirty seconds. He then started twitching the rod so the lure weaved back and forth in the water while Sonny reeled in the fishing line slack. "This action is called 'walk the dog.'" On cue, Milly jumped up from the deck and walked to the left side of Sonny.

"Wow, Milly seems very interested in your fishing!"

"Oh, you haven't seen anything yet. Wait until we actually catch a fish! Okay, your turn now. I can control the electric motor from anywhere on the boat so you take the bow." Sonny handed the rod back to Ava.

Ava stepped up to the bow. "Where should I cast?"

"Drum like to hide around structures like piers, logs, oyster beds, and the like. Do you see that downed tree ahead?"

Ava nodded.

"Cast near that tree."

Ava cast the lure about 10 feet from the tree.

"That's a good first cast, Ava. But try to get the lure on top of the tree. So cast it a little farther next time."

Ava appreciated how patient Sonny was with her. He didn't demean her in any way, despite her weak first cast. The next cast was a bit farther but not quite on top of the partially submerged tree.

"Much better, Ava. Reel it in and give it another shot."

Ava quickly reeled it in and cast it again. This time the lure landed on the water surface just above the end of the submerged tree.

"Perfect! Now leave the lure in place for a bit." About 30 seconds later Sonny whispered, "Okay walk the dog, Ava."

Ava then started twitching the lure back and forth as Sonny instructed. Milly was beside her now, laser focused on the lure.

Sonny continued, "If you get a bite, don't immediately set the hook. Make sure your rod is bent over and then set the hook."

"So about how long…" Before she finished, an explosion erupted on the water surface. Ava's rod bent over and she shrieked "What do I do now?"

"Set the hook! And I mean hard!"

Ava pulled hard on the rod.

"Now the fun begins," Sonny exclaimed. Milly was just as excited as Sonny, her tail wagging like a helicopter blade.

Line started peeling off Ava's reel and her rod bent over even more.

"It's running back toward the bank. It's trying to break your line around that tree. Start reeling harder. The drag is set so the line shouldn't break on your retrieve. But it will break if it wraps around that submerged tree."

Ava couldn't believe the force at the end of her line. Its will to live was overpowering.

"What is this fish?"

"Red drum most likely," Sonny replied.

As Ava pulled the rod up and to her right, the line gradually moved away from the tree.

"Way to go, Ava! You steered it away from that tree."

"What do I do now?" Ava asked excitedly, surprised by her desire to boat this fish.

"Just take what the fish gives you," Sonny replied.

"What does that mean?" Ava implored.

"You'll see…" Sonny laughed.

During the fish fight, Sonny took a closer look at Ava's face. Her green eyes glowed with excitement. She was truly enjoying this moment. She did not fake her enthusiasm. It was clear she wanted to capture this fish.

Ava was getting into a rhythm now. When the fish ran, she did not try to reel it in. Rather, she only reeled in slack when it ran to the boat or didn't pull as hard. After a few minutes, the fish was close to the boat. Sonny pulled a net down from the hard top canopy.

"Okay, here is where it gets a bit tricky," Sonny explained. "Try to guide the fish into the net."

After a few unsuccessful attempts, the fish finally found the bottom of the net.

Sonny placed the net gently on the boat. Without an invitation, Milly ran over to the fish and licked it.

Ava let out a shriek, "Yes!"

"Well done, Ava! That is a beautiful puppy drum!" Sonny raised his hand in a high-five gesture and she eagerly slapped it.

"It's gorgeous! How big is it?" Ava asked. Ava continued to gaze at the fish. She saw a glistening copper sheen across the fish plus three nickel-size brown spots near the tail. She marveled at its beauty.

"Let's check," Sonny said, pulling a fish gripper out of a hatch. He inserted the gripper in the fish's lower jaw and placed the fish on top of a measuring tape on the port side gunwale.

"He is 25-inches, which is a very nice size puppy drum."

"You said it was a 'he'. How do you know its gender?"

"Do you hear that sound?" Sonny asked.

Ava drew closer to the wriggling fish and could hear a croaking sound emanating from its throat.

"Yes, I do!" Ava replied. Milly heard it too and drew closer to the fish. She licked it again.

"Well, that croaking or drumming sound only occurs with male, not female drum. Sounds produced by male red drum are associated with courtship and spawning activity."

"You sound like a marine biologist. Oh, wait a minute, you ARE a marine biologist. You went to the University of North Carolina for your undergraduate degree and North Carolina State University for your graduate degree, right?"

Sonny raised an eyebrow, "How do you know that?"

"Have you ever heard of Google?" Ava laughed. "Plus, what kind of reporter would I be if I didn't research your background before writing a story about you? Okay, what shall we do with this fish?"

"Do you have a current North Carolina fishing license?" Sonny asked.

"As a matter of fact, I do. I bought it online last night when you said we were going fishing today. I wasn't sure what the rules were, but I didn't want to take a chance of either of us getting a fine."

"Excellent! Well, the fish is on the upper end of the legal 18- to 27-inch slot length so it is a legally caught fish."

"Is red drum good table fare?"

"It's my favorite tasting fish in these waters. If you keep it, I'll prepare it for you tonight at my place."

"Then let's keep it!" Ava said. She wasn't sure if her immediate acceptance of Sonny's dinner invitation was due to her curiosity about the fish taste or getting to know Sonny more. Perhaps both.

"Done!" Sonny then placed the fish on ice after a mercy killing.

Sonny took a closer look at Ava. She had a sparkle in her eyes that was…magnetic. She seemed unaware or at least modest about her beauty, which Sonny found compelling. Something stirred inside of him that he'd never experienced before. Her passion during the drum fight was undeniable. *"You just can't fake that enthusiasm. She gets it,"* Sonny thought to himself.

Ava matched his gaze and smiled. His knees weakened. He quickly regained his composure, shook his head slightly as if to break her spell, and said, "Shall we keep fishing?"

"Absolutely!" Ava laughed.

"Yup, she gets it," Sonny smiled to himself.

They spent the next few hours catching a variety of fish including two more under-slot red drum, some speckled trout, and a few flounder. None matched the size of Ava's first caught drum. Even though some of the other fish were legal size, Sonny did not keep any of them. He also decided not to use *Percival* on this trip, as he didn't want to risk losing it on a recreational adventure. Plus, he didn't want to draw Ava's attention to the fly at this time, or perhaps ever, for that matter. So, he used some flies that he tied instead.

Almost reading Ava's thoughts about the number of fish they put back in the river, Sonny explained, "I only keep what I eat. This fishery is already under tremendous stress from environmental factors and gill net fishing, that I don't wish to reduce the fish stock any further even if it is legal to keep some of the fish that we safely released this morning."

"Isn't North Carolina one of the few states in the Southeast that still allows gill netting in estuarine and brackish waters? Don't those nets indiscriminately kill everything in their reach? Why is this practice still allowed?"

Sonny grunted, "That is the $64,000 question. It's also a powder keg topic in this area, as the recreational fishermen have been at war for decades with the commercial fishermen and the Department of Marine Fisheries or DMF over the use of gill nets in these waters. The recreational anglers argue that juvenile fish such as striped bass are killed in gill nets, preventing a healthy stock for future fish generations. The commercial fishermen argue that if gill nets were banned, local restaurants and fish markets would suffer, as a good portion of their fresh catch comes from such nets."

Ava asked, "What are your thoughts on this topic?"

Sonny said, "It's not black or white. Several of my neighbors and friends are commercial fishermen. In some cases, their business has been handed down from generation to generation for almost one hundred years. It's not just a way of life for these people, but a strong sense of family pride. But I also understand the recreational fishermen's point of view as well. I have observed a steady decline of fish catches in these waters over the years. At the current rate, this fishery is not sustainable. So, something must be done to restore the fish stock. Otherwise, everyone will suffer, the commercial fishermen as well as the recreational anglers."

"So, if you were king, what would you do to improve the fishery?"

Sonny chuckled at the word 'king'. After a long pause, he said, "One solution would be to increase the cost of a recreational fishing license by another $10 per person. I believe about half a million recreational fishing licenses were sold last year. So that would supply an extra $5 million in revenue that could be used to subsidize these commercial fishermen to not use gill nets for most of the fishing season. They could still drop their nets, but only in restricted areas and certain times of the year. This would allow these fishermen to keep some semblance of their way of life while not sacrificing their income. It would also allow the fish stock to grow."

"Wouldn't a bunch of people rush out to purchase commercial fishing licenses to take advantage of this new subsidy?" Ava inquired.

"Well, you could have a grandfather clause that restricted the subsidy to only those commercial fishermen who had possession of a gill net permit for the previous 10 or 20 years."

"Interesting idea, Sonny. Why don't you propose this to the DMF?" Ava continued.

"Ha! Because I value my life and my friends," Sonny half-jokingly replied. He quickly changed the subject "Are you ready for some ice cream? It's almost noon and the bite has slowed down."

"Ice cream? Sure!"

Sonny stowed the fishing rods, pulled up the electric motor, and cranked the outboard motor. A few minutes later, they pulled into a quaint marina in Bath called *Teach's Marina*. After Sonny secured *Whisker* to the dock with the bow and stern lines, Milly leapt off the boat without an invitation. Ava laughed, "She's done this before hasn't she?"

"Once or twice," Sonny joked.

The three walked inside the marina. The bells above the door gave a jingle at their arrival. Given that it was October, there were only a few other customers inside. Like Pavlov's dogs, Milly started salivating at the sound of the bells.

"Milly!" shrieked a fifty-ish, medium build woman behind the counter. Milly bounded toward the woman and eagerly accepted a head scratch as she snuggled against her leg. "Oh, hi, Sonny."

Sonny turned toward Ava and laughed, "You can see who is more popular here. Ava, this is Bessie. Bessie, this is Ava."

Bessie smiled, "It's a pleasure to meet you, Ava."

Ava smiled in return, "Likewise, Bessie."

Bessie then opened the lid from a large jar on the counter and plucked out a doggie biscuit. Milly gently licked it off Bessie's outstretched fingers and proceeded to a corner of the store to munch on her midday snack.

"So, what I can get for you two?"

"We'd like some of your homemade ice cream, Bess. What are your flavors of the day?"

"Well, we have Bath Brittle and Pamlico Panache."

"What would you like, Ava?" Sonny asked.

"You pick," Ava responded.

"Okay. Bess, how about two cones with a scoop of each?"

A couple of minutes later, Sonny and Ava were licking their cones on the marina dock with Milly between them.

Ava said, "I passed through this town in my car yesterday and saw a brief movie about Bath at the Visitor Center. Can you tell me anything more about its history?"

"Believe it or not, Bath is the oldest incorporated city in North Carolina. It's over 300 years old. Did you ever hear of Edward Teach?"

"Yes, he's Blackbeard. The movie mentioned him." A lightbulb went off as Ava looked up at the Marina sign, "Ah, hence the name of this Marina."

Sonny nodded. "Well, Blackbeard did most of his pirating in the early seventeen hundreds. In fact, he lived in this very town for a short spell."

"What happened to him?"

"He got married and had a daughter who died young. But civilian life didn't take so he went back to his pirating ways. He pillaged waters from Ocracoke Island to Charleston, South Carolina. His infamous pirate ship *The Queen Anne's Revenge* ran aground off the coast of Fort Macon, North Carolina in 1718."

"Is that how he died?"

"No, he and the other pirates made it safely to shore. They eventually acquired another ship called the *Adventure* and continued pirating. In late 1718, a British ship captained by Lieutenant Robert Maynard engaged in a fierce battle with Blackbeard and his crew. Blackbeard died during this battle. His head was affixed to the bow of the British ship and brought to England as proof of his demise."

"Yeesh!" exclaimed Ava.

"Here's another interesting fact," Sonny continued. "The wreck of *The Queen Anne's Revenge* remained undiscovered for almost 300 years even though it lay in shallow waters just a mile off the coast of Fort Macon, a state park along one shoreline of Beaufort Inlet. It boggles my mind to think that tens of thousands of recreational and commercial vessels passed over that sunken ship over the years and didn't spot that wreck on their sonar."

"Did the treasure hunters find any treasure?"

"Not to my knowledge. It's possible that not much loot was aboard the *Queen Anne's Revenge* when it sank. Perhaps the treasure was buried somewhere else and has yet to be discovered. You've heard the expression 'spend like a sailor' right?"

"Of course."

"Well, maybe they spent their ill-gotten goods as soon as they were acquired. Afterall, the sinking occurred almost three centuries ago so no one really knows if the loot was spent or is still undiscovered. Believe it or not, I have a tiny connection to the discovery of the *Queen Anne's Revenge.*"

"Really? Do tell, Sonny."

While awaiting Sonny's response, Ava circled back to her cone.

Sonny said, "The day the treasure hunter was bringing the anchor from the *Queen Anne's Revenge* back to Beaufort in his ship, a friend of mine and I just happened to be returning from a fly fishing adventure at Cape Lookout. We wore ourselves out catching false albacore earlier that day and we were heading through Beaufort Inlet aboard *Whisker.* There was a flotilla of boats ahead of us plus a helicopter from a local TV station hovering above. Naturally, we hammed it up when they pointed the chopper TV camera in our direction. They probably thought we were part of the flotilla. In fact, my Raleigh friend Perry dropped his pants and mooned the camera!"

"Ha. I bet that shot didn't make the evening news," Ava said dryly.

"Quite the contrary. Even though we had no idea what was going on, we figured it was a newsworthy event given all the commotion. When we got back to Alan's bungalow in Beaufort, we turned on the evening news. Sure enough, there was the flotilla with a caption that read, 'Treasure hunter hauls Blackbeard's anchor to port'. The camera then zoomed in on *Whisker*. And there was Perry in all his glory with his ass pointing skyward. Of course, they blurred out the bare details but you got the drift."

"No way!"

"Yes, indeedy. After the moon shot, two news anchors were chuckling to one another. 'Well, I guess that's the end of the story, eh?'"

Sonny still laughed at the memory. Ava giggled as well.

After devouring their cones, they boarded *Whisker*, cranked up the motor, and headed out of Bath Creek toward the Pamlico River. Sonny steered *Whisker* left at the intersection of the two water bodies and headed down the Pamlico river. About 10 minutes into their journey home, Sonny slowed the boat down and said, "Ava, look over there."

Ava followed his pointing finger. She saw about a dozen large gray creatures easing in and out of the water with an occasional poof of spray shooting out of a blowhole.

"Are those...porpoises?"

"To be more precise, they are bottlenose dolphins. But close enough."

"Wow! I had no idea they could live in the river!"

"Yup, the downriver portions of the Pamlico and Pungo rivers are salty enough to support dolphin, a mammal, as well as some saltwater fish species such as red drum, speckled trout and flounder, the fish we caught earlier today."

"Can we get closer to them?" Ava inquired.

"Legally, we are not allowed to motor our boat to within 50- to 100-yards of them. But we may be able to attract their attention by slowing our boat down to a speed of 5- to 7-mph. Shall we try it?"

"Definitely!"

Sonny steered the boat away from the pod but throttled down the motor until the GPS read 6-mph. Sure enough, several dolphins peeled off from the pod and headed toward *Whisker*. The other dolphins followed suit. Soon they were swimming alongside the boat, some in pairs. One dolphin even swam under the bow of the boat while others swam on either side of the boat darting in and out of the water. There were some baby dolphins getting into the action as well.

Ava pulled out her cellphone and recorded a video of the show. "They're playing with us!" Ava giggled in delight.

"Yup."

"Have you ever hit one with the boat?"

"Never. They are smart and fast. Even so, I always slow the boat down when I encounter a pod just to be on the safe side."

Ava turned off the video recording and soaked in the scenery. Dolphins in a river! She shook her head.

"So how do we shake them?"

"We just slowly increase our speed until they can't catch up to us. Like so…"

Sonny gradually increased the speed of the boat until the pod gave up chasing them.

"That was amazing!" Ava marveled. "How often do you encounter dolphin?"

"There doesn't seem to be a pattern to their presence in these waters. I might go for a stretch where I see them every day for a two-week period. Other times, it might be a month or more between sightings."

Ava glanced at her watch and noted it was about 2 p.m. "So, what's the plan now?"

"We'll head back to Belhaven and give you a few hours break from me and then meet at my place for a fresh fish dinner--courtesy of your puppy drum," Sonny smiled.

"Sounds like a plan," Ava smiled back. A voice inside her said, "*Uh, oh Ava. You best be careful with this one.*"

Sonny then pushed forward on the throttle and *Whisker* forged ahead. A few minutes later, they made a left at Wades Point on the Pamlico River and worked their way up the Pungo River. About a mile up the Pungo, Sonny pointed to his right and said, "Do you see those birds diving on the river surface?"

Ava nodded.

"Those are probably bluefish devouring menhaden. Here, take a closer look." Sonny said, handing her a pair of binoculars. She peered into the binoculars and saw the commotion on the water surface. "There might even be something bigger underneath the bluefish" Sonny added. "Shall we investigate?"

"Of course!" Ava instantly replied.

After being on the water for more than six hours, Sonny was impressed with Ava's enthusiasm to extend their journey. "Terrific! Let's go!"

The Pungo River is not as wide as the Pamlico River, but it was still a good two to three miles from shore-to-shore where the birds were diving. When *Whisker* was about 200 yards from the birds, Sonny killed the outboard motor and dropped the electric trolling motor into the water. Reading her thoughts, Sonny said, "Like we did earlier today, we need to approach this school as quietly as possible in order to avoid spooking the predator fish beneath the surface."

As they got closer to the birds, Sonny started to pull out a big spinning rod for Ava. She said, "If you don't mind, Sonny, I'd prefer to make a video of you fly fishing."

Sonny paused and then said, "Okay, but there is a good chance I won't catch anything."

"That's fine. I'd just like to pay a bit more attention to your fly fishing technique. This morning was a lot of fun but I've got a job to do and, after all, you are the subject of this story."

Sonny shrugged and said, "No problem. Film away."

Sonny reached into the boat's rod rack and pulled out a fly rod. Ava pulled out her cellphone to begin the recording.

"Hey Sonny, isn't that a different fly rod than the one you used this morning?"

"Ding, ding, ding! Very good, Ava! Yes, this is a nine foot long, ten-weight fly rod. The one I used this morning was a lighter eight-weight fly rod." Sonny looked into the camera and shot a smile and a wink.

"Also, that is a big fly you've got tied onto your leader. Just what kind of fish are you expecting?" Ava inquired.

"Patience, Grasshopper," Sonny whispered as he held his forefinger to his lips for the universal quiet signal. Ava laughed quietly as she received the message loud and clear…or quiet-and-clear in this instance.

When *Whisker* pulled within 20 yards of the diving birds, Sonny peeled about 70 to 80 feet of line from the fly reel onto the deck and effortlessly began working the fly rod back and forth. For each of these "false casts," a fair amount of fly line on the deck of the *Whisker* disappeared into the rod and the arc of fly line above Sonny's head got larger and larger. Ava marveled at the ease of this action. After just three of these false casts, Sonny cast a fourth time but this time he gently laid the fly line across the water on the edge of the school of breaking bait fish. He then paused a bit before he began pulling or "stripping" the fly line in with his left hand as he held the fly rod with his right hand.

"Can you please explain what you are doing?" whispered Ava.

Sonny nodded and whispered, "After I cast the line out, I let it sink for about five to ten seconds before stripping the line in. I'm using a fly line called 'intermediate' because it sinks at a rate somewhere between a floating fly line and a sinking fly line. Hence the name 'intermediate'. I'm targeting fish at depths a few feet below the water surface so I can avoid the bluefish at or near the surface and target bigger fish below them."

Sonny repeated the casting routine a few more times without a hookup. He observed the school moving down river. Using the electric trolling motor, he positioned *Whisker* behind the moving bait school.

"Why did you move the boat behind the school instead of above it?" Ava queried quietly.

"Good question" he whispered in return. "Bluefish are savage predators but they don't usually eat their prey whole. They have razor sharp teeth. Like piranha, they can tear the flesh off the bones with just one bite. In other words, it's not an all-or-nothing proposition to get a meal. They can merely take a bite out of a fish and move on to the next one."

A lightbulb went off in Ava's head, "Got it! So, the bits and pieces of the damaged baitfish float down to a lower depth where a different, larger predator species lies in wait?"

"Exactly! Well, that's my theory anyway. Let's see if it works."

On cue, Sonny's fly rod suddenly went taut. Sonny at once pulled up hard on the fly rod in his right hand while simultaneously pinching down on the fly line between his left thumb and forefinger. The fly rod then doubled over.

"Got him! Game on!" Milly jumped up from where she'd been snoozing at Ava's feet and galloped over to Sonny's right side. She seemed to know exactly where to stand so as not to get in Sonny's way. The previously slacked fly line on the deck shot through the fly rod so Sonny was now playing the fish from the reel.

"What now?" Ava asked excitedly.

"Now the fun part begins. As you can see, the fish has peeled off at least 150 yards of my fly line backing. If I can't turn him soon, we're going to have to chase it or I might get spooled, meaning losing all my line. Do you know how to start and run a motorboat?"

Grateful that her dad let her operate rental motorboats on the Chesapeake Bay during her childhood years, Ava replied, "Of course. Just say when." She bolted back to the console, cellphone still in hand.

"When!" Sonny yelled back as more line peeled off his fly reel. "Just ease the throttle forward gently and point the boat toward the fish."

"This is like *Wicked Tuna*! We're chasing the fish!" exclaimed Ava. "By the way, what species of fish is this?"

"Hopefully, you'll see in a few minutes," Sonny replied. As *Whisker* got closer to the fish, Sonny cranked the fly reel quickly to take the slack out of the line. Ava continued to video Sonny with one hand on her cellphone while she steered the boat with the other hand.

"Okay, Ava, I've got about half my line back on the reel. Please put the throttle in neutral and then kill the motor."

After Ava turned the key to kill the motor, Sonny continued to fight the fish. If anything, the fly rod bent over even more. She was stunned that it didn't break in half. Then suddenly, the rod shot straight up and the line went slack.

"Ugh. We lost it," Ava said dejectedly.

Sonny turned to her and just smiled. "You think so?" He then started furiously reeling in the line. "Actually, the fish is still on. He's charging the boat!"

Sure enough, a few seconds later, the fly rod suddenly doubled over again.

"Here's the tricky part," Sonny exclaimed. "We need to keep the fish away from the trolling motor and outboard motor propellors. Otherwise, the line will be cut like a hot knife through butter." Sonny then pulled up the trolling motor with his left hand while holding onto the fly rod with his right. Sure enough, the fish went straight under the bow of the boat and charged toward the opposite direction from where it was initially hooked. More line peeled off the reel.

"Shall we chase it again?" Ava said as she hurried back to the console.

"I don't think so. I've got enough line back on the reel and, believe it or not, it is finally starting to tire." Ava wasn't sure who was more tired—the fish or Sonny, as beads of sweat were now streaming down Sonny's face. She couldn't ignore, nor did she particularly want to, his strained but toned biceps as he was fighting the fish.

Ava was a bit anxious now because she really wanted to see this fish. She had no idea what it was other than it wasn't like any of the fish they caught earlier today.

After a few more minutes, Sonny drew the fish close to the boat. Both Milly and Ava peered intently in the direction of the fish. It finally came to the surface.

"Oh my God! It's huge! What is it?" Ava asked.

"Believe it or not, it's a red drum."

Ava was incredulous. "What a minute. THAT is the same kind of fish that I caught earlier today?"

Sonny smiled, "Yep. But we're still a long way from boating it. I could use your help. Please grab the net and stand to my right." Sonny nodded toward the net.

Ava propped her cellphone against the front seat, pointed it toward the bow, and continued recording the action. The fish was on its side now. It was a magnificent looking fish with a shiny copper hue and a large spot on its tail.

"Now dip the net all the way under the water surface with the opening toward the fish. I'm going to lead the fish toward the net."

Sonny did just that. After the fish found the bottom of the net, Ava tried to lift it out of the water. But it was so heavy that she struggled to pull the net out of the water. "Here, let me help. It's a big fish." Sonny quietly stood beside her, putting both hands just below Ava's hands. "Okay, on three. One, two, three!" they both hoisted the netted fish onto the deck.

Ava could hear and feel the drum sound resonating through the boat.

"Yes!" they simultaneously screamed and high fived each other.

"Wow! That's a male drum, right?" Ava asked breathlessly. She noted the fish was moving but not thrashing as aggressively as the smaller drum caught earlier in the day.

"Indeed, it is. It's a bull drum. Now we must work quickly because we want to release it as fast as possible so it has a good chance of surviving. So, if you'd like to take some pictures, now is the time. I'm going to unhook it and get a measurement now."

Ava grabbed her cellphone, and with the video still rolling, alternately pointed the camera at the fish and Sonny. She took some still photos as well. As promised, Sonny quickly removed the fly from the corner of the drum's mouth, pulled a tape measure out, and measured the length of the fish.

"Forty-eight inches" Sonny said calmly. Milly walked over and licked the fish.

Ava laughed "I'm guessing the two of you have done this dance before, eh?"

"Yes, once or twice," Sonny laughed back.

Sonny then lifted the fish, went to the stern, and gently placed the fish in the water while still holding onto it. With both hands, he then moved the fish forward and backward.

"What are you doing, Sonny?"

"Before releasing a fish this size, it's important to give them a charge of oxygen across their gills. This back-and-forth motion allows this to take place. If I do this right, it will eventually start fighting again…like so." And just like that, the fish wriggled out of Sonny's hands and bolted into the depths of the river.

"Well done, Ava! I couldn't have boated that fish without your assistance. Thank you!"

Ava doubted that was true but she appreciated the compliment, nonetheless. She also appreciated how respectful he was throughout the day. He wasn't the least bit condescending toward her. He made her feel more like a teammate than an apprentice. Another thing she noted was the look of enthusiasm on Sonny's face throughout the entire process of stalking, casting, hooking, fighting, boating, and releasing the fish. Even though he'd probably caught dozens or more of these huge fish, she could sense he never got bored with this ritual. It was clear that Milly didn't either!

"My pleasure, Sonny. About how old is a 48-inch bull drum?"

"That fish is probably 30 years old."

"Wow. I can see why you were so careful in releasing it. I noticed there was some white gunk on the boat deck near the drum. Is this its sperm?"

"Quite right, Ava. But don't worry, it will produce more sperm so it can still do its thing."

"Good. It's early October now. Do these guys migrate? How long do they stay in the rivers?"

"Once their eggs are hatched in these brackish waters, the hatchlings stay in the general area until they reach sexual maturity at three years post-hatch. In the fall, they then migrate through the Pamlico Sound into the ocean, through several inlets like Ocracoke, Hatteras, and Oregon Inlet to mention a few. They then migrate up and down the North Carolina, Virginia, and South Carolina coasts and return to these waters again in the late summer and early fall to spawn."

"Sort of like salmon?"

"Similar, except red drum don't die after they spawn. And their spawning takes place in brackish waters as opposed to freshwater where salmon spawn."

"So just how big can red drum get?"

"They can grow to 60-inches and 100 pounds."

"Unbelievable! So, what now, Captain?" Ava cut off the video recording.

"Ha! I love your spirit, Ava, but I'm taking you back to Belhaven now. Our little side adventure kept us longer than planned, it's almost 4 o'clock."

Sonny was pleased that Ava looked a bit disappointed when he told her the adventure was over. "*She's got game,*" Sonny thought to himself.

Fifteen minutes later, Sonny eased *Whisker* up to the Belhaven town dock. Ava hopped off the boat onto the dock, turned and said, "What time shall I arrive tonight?"

"How about 7:30? I'll text you my address."

"Sound great. I'll see you then!"

IX. October

Five minutes later, Ava waltzed through the front door of R&R, waved to Rita in the living room, and walked up the stairs to her room. After showering, she lay across her bed, gazed through the window at the river, and reflected on her day. Although physically tired, she felt mentally exhilarated. She couldn't recall the last time she had this much fun. The wildlife viewing was insane: eagle, osprey, pelicans, and dolphin -- not to mention the fish. And Sonny was a perfect guide, companion, and captain. *"Despite his prowess with the fly rod"* Ava thought to herself, *"he seemed more interested in ensuring I had a good time than showing off. He stayed humble throughout the day, even after landing that monster red drum. And those deep blue eyes don't hurt either,"* Ava smiled.

The soft, early evening light cast a cozy blanket across her body and she slipped into a deep sleep. At 6 p.m., Ava awoke to a rapping at her door. She bolted upright and said, "Yes?"

"Would you like to join our other guests for some wine and words?" Rita inquired.

Not wanting to appear rude, Ava said, "Sure, I'll be down in five minutes. Thank you, Rita." Ava donned a powder blue sundress, brushed her hair, stepped into her sandals, and joined the other guests in the parlor.

After arriving home from the fishing adventure with Ava, Sonny washed down the boat and secured it in the boathouse. He then filleted Ava's puppy drum and placed the fillets in the fridge and the carcass in the crab pots at the end of his pier. Before submerging the pots back into the river, he plucked out four large male blue crabs, known as "Jimmies", that had been lured there from the previous 24-hour soaking. Using tongs, he placed the crabs in a large paper bag and put them in the fridge for future steaming.

Milly was intensely interested in these crabs. When she was a puppy, she made the mistake of getting her nose too close to a very angry crab as it was scuttling across the pier after Sonny dumped the crabs from the pot. The large Jimmy was not amused with Milly's curiosity and managed to get one of its sharp claws imbedded in Milly's nostril. Milly let out a yelp and flung her head skywards, releasing the crab's grip on her nose and sending it airborne and then safely into the river. Sonny was not happy about this canine-crustacean encounter either as that particular crab was the biggest one by far that season. That crab alone would have made a delicious crabcake.

Sonny didn't have the heart to yell at Milly because she really didn't do anything wrong. But Milly was a smart dog and never got pinched again. Unfortunately for the crabs, Milly held a life-long grudge against them. Every subsequent close encounter with a crab ended poorly for the crab. Milly would avoid the claws and bite through the carapace, mortally wounding the crab. Interestingly, Milly was otherwise a total beta creature with every other animal including canines and people. She wouldn't hunt or harm a living soul besides crabs. Due to Milly's hatred for crabs, Sonny carefully extracted each crab from the pot using tongs rather than dumping the crabs onto the pier. If he missed the bag and the crab hit the pier, Milly lay in wait and would at once pounce upon the poor creature.

Fortunately, Sonny was successful in bagging all four Jimmies today. He then steamed the crabs in Old Bay, vinegar, and beer. After picking the crabmeat from the hard shells, he stored it in the fridge for dinner later than evening. He then turned to the drum fillets, adding a bottled marinade before he hopped in the shower.

At 7:30 p.m. sharp, Sonny heard the crunching of gravel on his driveway. He glanced out the kitchen window in time to see a lithe blonde gracefully easing out of her white sedan. The transformation from Ava's tomboy-like outfit this morning to a simple blue sundress this evening was remarkable. Her shoulder-length blonde hair was no longer in a ponytail and flowed freely around her. Sonny gathered himself.

Before she could knock on the screen door, Sonny yelled, "Come on in, Ava." She walked inside with a smile on her lips and a bottle of wine in her hand.

"Hi, Sonny! I wasn't sure what you drank, but I figured it was safe to bring a bottle of Sauvignon Blanc from New Zealand since you are preparing fish for dinner."

"Perfect! How about you pour us a glass while I finish cooking some mini-crabcakes as an appetizer?"

"Wait a minute. You're making crabcakes? Be still my heart!" Ava exclaimed. "Where did you get crabmeat in October?"

"Remember, we are a bit farther south than you so we often get crabs until mid- to late-October. Oh, these came from my pier earlier today."

"So, you couldn't find any fresher crabmeat than that?" Ava joked.

"Ha! Only if you'd arrived an hour earlier," Sonny replied softly.

The aroma of the crabcakes placed gently on the hot iron skillet hit Ava with a pang of nostalgia. She drifted back in time to the Eastern Shore of the Chesapeake Bay. Before Ava discovered boys, she used to spend summers at her aunt and uncle's fishing "shack" in Oxford, Maryland. She and her Uncle

Jack would entice blue crabs in the marshes using chicken necks tied to a string. A long-handle net would then be used to capture the critters. After they acquired a couple of dozen crabs, they would later steam and pick them in a multiple-hour ordeal while listening to music and drinking beer (Uncle Jack) and lemonade (Ava). The steamed crabs were complemented by boiled locally grown Silver Queen corn.

"You seem lost in thought," remarked Sonny.

"Yeah, the smell of those crabcakes reminded me of my childhood," Ava replied.

"Care to elaborate?"

"Maybe later. I'm starving. When can we eat?"

"How about now? Belly up to the bar!" Sonny shot back.

Sonny placed several mini-crabcakes in a circle on a large plate with a bowl of home-made cocktail sauce in the middle.

He sat on a barstool beside Ava, grabbed a crabcake with his fingers and said, "I just dip it into the sauce and eat it whole, like so."

Ava followed suit. Before placing the crabcake in her mouth she said, "I must warn you, Sonny. My uncle made pretty good crabcakes." She then popped one into her mouth.

After consuming the crispy morsel, Ava's eyes opened wide, "Oh my God, Sonny. These are incredible!" And she meant it.

Sonny smiled humbly, "Thanks, ma'am. All in a day's work."

They made quick work of the mini-crabcakes. Ava's eyes drifted to the river. The autumn sun had already set, but the remnants of pink sunlight lingered across the Pungo.

"You have a spectacular view here. What is the history of this property?"

"Well, it was owned by a family of crabbers. The most current generation had no interest in carrying on the family tradition so I purchased it from the owner for a very reasonable price about five years ago. In fact, the price was so low that I made an offer higher than his asking price. Charlie, the owner and last remaining crabber in the family, shook his head at my higher asking price. He said, 'Sonny, my kids and grandkids have no interest in crabbing. I know you don't commercially crab full time either, but my gut tells me that you love it here and won't sell it for a quick buck. Is that right?' I assured him that I had no intention of selling this property. Even though Charlie died a few years after I bought his property, I've continued to honor that promise. In fact, I've purchased a couple of more acres immediately adjoining the property."

"So how many acres do you own now?" Ave asked.

"Just four acres," Sonny replied,

"Just four acres? Are you kidding me? Do you know how much that amount of waterfront acreage would be worth on the Chesapeake Bay?"

"It's a moot point, Ava. It wouldn't matter if it was worth a million or five million dollars. I made a promise to Charlie not to sell it and I intend to keep that promise. Besides, where else on the East Coast can you get this type of view?"

Ava's eyes drifted back to the river and she had to admit that it was indeed a unique property with a spectacular view.

"Okay, enough real estate talk. I'm going to go grill the puppy drum you caught this morning. Feel free to pour another glass of wine and make yourself at home. I'll be back in 20 minutes."

While Sonny was grilling the fish, Ava walked around the living area and noticed several framed photos of Sonny and presumably some family members hanging on the wall. One photo caught her attention. It was a man and a boy standing by a pond, each with a fly rod in hand. The man appeared to be in his middle or late thirties and the boy about 10- or 12-years-old. Each wore a half smile like they shared a secret. With that square jaw, deep blue eyes, and dimples, the boy had to be Sonny. She guessed the man was Sonny's father given his similar physique and facial features compared to present-day Sonny. She made a mental note to ask Sonny about the photo later.

Sonny returned 20 minutes later and prepared two plates of sizzling hot grilled drum fillets topped with lump backfin crab with a dill-speckled white sauce drizzled across the crabmeat. Beside the drum were several sprigs of grilled asparagus along with grill-roasted red potatoes.

"Wow! Do you eat like this every day?" Ava marveled.

"Not every day, but a couple of days a week. I vacuum seal and freeze the fillets from fish I catch during the spring, summer, and fall so I have fresh fish even during the winter months."

"I could get used to this…" Ava said after she took her fist bite. "Mmmm…this practically melts in your mouth." Ava closed her eyes and savored each subsequent bite.

"The wine you brought goes well with this meal. Thanks again for bringing it, Ava."

"Of course. It's the least I could do after such a spectacular fishing trip plus this fabulous meal."

Sonny smiled in appreciation of her compliments. As they ate their meal, the conversation centered around the events of the day. Ava observed that Sonny didn't embellish anything about their fishing adventure and, if anything, offered more praise about her puppy drum catch than the monster drum he caught. *Who is this guy*" Ava thought to herself. Most of the subjects of her articles focused on their own accomplishments not anyone else's.

After their meal and shared cleanup, Sonny poured them both a glass of wine and invited Ava to join him on the couch. They sat a few feet apart.

After a sip of wine, Sonny asked, "So you asked me a bunch of questions about my life. How about you tell me about yourself?"

"What would you like to know?"

"Well, for starters how about you tell me about your family?"

Ava paused. "I have fairly normal parents...well I did. My dad passed away about a year ago from lung cancer.

Sonny said softly, "I'm so sorry, Ava."

"Thank you," she said quietly. She paused, but Sonny could sense that she wasn't ready to talk in detail about her father yet so he just listened.

"I've got two older brothers," she continued, "which is probably why I was a bit of a tomboy growing up. I played field hockey, tennis, and basketball in high school. As you can see, I'm only five foot six inches so I played point guard on our varsity high school team."

"Was your team any good?" Sonny asked.

"Not really. But it was fun being part of a team. I also enjoyed the diversity aspect of the game – it was a chance to get to know teammates I never had the chance to be friends with otherwise."

Sonny nodded thoughtfully recalling his time playing intramural basketball during his years at UNC-Chapel Hill.

"Do you think being a jock helped you become a good sports reporter?"

Ava laughed at the word 'jock'. "Well, I'd like to think it helped me some. Even though my teams never won any championships, the commitment to being a good athlete on an average team is more-or-less the same amount of effort as athletes on championship-caliber teams. The difference is often DNA rather than effort. There are many other factors, of course, like the amount and type of competition, quality of coaching, how soon an athlete started their sport, and so on."

"Interesting. So why did you choose sports reporting as your career?"

"Good question!" she laughed. "But seriously, there are several reasons. My father got me into sports at a very early age, probably because my brothers played sports as well. Like you, he was also an outdoors person and enjoyed fishing, particularly on the Chesapeake Bay."

"Ah, that explains your proficiency with the spinning rod."

"Thank you, Sonny. My dad used to rent row boats with small outboard motors at Sandy Point State Park on the Bay. We would first catch a bunch of spot, a local baitfish, in the shallows with blood worms. We'd then move to deeper water, anchor, and live-line the spot using spinning rods. We'd catch some decent size stripers. It was a lot of fun." Ava smiled at the memories.

A shadow crossed Sonny's face upon hearing of the fond memories of Ava with her dad.

"Oh shoot. I'm sorry, Sonny. That was insensitive of me to bring up my dad given how young you were when you lost yours."

"Not at all," Sonny countered. "I enjoy hearing about your family. How about your mom?"

Ava smiled, "She is a teacher, like my dad was. She is super supportive of my career path, although not so much at my choice of earlier boyfriends."

Sonny's brow raised, "Do you have one now?"

"Not at the moment. Anyway, enough about me. If you don't mind, I'd like to learn more about you. Afterall I'm getting paid to write about you, not me!" she laughed.

Sonny loved her laugh. It was a blend of giggle and guffaw. She didn't mask her laugh either, which Sonny appreciated.

"Sure, what else would you like to know."

"I'm curious why you decided to make a career out of bass fishing rather than saltwater or brackish water fishing, especially since you grew up in these waters?"

"It's a money thing. As I mentioned to you last night, there are only a handful of professional fishing tournaments in brackish water environments. And those few tournaments don't pay much money. Conversely, there are a ton of bass fishing tournaments throughout the United States with big prize money for the top five finishers, not to mention the endorsements from various sponsors like manufacturers of boats, fishing equipment, and the like."

"Yeah, I have noticed the attire of bass fishing contestants look like those worn by professional race car drivers. Every square inch of their jackets and hats is plastered with different sponsor logos. How come your attire doesn't have any such 'artwork'?"

Sonny laughed, "Mainly because I haven't been that successful in landing sponsors! Also, I don't feel like walking around like a human billboard. It's a sore point with Dan because he claims I'm losing a lot of potential sponsors by refusing to wear such 'artwork' as you say."

"Can you afford that luxury?"

"Not really but it's just not my thing."

Ava peered closely at Sonny and tried to read him. He looked nothing but genuine. It was subtle, but somehow the two were now closer to each other on the couch.

"How about we circle back to the Big Rock Tournament in Morehead City next spring?" Ava asked.

"Okay, but how some more wine first?" Sonny offered.

"Absolutely!" Ava smiled.

After topping off both glasses, Sonny sat just a wee bit closer to Ava on the couch. They clinked glasses and took a sip. Sam Hunt, Jackson Dean, Kane Brown, and Chris Stapleton joined them in the background. As the country music wafted throughout the room, the two settled into a comfortable silence. They locked eyes and a slight smile formed on Ava's lips. Her ocean eyes were hypnotic. "*Gawd, she's beautiful*" Sonny thought wistfully.

"This could get complicated, Sonny," Ava said quietly reading his primal thoughts.

Understanding her meaning, Sonny smiled back, "I like complicated. Besides, I feel something that I can't explain when I'm around you, Ava. Unless I'm reading the tea leaves wrong, you feel it too."

Ava gazed into Sonny's azure eyes and had to admit to herself that she felt something, too. But she'd been hurt too many times in the past with men who were charming at first, until the horns eventually surfaced. Still, there was something about Sonny that seemed different.

"Maybe, Sonny, but…."

Before she could continue, Sonny slowly moved his lips to mere inches from hers.

"I'll take your maybe as a yes…" Sonny confidently whispered.

They closed the gap. The kiss was soft, but electric. The day's events were a slow burn to the story now unfolding. Their first kiss led to dozens more, each one successively more passionate than the previous one. At one point, Sonny pulled back to look briefly at her face. Her cute button nose and the splash of freckles on her nose were simply too much for him and he quickly closed the gap. She was just as hungry for his lips as he was for hers.

He then took her hand and she followed him to the bedroom. Standing beside the bed, Sonny deftly unbuttoned Ava's sundress revealing a slender, natural physique. She could no longer hide her natural beauty from him. She unclothed him as well. The two stood naked mere inches apart. Kane Brown serenaded them from the living room:

> *I don't wanna love you just for one night only*
> *This ain't just a take you home thing*
> *Pick you up and buy you one more, whatever you're drinking*
> *That ain't my style, Ain't what I'm thinking*
> *Thinking every morning with you, baby,*
> *Coffee pourin, talkin' bring you breakfast in bed*
> *A kiss on your head, again and again*
> *Girl I don't wanna love you just for one night only*
> *I don't wanna love you just for one night only…*

Sonny tenderly wrapped his arms around Ava and she eagerly accepted them. Their skin seemed to soak in the presence of the other. She tilted her head up and Sonny softly pressed his lips to hers. They kissed for several minutes until their legs became too unsteady to continue standing. They simultaneously collapsed on the bed still wrapped in each other's arms. He extracted his lips from hers and began kissing her neck, breasts, and below. As he kissed and licked his way down her body, she moaned in pleasure. He hovered between her thighs for a moment before gently licking her. The teasing was too much for Ava so she tried to pull Sonny closer but he would have none of that. She recalled his words earlier in the day, "Patience Grasshopper…" She almost laughed but didn't want to ruin the moment.

Sensing Ava's near frustration, Sonny finally applied more pressure and motion. He was a patient lover and continued pleasuring her until she could no longer hold back. So close, so close until…her back arched and she let out an explosive moan. She immediately pulled Sonny up to her face, kissed his mouth hard, and guided him inside her.

He did not resist. And yet, he was in no hurry to finish their dance. On the contrary, he wanted this sensual waltz to last all night long. He kissed her lips, nose, ears, neck, and breasts. They interlocked fingers as he thrust slowly in and out of her. He pulled apart to gaze into her dreamy green eyes. She smiled, then put her arms around Sonny's neck and drew his lips toward hers yet again. That did it. He simply could not hold out any longer…nor did he try. In a thundering moment, he released a year's worth of tension and screamed in ecstasy. He collapsed into her outstretched arms.

They lay together in stillness without a word spoken for several blissful minutes. One of Ava's arms was casually drooped over the bed. Suddenly, she felt something wet touch her fingers. She yanked her hand back up and yelled, "Yikes! What was that?"

"Milly!" Sonny said firmly. Milly slinked out from under the bed with a guilty look on her face.

"Sorry about that, Ava."

Ava laughed as she extended her hand to Milly's head. Milly eagerly licked it again, all guilt wiped clean from her face. Ava continued scratching Milly's head and said, "It's okay, Sonny. She just surprised me. Does she always do this during your um…trysts?"

"To be honest with you, I'm a bit rusty in that department. It's been quite some time," Sonny laughed.

"You could have fooled me," Ava said coyly, then kissed him softly to punctuate her thoughts.

"Anyway, Milly has a connection with you that I can't really explain. It usually takes her a lot more time to feel comfortable with a new person in my life. And sometimes she never feels it. But it was instant with you."

"I'll take that as a compliment!"

"As well you should. Dogs are excellent judges of character."

"How about you? Did you feel the same way when we first met?" Ava asked quietly.

"It's probably not very manly to admit this, but I did."

"Me, too" Ava replied in relief.

"So, where do we go from here? I mean, you're heading back to D.C. tomorrow after breakfast, right?"

Ava nodded sadly.

"I don't want this to end, do you?"

Ava shook her head and said, "No, but we live five hours apart. I'm not fond of long-distance relationships. Been there, done that."

"Understood. I had one that didn't turn out so well myself," Sonny reflected. "So, what do you think we should do?" he asked hopefully.

Ava paused long enough to provide a thoughtful response. She finally broke the silence.

"Here's an idea. How about we meet with Dan tomorrow morning, as scheduled, to discuss the idea of your participation in the Big Rock Tournament next June? If he likes it, I'll then talk to my editor -- your uncle -- and see if he'll let me continue building the story on you. If I get the green light, we can continue seeing each other during the next several months as you prepare for the tournament. I'll write several pieces on you during this period to include your training regimen, sponsorship challenges, and the like. It's October now so that would be what..." Ava started counting the months on her fingers "seven months before the Big Rock Tournament in June."

Sonny let her idea soak in. "I like it! This will give me added incentive to learn a new style of fly fishing. You do understand I have absolutely no chance of winning this tournament, right?"

"I suggest you don't volunteer those thoughts to our readers or your potential sponsors!" Ava laughed.

"Just trying to be honest, ma'am," Sonny chuckled. "I have one more important question for you."

"What's that, Sonny?"

"I was wondering if you'd like to stay the night?"

In response, Ava wrapped her arms around Sonny, pressed her naked body against his, and whispered in his ear, "I thought you'd never ask" and then lightly bit his ear lobe. They did not get much sleep that night.

The next morning, Dan was reading the local paper while sipping coffee in a booth at the Belhaven Diner. He glanced up to see Sonny and Ava saunter through the front door and sit across him in the booth with cat-ate-the-canary smiles on their faces.

"My oh my, aren't you two a sight?" Dan teased. "Rough night?"

"Is it that obvious?" Sonny asked sheepishly.

"Let's see…blood-shot eyes, and could you be sitting any closer to each other?" Dan continued, "Oh, and the knowing smiles on your faces. Neither of you should quit your day jobs to play professional poker."

"Okay, Sherlock. Do you want to hear our idea or would you rather gossip?" Sonny asked playfully.

"Oh gossip, most definitely!" Dan instantly replied. All three laughed.

Just then a middle age black woman walked up to their booth. "Hey Sonny. Coffee for you and your friend?"

"Most definitely. Crystal, this is Ava. Ava, please meet Crystal, the owner and operator of this fine establishment."

Both women smiled at each other.

After Crystal delivered two steaming cups of coffee, Sonny said smiling, "So, what were you saying, Dan?"

"About last night between you two?" Dan replied laughing.

"Okay, but no details. The Cliffs Notes version is we had a wonderful fishing adventure yesterday and hit it off over dinner last night."

"That's all I'm getting?" Dan pleaded.

"Yup," Sonny and Ava simultaneously replied.

Dan sighed, "Okay, okay. So, what is your grand idea?"

Over coffee and pancakes, Ava spelled out the plan. To his credit, Dan listened to every detail of the plan without laughing at the absurdity of it. After Ava finished, she said, "What do you think, Dan?"

"Let me answer that question with a few of my own. First, Sonny, do you think you can win that tournament?"

Sonny said, "Probably not. In fact, I doubt I'll be able to catch and boat a qualifying 400-pound blue marlin. In fact, a 300-pound blue marlin caught on a fly rod would be a world record. And the Big Rock Tournament rules wouldn't even let me take a 300-to-400-pound blue marlin to the scales."

Dan did not appear deterred. "How much are the entrance fees and expenses?"

"About $50,000," Sonny replied. Dan let out a long whistle of astonishment upon hearing that harsh financial reality.

"Do you have that kind of money?"

"You know my finances, Dan. Do I have that kind of money?"

"Nope." Dan replied flatly. "As you know, most of your recent winnings went toward your outstanding debts."

Sonny nodded sadly.

"Let's skip past the financial barriers for a minute and assume that we somehow come up with the money. What do you hope to accomplish by entering a tournament that you say, in your own words, Sonny, have almost no chance of winning?"

Ava answered on behalf of Sonny, "The publicity alone could put Sonny on the map. According to Sonny, no fly fisherman has ever entered the Big Rock Tournament. I'm guessing he could get sponsorships from fly rod and fly reel manufacturers, not to mention manufacturers of related gear."

"So how can I help?" Dan asked.

"I was thinking that you could negotiate contracts with the manufacturers and I'll continue writing stories about Sonny's training and preparation for a tournament that he has no business entering in the first place."

"Thanks for your confidence," Sonny smirked.

"You're welcome," Ava replied, ignoring Sonny's sarcasm. Speaking to Dan, she said, "Given the longshot odds here, I think we'll need some additional people on our team."

"Agreed," Dan said.

"Hello? I'm right here." Sonny cut in.

"And we're so glad you are," Ava smiled sweetly at Sonny. Looking back at Dan, Ava continued, "PR is going to be critical to get sponsors, right?"

"Yes," Dan agreed. "But won't your articles help gain some attention?"

"Hopefully, but we're a small paper compared to our competitors, so that probably won't be enough to land any serious sponsors. Do you have any contacts at fishing trade magazines?"

"I've got a few I could reach out to."

"Great!" Ava finally turned to Sonny, "So who else do you need on our team?"

"Finally," Sonny laughed, "She seeks my opinion!" But Sonny was secretly pleased that she referred to their little group as 'our team'.

"For starters, I know very little about big game fly fishing. So, I'm going to need to reach out to my offshore fly fishing friends and get a crash course on that type of fishing."

"Do you have anyone in mind?" Ava asked.

"Actually, I do but he's a bit unorthodox," Sonny said.

"Pipes?" Dan queried.

"Yup," Sonny replied.

A shadow crossed Dan's face.

"When you say 'unorthodox', can you expand on that? Also, is 'Pipes' his real name?" Ava asked.

"The reason he's called 'Pipes' is because he snores as loud as a set of bagpipes."

"And the unorthodox part?"

"He's a bit like Boo Radley from 'To Kill a Mockingbird'. He absolutely abhors the limelight. He's caught more big game fish on the fly rod than anyone I know. But here's the thing. You'd never know it because he doesn't bring attention to himself. He's not on social media of any kind. And you never hear him brag about the impressive fish he's boated. In short, he loves fly fishing for the pure joy of it."

"So, if he's so reclusive, how did you meet in the first place?" Ava asked.

"It was pure accident, really. We met about 10 years ago in Weldon, North Carolina. Every spring, striped bass, or rockfish as you call them in your region, migrate up the Roanoke River from the Albemarle Sound and Atlantic Ocean. They often spawn near Weldon. It's a fantastic fishery and it's not unusual to catch more than a hundred stripers on the fly rod in a single day. Seeing the stripers erupt on the surface during the spawn is an unforgettable sight. My friends refer to this event as 'sex on the water'." Dan did not miss the knowing glance that Sonny and Ava briefly exchanged.

Sonny continued, "Anyway, I was backing an old skiff down the boat ramp in Weldon to begin my fly fishing adventure for the day. I co-owned that boat with a Marine friend of mine named Gordo. He couldn't make that trip so I went solo that day. We affectionately named the boat *The Minnow* because something always seemed to go wrong with that boat. Sure enough, when I tried to start the outboard motor, nothing happened. I tried repeatedly, but no luck. After about 10 minutes of this futile effort, I heard a quiet voice in the next ramp over say, 'May I help you?'. I looked over and saw this large, forty-ish teddy bear of a man with a full beard. His appearance did not match his subdued voice. I said, 'Sure, have at it!'. He opened the motor cowl and gave a quick glance inside the motor works. He gently pulled on a wire and said, 'The battery wire is loose. It probably came loose on your drive here. Do you have a wrench?' I handed him a wrench from a boat compartment and he tightened it. 'Now try cranking the motor.' Sure enough, it fired right up!

"I thanked him and asked him if he had a boat. He said no, he was just fishing from the bank with his fly rod. I asked him if he'd like to join me for the day and he said, 'that would be lovely.' I almost laughed because those words did not seem to fit with this big burly man.

"After parking my truck, we hopped on the *Minnow* and motored down river. He extended a huge hand and said, 'I'm Pipes.' We spent the next 10 hours catching stripers with our fly rods. For a large man, he was surprisingly elegant with his fly-casting. Even though it was keeper season for stripers, we released every striper we caught. His flies were a work of art and it was clear how meticulous a fly-tyer he was. He was out-fishing me about two-to-one and rather than brag about it, he did his best to help improve my catch rate. He offered some of his flies to me which I gladly accepted. My catch rate instantly improved! I'm not sure that's a testament to how ugly my flies were or the high quality of his flies. Probably both.

"The more we fished, the more he opened up. He was going through a rough patch in his personal life at that time. I offered him no advice because who the hell am I to offer advice to a stranger, right? Anyway, I just listened. Pipes seemed to appreciate that. As the sun went down, I asked him if he'd like to go back to the boat ramp. Even after fishing all day, he looked a bit disappointed when I suggested we head back. He then asked me, 'Would you like to continue fishing, Sonny? The big ones often come out after dark.' I replied, 'Is the Pope

Catholic?' to which Pipe laughed out loud for the first time that day."

"This is very interesting, Sonny" Ava jumped in, "But is this story going anywhere?"

"Patience, Grasshopper." Sonny replied.

Ava rolled her eyes. She then shot a pleading look at Dan for help.

"Don't look at me, Ava. When Sonny gets on a roll with his stories, there's no stopping him."

Sonny barreled on. "I'm near the end, okay? It was pitch black but we were still catching stripers. Our boat was the only one remaining on the river -- all the other boats left at sundown. As Pipes predicted, after sundown, the stripers were mostly bigger than the ones we caught during the daylight hours. During the day, most of the stripers were between 18- and 20-inches. But some of the stripers at night were up to 28-inches in length. At about 9 p.m., Pipes said, 'How about we catch one more striper each and then call it quits?' I was tired by then, so I agreed. Almost at once, I caught a 25-inch striper and safely released it like the others caught that day.

"I then glanced over at Pipes and saw his fly rod double over. I asked him if he snagged a rock on the bottom. He replied, 'I don't think so. Look at my rod'.

"I aimed my headlamp at his rod tip and noticed it was dancing up and down. 'Holy shit! That's a big fish, Pipes!'

"Pipes was grinning ear to ear and said, 'Yes sir, it certainly is!'. Pipes's rod was clearly under matched for that size fish, but Pipes was not. Instead of horsing that fish in like most anglers would, including myself, Pipes patiently played that leviathan for 45 minutes. When Pipes finally got the fish close to the boat, it made another run and started circling the boat. On the second circle around the boat, Pipes calmly said, 'I'm hooked'.

"I replied, 'I know you are. It's a big fish'."

'You don't understand. My ass is hooked to your fly rod.'

"I glanced down with my headlamp and sure enough, a fly from one of the fly rods stored in the rod rack was hooked deeply into Pipes's ass. Pipes was literally tethered to the rod. Meanwhile the striper found its second wind and took off again, pulling more fly line from the reel so the fish didn't break the 17-pound test tippet. I quickly leaned down and bit the line connecting the fly and Pipes's ass with my teeth thus freeing up Pipes to continue the fight. About ten more minutes passed until the fish finally surfaced near the boat. I took one look at that fish and said a bit nervously, 'That fish will NOT fit inside my net!'

"To which Pipes confidently replied, 'We'll make it work, Sonny.' And amazingly, we somehow managed to net that fish. And she was indeed a beast weighing 43 pounds on my electronic scale. Eggs were spewing out all over the deck. I took some quick pictures of the fish and asked Pipes if he would like to keep her since it was still keeper season. Pipes looked almost insulted by the question and replied, "Not on your life. Look how many eggs she's kicking out right now. I'm going to revive her and safely release her so she can do her thing.' And that is exactly what he did. Without a grimace, he then plucked the fly that was imbedded in his ass during the fight," Sonny laughed.

He continued, "After arriving home, I did some research and discovered if Pipes sacrificed that fish and had it weighed on a certified scale, it would have been a North Carolina state record for the largest striper ever caught on a fly rod. After my research, I called Pipes and informed him of my discovery. I asked him if I could submit the striper pictures to some local papers and national fly fish magazines. His instant reply was 'Absolutely not!'.

"Puzzled by his response, I asked him 'Why not? This is a significant catch. If we don't do this, no one will know about your achievement'."

'Not true. You know about it. I fly fish for several reasons, but publicity is not one of them.'

"We became instant friends and from that day forward, we've met every year in April or May for a day or two on the Roanoke. He also visits me at my Belhaven cottage to fly fish for the big drum every fall. He's traveled all over the world in search of expanding the number of species to catch on a fly rod. God knows how many potential world record species he's caught. But no one knows this because he's so averse to publicity. But I do know blue marlin is one of the fish species he's caught because he sent me a picture of one that weighed about 300 pounds."

"Wait a minute," Ava interrupted, "Wouldn't that have been a world record blue marlin on the fly rod?"

"Absolutely! You remembered our conversation last night!" Sonny beamed.

"Well, most of it, anyway," she trailed off. Now it was her turn to blush.

Dan jumped in "Okay, now I get the point of your story, Sonny. You want Pipes to be part of our team because of his expertise catching blue marlin, right?"

Sonny nodded, "Exactly. There's only one problem."

"Yes?" Ava and Dan asked simultaneously.

"He has a phobia about the press. For that matter, he's pretty gun shy about being around people in general."

"It's true, Ava. I've never met Pipes either, although I knew a man who shared the same nickname," Dan said quietly.

"How about you let me work on that angle?" Ava smiled confidently.

"I have to admit, if anyone could convince Pipes to change his stance on that issue, it would be you," Sonny laughed.

"Agreed," Dan added.

"Okay then, we've got a good start here. There's seven months before the tournament," Ava said. "Sonny, how about you talk to Pipes to see if he's willing to join our team? Dan, can you start working on some sponsors? And I'll write an article about my fishing trip with Sonny yesterday with a teaser at the end about the Big Rock Tournament. Anything else?"

"I like this gal, Sonny," Dan smiled.

"Yeah, me too," Sonny agreed.

"Hey guys, I'm still in the room!" Ava giggled.

Dan raised his coffee mug and said, "To Team Sonny!" All three clinked mugs, "To Team Sonny!"

X. March

The next few months were a whirlwind of activity for Team Sonny. Ava's article on her October fishing adventure with Sonny on the Pamlico and Pungo Rivers and plans to participate in the Big Rock Tournament did indeed attract some publicity and sponsor interest. Dan used Ava's article to successfully land sponsors from a fly rod manufacturer, a fly reel manufacturer, a fly line manufacturer, and even a local pork rind company. Afterall, North Carolina is the second largest hog producing state in the country, so Dan figured it was worth a shot.

The biggest challenge in landing these sponsors was Sonny's reluctance to plaster patches and decals over his attire and boat. He was adamant about not looking like a human billboard. They reached a compromise when Sonny reluctantly agreed to allow the strategic placement of a few tasteful sponsor patches on his shirt and hat. Besides, there was no point in adding decals to Sonny's boat because he would be chartering a larger, ocean worthy boat for the Big Rock Tournament rather than his smaller bass boat.

Despite landing these sponsors, Team Sonny was still about $25,000 short of their $50,000 goal to enter and take part in the Big Rock Tournament, which was just three months away. Sonny, Ava, and Dan met virtually on Zoom every week or two to check on the team's progress. Ava started the conversation tonight from her apartment in Georgetown.

"Good evening, gentlemen! So, how's the sponsorship game going, Dan?"

"We've seemed to hit a brick wall," Dan answered. "The few sponsors that have signed on will only put a minimum stake in our team because of Sonny's unproven track record with offshore fly fishing."

"Hmmm…so what are our other options?"

"I might have another funding option," Sonny volunteered.

"What's that?" Dan asked.

"I'm not exactly sure, but Alan invited Ava and me to his cottage this Saturday night to discuss it over dinner. Ava, are you still a go to visit me this weekend?" Sonny asked hopefully.

"Of course! I'll be at your place by early Friday evening if that works for you?"

"Absolutely!"

"Don't mind me," Dan cut in playfully.

Milly barked in support of Dan's slighting comment. She was standing next to Sonny and was transfixed to the computer screen since tiny versions of two of her favorite people were side-by-side on the screen.

"Hush yourselves," Ava laughed. "And, Milly, I'll see you soon!" Milly barked again. But her tail did what it always did at the sound of Ava's voice – it spun like a helicopter blade.

"I'll check in with you two next week. Good luck with Alan on Saturday night!" They all signed off.

Friday night couldn't come too soon for both Ava and Sonny. As soon as Ava pulled onto Sonny's gravel driveway, Milly burst out the screen door and greeted Ava before she could even open the car door.

"How do you like my burglar alarm?" Sonny called out from the porch.

"Oh, it's a fierce one for sure," Ava laughed. After easing out of the car, she stooped down, scratched Milly's head, and said, "How's my girl doing? Did you miss me?" Milly responded by licking Ava's nose and wagging her tail.

Sonny walked down the steps toward Ava and said, "I can't speak for Milly, but I can tell you one thing. I certainly missed you!" He then wrapped his arms around Ava and planted a long passionate kiss on her lips.

"Me too!" she agreed and initiated the next kiss. She pulled apart from Sonny's lips and said, "Let me freshen up, okay?" Sonny nodded as they held hands and walked inside.

A few minutes later, Ava walked out of the bathroom wearing nothing but her panties.

"How about a drink?" Sonny offered from the kitchen. He then glanced up and froze at the beautiful sight in front of him.

"I've got a better idea," Ava said coyly. She then took his hand and led him to the bedroom. Sonny did not resist.

An hour later, they lay naked and satiated on Sonny's bed. Still out of breath, Sonny panted, "Damn, I missed you!"

Ava laughed, "That makes two of us, cowboy."

She snuggled up to his chest while he gently stroked her head. They lay in comfortable silence for several minutes before Ava whispered, "Do you know one thing I really like about you, Sonny?"

"Just one thing?" Sonny chided.

"Oh, stop it. I'm trying to say something nice here," Ava laughed.

"I'm sorry, please continue," Sonny replied.

"We've been seeing each other for about four months now and you have yet to ask me about any previous boyfriends. Why is that, Sonny?"

"Look. We both have a past, Ava. I don't want to judge you on any of your previous relationships, just as I hope you don't judge me on mine. I'd prefer to focus on the present, not the past. I'm just grateful that, for whatever reason, you have decided to see me."

"Are you curious if I'm seeing anyone else?" Ava queried.

"I don't feel it's my place to ask you that question. Afterall, we live five hours apart. You're a beautiful, intelligent woman who interacts with celebrities far richer and more famous than me as part of your job. I'm sure you get many offers."

"So, you're a celebrity now?" Ava teased.

"Hardly. And you KNOW I'm not rich," Sonny laughed. "But I think you get my drift."

"I do. How would you feel if I told you I wasn't seeing anyone else?" Ava asked.

"I would feel pretty damn good to tell you the truth. And a bit surprised," Sonny admitted.

"Don't sell yourself short, Sonny" Ava said encouragingly. "You have a lot more going on than you give yourself credit for."

"Hey, didn't you just end your sentence with a preposition? And you call yourself a writer?" To which Ava responded by playfully pinching his arm.

"Ouch! That hurt!" It's time for me to punish you for that" after which he started tickling Ava mercilessly.

"No please, Sonny." She giggled, squirming to get away. "I'll do anything if you just stop tickling me!"

Sonny stopped tickling her. "Anything?" Sonny asked hopefully.

"Anything," Ava whispered, as she wrapped her arms around Sonny's neck and drew his lips toward hers.

The next morning, a beam of sunlight crept across Ava's closed lids. She slowly pried her eyes open and absorbed the river view. A cacophony of sounds greeted her as gulls, cormorants, osprey, and pelicans danced above and under the water. In the four months she'd been seeing Sonny, she had yet to tire of this view. Nor did she think she ever would. She turned around in bed to face Sonny, but he was gone. Just then, the aroma of fresh coffee stirred her olfactory senses into a blissful awakening. She smiled and said to herself, '*Bless you, Sonny!*' She donned one of Sonny's T-shirts, poured a hot cup of coffee, and joined him on the deck.

"Good morning, Sunshine!" Sonny smiled.

"Good morning, Fisherman," Ava said as she softly kissed his lips.

She sat in the porch chair next to Sonny, took her first sip of coffee, and asked "What's the plan for today?"

"As you can see, it's a beautiful morning. How about I give you a fly fishing lesson from the pier, we grab some lunch, make love, and then head over to Alan's for dinner?"

"Ha! I like how you subtly squeezed in that afternoon activity as just another punch list item," Ava laughed.

"Do you mean lunch? Hey, a guy's gotta eat, right?" Sonny shot his most innocent look toward Ava. "Oh, you mean that other thing," Sonny chuckled. "Speaking of food, how about some breakfast?"

"Yes please. I'm famished!"

Over a hot breakfast of scrambled eggs, bacon, grits, and toast, Ava asked, "Do you have any idea what Alan has cooked up for our team as far as fundraising goes?"

"Not a clue, but I trust his judgment. I suggest we go there tonight with an open mind and see what he has to say, okay?"

"Sound good to me. He seems like a straight shooter."

Sonny nodded in agreement. "Almost too much so at times."

"How do you mean?"

"He's been accused of not having many social filters. But at least you know where you stand with him, which I really appreciate. And if he gives you his word, you can bank it."

"You mentioned that he has two children, Holly and Colt, right" Ava asked.

Sonny nodded.

"Does Alan have a wife?"

A cloud crossed Sonny's face. After a long pause he said "Alan was married to a wonderful woman named Jean. But sadly, she died about twenty years ago from pancreatic cancer. She never smoked, took drugs, or consumed much alcohol. But, as you know, cancer can hit anyone regardless of their age, gender, race, or lifestyle. Alan is in his sixties now and, despite the encouragement from his kids to find another partner, he has yet to find or even seek one for that matter. Whatever religious beliefs Alan may have had prior to Jean's death, they seem to have evaporated the day she died."

"That is so sad," Ava commiserated.

"Yes, but Alan had two kids to raise so he pushed aside his grief so he could focus on them. Of course, they were devastated as well. Alan did his best to provide help for them. He ensured they were offered counseling support and he made sure they maintained family traditions with both sides of the family. Alan has since drifted a bit apart from Jean's side of the family, but the kids are still very much involved with their mom's siblings and all the cousins. Even though this extended family is filled with wonderful people, I think it hurts Alan too much to be around Jean's side of the family without her."

"Wait a minute," Ava searched her memory. "Isn't Jean's death about the same time as your father's?"

Sonny looked down and quietly answered, "Yes it was. Jean died about six months before my dad."

"Oh, so that probably explains why Alan took you under his wing, eh?" Ava asked.

"Perhaps, but he never tried to insert himself into my life or my brother's for that matter. Alan was more like an uncle than a father. I always appreciate that about him. And since his kids were near my age, we were like cousins and hung out a good bit during my childhood. This is a small town, Ava. When people need help, it often just arrives, unasked. Alan was like that. Despite his own tragic loss, he just showed up at our doorstep shortly after my dad died and took me fishing. Instead of pitying me, he didn't mention one word about my dad. We just fished. It was the perfect antidote for where I was."

"And how did your younger brother handle the loss of your dad?"

"Dill was always closer to our mom than our dad so, while devastating, he seemed to manage the loss better than I did."

"Plus, you were…right…there…when it happened, Sonny." Ava said empathetically. "I can't imagine the impact that had on you." She held his hand while saying this.

Sonny's eyes clouded over as he reflected on that terrible day. He shook his head briefly to cast off the memory. "It's okay, that was a long time ago." But Ava could sense the wound was still deep.

Sonny continued, "You lost your dad about a year ago, right? That's still pretty fresh. How are you handling that?"

Tears welled up in Ava's eyes, "Honestly, I'm still processing it. While I miss him terribly, it was horrible to see him wither away toward the end. Do you know when I miss him the most?"

Sonny shook his head

"Right after a Skins game. Win or lose, we would call the other and either commiserate with their loss or rejoice in their victory." Ava smiled at the memory. Sonny smiled, too.

After a long pause, Ava said, "Enough gloom and doom. How about that fly fishing lesson you promised?"

"Most definitely!" Sonny replied, grateful for the topic change. He added, "Just so you know, people make a big deal about how complicated fly fishing is, but it's not that hard once you learn the basics. Come on, let's go!" Sonny said encouragingly.

After a quick cleanup of the breakfast dishes, Ava and Sonny were standing on his private pier on the Pungo River. He held a fly rod in his right hand so comfortably, Ava observed, that it appeared to be an extension of his arm. He began the lesson.

"Fly fishing can be as simple or complicated as you wish."

"I like simple," Ava cut it with a grin.

"Ha! I thought you might" Sonny laughed. He continued, "For simplicity's sake, I'm going to focus on some fly fishing techniques I use to catch puppy drum, speckled trout, and flounder. As you know, one can often find those species in these brackish waters. We'll start with the equipment and types of flies and then move on to fly-casting, retrieving the line, hooking, and landing the fish. Sound good?"

"Aye aye, Captain!" Ava playfully answered.

"Okay then. Here we go…"

Several hours after checking off all the boxes on Sonny's activity list including some bedroom fun, they pulled into a long dirt driveway leading to Alan's rustic cottage on the Pamlico River. Dusk was approaching, but they could still make out three figures near the river bulkhead throwing some bean bags.

As Sonny's pickup inched closer to the river, it was clear that a spirited cornhole game was underway with Alan and two thirty-something adults. The funny thing was the most animated of the three players was Alan! He threw his arms up in protest. Ava and Sonny could hear Alan say, "the bag did NOT hit the dirt before landing on the board!" Simultaneously the other players said, "Dad, yes it DID!"

Ava turned to Sonny with a broad smile and said, "So Alan has no social filters AND he's competitive, right?"

"Yup," Sonny laughed.

After parking the truck, the young woman ran over to Sonny and wrapped her arms around him for a long hug. "Boy, am I glad you all showed up. Dad is NOT happy right now!"

"Let me guess. Your dad is losing to you both?"

"You got it." Turning to Ava, the woman smiled and said, "You must be Ava. Hey. I'm Holly. Nice to meet you."

Ava smiled in return, "It's a pleasure to meet you as well, Holly." Ava extended her hand but Holly brushed it aside and, instead, wrapped her arms around Ava. "Sorry, but I'm a hugger."

"That's quite alright." as she readily accepted Holly's hug. Ava accurately sensed the relationship between Holly and Sonny was platonic rather than romantic, despite their closeness in age.

The other men finally caught up to Holly. The young man was tall and slender, about 6 foot 4 inches.

"Hey, Sonny" they said.

"Hey, Colt. Hey, Alan," Sonny replied as he shook their hands. "Alan, you know Ava." Alan dropped his competitive facade for the moment and shot Ava a big smile which she instantly returned. "Colt, this is Ava. Ava, this is Colt." Colt extended his hand which she warmly accepted.

Stirring the pot Sonny asked, "So who's winning the game?"

"Don't go there, Sonny!" Holly hissed.

"Just kidding," Sonny quickly replied.

They all laughed, even Alan.

Ava soaked in her surroundings for the first time and was astounded at the view. They stood under a canopy of mature live oak trees. The sun was just setting on the river and cast an orange and pink hue above it. Pelicans were diving halfway across the river which had to be four or five miles wide from where they stood.

Ava exclaimed, "My God, Alan. Do you ever tire of this view?"

"Never," Alan replied softly. "Just wait. It gets even prettier after the sun goes down."

"I can't imagine it looking any prettier than this." Ava said wistfully. She was tempted to pull out her cellphone and take some pictures, but something held her back. Perhaps, she wanted to remember this view from her mind rather than a photo. She wasn't sure why, but she was confident it was the right decision.

"We've got enough daylight for another game of cornhole" Alan offered.

"Okay, but you're going to ref, Dad," Holly replied with conviction.

Alan visibly slumped but begrudgingly agreed, "Alright. Teams?"

Ava volunteered, "Holly and me against the boys?"

"Done!" Colt instantly replied.

Knowing her brother's athleticism, Holly glanced at Ava as if to say, "Are you crazy?" but caught Ava's wink. She shrugged and said, "Okay."

Colt then mumbled to Sonny, "This will be a massacre."

Hearing this, Ava suggested, "Loser does dishes?"

"Absolutely!" Colt replied. "Would you two like a few warmup tosses?" Colt asked Sonny and Ava.

Answering for both, Ava said, "That's okay, Colt. We'll warm up during the game."

"How about we adjust the distance between boards by gender to make it fairer?" Colt teased.

"So, you boys want to stand closer to the boards than us? Nah, that wouldn't be fair, would it?" Ava shot back.

Holly laughed, "I like your spirit, Ava!"

"Yeah, me too," Sonny smiled. "You heard the lady, Colt. Let's go!"

A few minutes later, Sonny and Ava stood by one Cornhole board while Holly and Colt stood by the opposite board.

Holly and Colt threw the first set of bags. Holly landed two bags on the board but Colt landed two of his bags on the board plus one through the hole. Score: Boys 3, Girls 0.

Sonny's first toss landed on the board just in front of the hole. Ava's first toss hit the dirt just in front of the board. She did not account for the stiff breeze coming off the water.

Talking a bit of smack, Sonny said, "It's not too late to cancel the bet, Ava".

"Not on your life!" Ava replied with a grimace.

Sonny's next toss found the board just above the hole.

Ava then calmly threw the next bag which landed on the board just left of the hole.

"Nice toss, partner!" Holly yelled.

Sonny's third toss found the hole. As did Ava's.

Sonny's fourth toss slid by the hole and crept off the board. Ava's fourth toss whooshed through the hole. Holly whooped, "Yay, girl!"

Alan announced the score: "Boys 3, Girls 2"

Sonny glanced at Ava, "Hmm, something tells me that you've played this game before."

Ava smiled sweetly and replied in a faux Southern accent, "Now whatever do you mean, Darlin'?"

The game went back and forth until the score was 20 points Boys to 19 points Girls. Sonny and Ava were up for the next tosses.

Alan announced the score and reminded the teams that the first team to score at least 21 points wins.

Sonny tossed first. His bag sailed right through the hole.

"Game, set, match," Colt goaded.

"Not so fast, cowboy," Ava replied and threw her bag through the hole as well.

"Yes!" Holly exclaimed.

Sonny's next toss found the hole as well. Ava matched his toss.

Sonny's third toss hit the board and slid into the hole.

"Way to go, partner!" yelled Colt.

Although Holly visibly slumped, she said encouragingly, "Come on, partner!"

Ava did not disappoint. Her third bag hit the left side of the hole and barely slipped through.

"Yay!" Holly screamed.

Alan announced, "The score remains 20 to 19, Boys."

The fourth bag that Sonny tossed hit the front of the board and slid right up to the hole and hung about halfway over.

"Great toss, Sonny" Colt yelled. "Your bag is virtually blocking the entire hole. If Ava's bag even touches your bag, it will slip through. The best they can score is one point which would give us both zero for the round. I'll take care of business on my end," glancing cockily at his sister. Holly glared back at her 'little' brother.

Ava started casually tossing the final bag from one hand to the other while she stared at Sonny, "Do you remember me telling you about picking crabs on the Eastern Shore of the Chesapeake Bay during my youth?"

Sonny looked puzzled at the topic change but nodded.

Ava continued, "Well, they had cornhole boards for kids who filled up on crabs before their parents did. I became quite good at the game. I not only beat the other children but also most of the adults. In fact, I played on cornhole club leagues during my college years and won several tournaments." Still looking at Sonny, she then tossed her final bag high in the air and turned her head just in time to see her bag sail through the hole missing Sonny's bag entirely.

Alan announced in a formal voice, "Final score: Girls 21, Boys 20."

Stunned silence ensued for a moment before Holly yelped, "WHAT? Yes!" She immediately ran over to her partner and high fived, fist-bumped, and hugged her. They then did a little victory dance because Holly rarely beat her brother at anything remotely athletic.

Sonny shook his head and just laughed. Colt did not like to lose, but begrudgingly congratulated both women on their victory.

"Who's hungry?" Alan asked the group.

"I'm famished!" Ava replied.

"Well, you've come to the right place then. Afterall, 'Pamlico' is an Algonquian word that means plentiful." Alan said.

"I did not know that" Ava said sincerely.

Alan continued, "For many centuries, the Algonquian people lived right here along this riverbank. In fact, two of our neighbors, Robbie and Kimmy, found some Algonquian pottery shards buried in the sand of a nearby beach and sent them to an archaeology professor at East Carolina University in Greenville for analysis. He figured out the pottery was over 2,000 years old!"

"Wow!" Ava exclaimed.

"Yeah and…."

Exasperated, Colt cut in," How about we delay the history lesson until after dinner, Dad? I'm starving."

"Of course. You're right, son. Everybody, please come inside."

Ava, Sonny, and Colt grabbed seats around a large round table in a glass sunroom overlooking the river. In the kitchen, Holly prepared appetizers and a pitcher of margaritas while Alan stirred a large pot on the stove and put something in the oven. Heavenly aromas of fresh baked bread and seafood permeated the cottage. Ava smiled to herself as she noted how well Holly and Alan worked together in the kitchen. She rightly figured this father-daughter cooking team was solidified after the loss of Alan's wife during the kids' teen years.

Alan and Holly joined the others with apps and drinks. After pouring everyone a margarita, Alan raised his filled glass and said to the group, "To Team Sonny!" and they all clinked glasses and took a sip.

Ava said, "I don't know if your dad mentioned this, but we caught your Brother-Sister act at Tommy's Tavern a few months ago."

Holly cut in, "I prefer to think of us as a Sister-Brother duo. Afterall, I'm five years older than Colt."

Ava laughed, "I stand corrected. You two are terrific! Did you write that Pamlico song?"

Holly beamed, "Yup, I did.."

"Well, I think it's really good -- good enough to be sold commercially" Ava declared.

"Thanks for the compliment, but I'm not sure there is a market for something so specific to this area. But speaking of markets, I've got a fundraising idea to help Sonny raise money for the Big Rock Tournament in June. Afterall, that's why we're here tonight, right?"

Everybody nodded.

"Okay, let's hear it, Holly," Sonny said encouragingly.

Holly continued, "You've heard of 'Go Fund Me', right? Well, there is a new fundraising operation called "Sports Support Now" or SSN that is geared specifically to help raise money for promising sports men and women without means for things like training, sports camps, tournament entrance fees, travel expenses, and the like."

"Sports Support Now? Sounds like a jock strap," quipped Colt.

Ignoring her brother's snide comment, Holly continued, "Anyway, SSN might be a legal way for us to raise money for Sonny's participation in the Big Rock Tournament."

"Exactly what does 'without means' mean?" Sonny asked.

"From what I've read so far, it sounds like the average income for eligible participants needs to be less than $80,000 for each of the prior three years. And I'm pretty sure you meet this qualification. If you agree to pursue this, Sonny, I'll take care of the SSN paperwork and ask Dan to help with marketing."

Looking at Ava, Alan said with pride, "Holly is an excellent grant writer. She's won several grants on behalf of Belhaven

High School where she teaches English." Both Sonny and Colt nodded in agreement.

"Thanks, Dad. So, what do you think, Sonny?"

"Sadly, I do meet the income requirements. I don't really see much downside, do you?" Sonny glanced at Ava.

"I don't either," Ava agreed. Then, turning to Holly, Ava asked, "What happens if we don't reach our goal? Can we still use the money that was raised?"

"There's the rub," Holly replied. "If the goal is not achieved, then all the money must be returned to the donors. But if you exceed the funding goal, you can't accept any money above it. This prevents people from picking a ridiculously low funding goal."

Sonny nodded thoughtfully, "So the bottom line is we need to pick a financial goal that covers our expenses but can still be achieved, right?"

"Exactly," Holly responded.

"Seems fair to me," Sonny added. He then turned to Alan and asked, "Alan, do you still own that cottage in Beaufort?"

Alan nodded. Sonny continued, "I'm going to need a place to stay a few weeks before plus the six days during the tournament. Since Beaufort is only 10 minutes from the Big Rock weigh-in site in Morehead City, I was wondering if I could rent it from you during this period?"

Alan shook his head, "Absolutely not!"

Sonny hid his disappointment and just nodded his head. "I understand."

Now smiling, Alan said, "No you don't. I won't rent it to you, but you can stay at the cottage at no charge."

Sonny held his hands up in protest, "No way, Alan. That is a prime rental period for you."

"Too late, Sonny. I've already reserved the cottage for you for those dates. There will be no more discussion on this topic."

Stunned, Sonny said, "Thank you, Alan."

Mostly silent to this point, Colt said quietly, "I'll so some research on your Big Rock Competitors to determine the most likely winning boats."

"Colt is an absolute genius with analytics and numbers in general," Alan said pridefully.

Colt brushed aside the compliment with a wave of his hand.

"That would be terrific, Colt. Thanks!" Sonny said.

Just then, the kitchen timer started beeping.

"Ah, dinner is ready!" Alan chimed in enthusiastically.

A few minutes later, they all dined on hot seafood bisque, warm bread, and salad. After her first spoonful of soup, rich in shrimp, backfin crabmeat, fish, bacon, potatoes and savory spices in a creamy base, Ava exclaimed, "My God, Alan. This soup is incredible! How did you get your hands on this much fresh seafood in March?"

Alan smiled at the compliment, "Strictly speaking it's not truly 'fresh', as the seafood was caught or trapped last summer. But I vacuum-sealed and froze the seafood shortly after harvesting."

"Well, it tastes fresh to me. Mmm...so good!" after sipping another spoonful of the creamy nectar.

Ava's eyes then drifted to the river. Although the sun was well past setting, an orange-indigo painting covered the horizon above the water surface. She couldn't recall a time in her life where she felt this calm and comfortable with a group of people in such a magnificent environment. She fast-forwarded for a moment dreading the thought of fighting D.C. traffic the next day. Just as quickly though, she pushed those stressful thoughts aside and decided, instead, to focus on this evening, Sonny, and these fine people.

After the dishes were cleaned by the Boys, the five adjourned to the pier with two fingers of Buffalo Trace Bourbon in each tumbler. There was a spring chill in the night air and the stars and planets popped out like beacons of light. Ava turned to Holly and said, "I can see where you get your inspiration for your songs."

"Yup. If this doesn't move you, I don't know what will."

Ava nodded.

Sonny quietly addressed the group. "As many of you know, I've had a few knocks in my life. But I can't recall a time in my life when I've had this many people in my corner. Win or lose the Big Rock, I'd like to thank each of you for your support on this journey," Sonny held up his tumbler and the others clinked theirs against his. Although it was dark, Ava caught a glimpse of a tear inching down Sonny's face. If anyone else noticed, they didn't let on.

XI. May

"Damn it!" Sonny yelled. Turning to Pipes, Sonny pleaded, "Why can't I get that beast to hit my fly?" He peered at the frothing ocean water behind their chartered 42-foot offshore boat, fittingly named *Fly Knot?*, as first mate Mason scattered bait in the froth behind the stern to entice blue marlin to the surface. This strategy was working, too, because a small blue marlin was indeed popping up and down devouring the bait near the surface just behind the boat. However, it completely ignored Sonny's fly. He was reluctant to tie *Percival* to the leader of his fly rod just yet, as he did not want to risk a break-off. Plus, no one else knew about the magic fly, including Pipes. But if he didn't get the experience of a hooking and boating a blue marlin soon, he would have virtually no chance of boating one during the tournament next week. "*One week!*" Sonny thought grimly.

Laughing, Pipes said, "You're trying too hard, Sonny. Slow your retrieve down."

Frustrated, Sonny reflected on the past two months. Everyone on his team was doing their jobs but him. It wasn't for lack of trying, that was for sure. As Pipes implied, perhaps he was trying too hard. The day after the team departed from Alan's Pamlico River cottage in March, Holly started the funding ball rolling by completing the paperwork for SSN. Ava wrote a couple of nice pieces in the *Tribune* on Sonny, including her fishing day on the Pamlico and Pungo Rivers with a few important omissions, of course. He smiled briefly at those omissions. Each article was gaining more and more traction. When she finally disclosed Sonny's intentions of taking part in the Big Rock Tournament, the response was explosive. The fact that no fly fisherman had ever taken part in the Big Rock

Tournament was compelling enough. Combine that with the human-interest story that Sonny was just a hard-luck, regular guy from a small North Carolina coastal town with no big game fishing experience created a David and Goliath story that resonated with many readers and viewers, whether they were fishing fans or not.

Newspapers, magazines, and even some TV stations up and down the East Coast picked up the story. Dan's phone was ringing off the hook because Ava included the funding link plus Dan's cell number at the end of her article. Dan did his best to limit the calls, but he allowed reporters from some of the bigger news outlets to contact Sonny directly to stimulate more funding. This strategy worked because several fly fishing enthusiasts, as well as conventional freshwater and saltwater anglers alike started kicking in money to the fund. Within a month after Holly started the fundraising effort, Team Sonny achieved the $25,000 SSN goal. The SSN money combined with the sponsorship money supplied the $50,000 overall funding goal for Team Sonny.

As promised, Alan let Sonny stay in his rustic two-bedroom Beaufort cottage for May through the end of June. One of the biggest challenges was finding an offshore boat, captain, and first mate not already scooped up by the other Big Rock contestants. Sonny reached out to his saltwater fly fishing friends in the Crystal Coast region for help. One captain's name kept popping up: Eli Moore. His friends described him as a bit quirky, but one of the best light tackle saltwater fishing captains in the business. To Sonny's surprise, Eli was not booked for the Big Rock Tournament. When Sonny asked if he could book him for the tournament as well as a few days leading up to the tournament, Eli said, "I'd like to meet you first. How about you come to the Beaufort Marina where my boat is moored – say at 8 a.m.?" Sonny readily agreed.

Sonny arrived spot on time the next morning. When Sonny saw Eli's boat, he tried to hide his disappointment. It was an old 42-foot center console boat with twin 300-horsepower outboard motors. A slender and fit fifty-ish man with a long, salt-and-pepper ponytail laughed when he caught Sonny's glum look.

"She doesn't look like much, but she's fast and reliable. You must be Sonny. Hi, I'm Eli," he extended a strong, weathered hand to Sonny.

"It's a pleasure meeting you, Eli," Sonny shook Eli's hand in return. He then handed Eli a steaming cup of coffee.

Eli eagerly accepted the coffee with thanks.

Sonny said, "I'm sorry if I looked disappointed by your boat. It seems like a fine boat, but it looks pretty small compared to some of the other offshore boats I've seen. Can it handle rough seas leading up to the Gulf Stream? Afterall, it's about 50 miles to the blue water, right?"

Eli nodded, "It is indeed. But *Fly Knot?* is more than capable in these waters. Plus, the relatively small size and powerful motors give us a speed edge compared to the larger offshore boats," Eli said nodding toward the outboards.

"So, let's say we get lucky and hook a blue marlin. How are you going to boat it? Is there enough room on this boat to properly store it?"

"Fair questions, Sonny. Do you see that block and tackle setup on the portside gunnel?" Eli said pointing to a large L-shaped device. Sonny nodded. Eli continued, "If we can somehow get the marlin to the portside of the boat, we can then hook the fish in the mouth and lift it up and over the gunnel with that block-and-tackle setup."

Sonny then asked, "And then what? Do you have storage under the deck for a big marlin?"

"No, we don't," Eli admitted. "But we have room on the deck for a blue marlin. We would have to immediately wrap it with a blue fin tuna blanket and keep it on ice for the return to the weigh-in dock at Morehead City so it doesn't lose much weight."

"Have you ever participated in the Big Rock Tournament before?" Sonny asked quietly.

"Nope. Have you?" Eli shot back.

"Touché," Sonny laughed.

"To give you some comfort, my mate and I have considerable offshore fishing experience, including some light tackle spinning and fly fishing for gamefish like mahi, yellowfin tuna, sailfish, and even some small blue marlin. Many of my customers grew tired of plowing the ocean with heavy conventional trolling gear. By using light tackle, they traded fish size for fight quality. As a fly fisherman, I'm sure you can appreciate what I'm saying."

Sonny nodded.

"But I'm not going to lie to you, Sonny," Eli continued. "As you know, the world record blue marlin caught on a fly rod is only about 300 pounds. And a blue marlin that size wouldn't even qualify for the tournament. So, I'm in unchartered waters catching one over 400 pounds with light tackle."

Just then, a short, muscular thirty-ish black man walked up to Eli. "Hey Captain. Is this Sonny?" Eli nodded.

"Sonny, I'd like you to meet the best first mate on the Crystal Coast, Mason Bridger."

Mason smiled broadly and extended a catcher's mitt hand which Sonny at once accepted.

"So, Mason, how do you like working for Captain Bligh…I mean, Eli?" Sonny queried in jest.

"Ha! He's a tough nut but a fair one," Mason laughed.

"Hey, guys, I'm right here!" Eli said lightheartedly.

"One more thing. Would you guys be okay with me bringing a friend and my dog on our pre-tournament fishing trips?" Sonny asked hopefully.

"As long as they don't get in the way, I'm fine with that. How about you, Mason?" Eli asked.

"Works for me," Mason replied.

"Thank you. So let me see if I've got this right," Sonny mused. "We'll have the smallest boat in the tournament. None of us has any experience catching blue marlin remotely close to the qualifying weight minimum. We have the smallest crew and the lowest budget. On top of this, we'd have to catch a world record blue marlin on a fly rod to even qualify for the minimum keeper size. Does that sum it up?"

"That's about right," Eli agreed. Mason nodded as well.

"Sounds like a perfect fit to me. I'm in!" Sonny said.

All three men laughed and shook hands. Sonny worked out the financial details with Eli and then left.

Milly's bark jolted Sonny back to the present. Until now, only Sonny had ever seen *Percival*. But he was left with no alternative now. He pulled in the fly line.

"What are you doing, Sonny? There's a blue marlin right there," Pipe's said pointing behind the stern.

"I'm changing flies. As you can see, that fly is not working. If anything, the marlin seems repulsed by it," Sonny replied.

A few minutes later, Sonny cut the old fly from the leader and tied on *Percival*.

"Whoa! What the hell is that?" Pipes exclaimed. "I've tied a lot of saltwater flies in my time. But I've never seen anything like that. What do you call it?"

"I call it *Percival*."

"As in King Arthur's *Percival*?" Pipes asked, raising an eyebrow.

"I'm impressed, Pipes! You actually read!" Sonny laughed.

Ignoring Sonny's slight, Pipes continued, "If memory serves, *Percival* was only one of two knights to find the Holy Grail. Didn't he also kill the Red Knight?"

"Right on both counts, Pipes."

"Look how that fly catches the light. It seems to glow and change colors. What materials did you use to tie it?"

"I don't know because I didn't tie it."

"Then who did?" Pipes probed.

"I don't know that either. I picked it up in a local tackle shop in Belhaven. Let's give it a shot, okay?"

"Why not? We can't do any worse than we've been doing," Pipes agreed.

Sonny gave a few false casts with the stout sixteen weight fly rod before gently placing the 100-pound test leader and *Percival* on the ocean surface. Mason continued throwing bait in the water to hold the attention of the small blue marlin still hanging around. In less than a minute, the marlin veered suddenly to his right and inhaled *Percival*. Sonny was so shocked at the suddenness of this bite that he almost lost his grip on the fly rod! Fortunately, instinct took over and he grabbed tightly on the rod and jammed *Percival* into the mouth of the marlin. Game on!

Simultaneous shrieks from Eli, Mason, and Pipes supplied the fuel for Sonny to battle this beast. Milly barked encouragement as well. Eli at once cut the engine to decrease the tension on Sonny's leader.

"Now what, Pipes?" Sonny shrieked as the 500 yards of fly line and backing started peeling out of the large arbor reel. Sonny had never hooked a fish this big before…by a mile. The adrenaline charge pulsing through his veins was unlike anything he'd ever experienced.

"Let him run. Trust your equipment. Now gently tighten the drag," Pipes calmly instructed.

Just then, the marlin leapt clear out of the water shaking his head in a fruitless attempt to unhook *Percival*. Sonny braced for impact as the fish crashed back onto the ocean surface. It now charged into the depths of the sea. As Pipes instructed, Sonny kept steady pressure on the fish but not so much as to risk a line breakage. After about 30 minutes of relentless fighting, Sonny was finally starting to gain some line back onto the reel. In another 20 minutes, the marlin was beside the boat.

"Now what?" Sonny breathlessly asked the group.

"I got this," Mason offered. He put on a glove, grabbed the leader, and gently pulled the fish closer to the boat. He then grasped the bill of the marlin with one hand and unhooked *Percival* with the other. With the bill still in his gloved hand, Mason gently moved the marlin back and forth to ensure it would survive after its release. To everyone's great relief, it yanked its mighty head, freeing itself from Mason's strong grip. In a flash, it darted below the surface.

Everyone screamed or barked after its safe release. They all high fived including Milly.

"Wow! That was incredible!" Sonny yelled. "How big was that marlin, Captain?"

"I'm guessing 250 pounds," Eli replied.

"That's all?" Sonny said disappointedly.

"You're missing the point, Sonny." Eli said. "You just hooked and boated your first blue marlin on a fly rod! That alone puts you in an elite group. Congratulations!"

"You're right, Captain. I'm very grateful to all of you for your help. There is no way I could have hooked, fought, and boated that fish without each and every one of you. And that includes you Milly," Sonny said petting his canine companion. Milly's tail wagged as if to say, "You're welcome."

Pipes then whispered to Sonny, "I suggest you put that fly away until the tournament begins and don't tell anyone else about it." Sonny nodded in agreement.

Meanwhile back in D.C., Ava was trying to balance helping Sonny and keeping up with her other reporting assignments. It was spring training for the Skins which she would normally cover. Fortunately, her editor and boss, Ed Gray, had a bone in this fight as he wanted to help his nephew as much as possible without crossing a professional line. Since Ava's articles on Sonny were gaining more and more readers, it was an easy call to have her continue covering the Sonny Blue Big Rock story.

In one of Ava's backstory pieces in April, she reached out to some professional bass anglers to supply some background on Sonny. After some cursory research, Ava discovered that Etlas LeBleu from Louisiana was one of the most successful professional bass anglers currently on the circuit. He readily agreed to a video interview.

"Mr. LeBleu. Thank you for agreeing to talk to us about Sonny Blue," Ava began.

"Not at all. And please call me Etlas," he replied in a slight Cajun drawl.

"So how do you know Sonny?" Ava continued.

"Sonny and I started on the circuit at about the same time. We had an instant connection, probably because we were both rookies on the circuit in the same year. Because our last names are similar, our fellow anglers would jokingly refer to us as the 'Blues Brothers'. Of course, I would always correct them with the spelling and say we were the 'LeBleu Brothers'," he laughed at the recollection.

"Did you stay close to each other over the years?" Ava probed.

"I tried to; I really did. But we took diverging paths after a few years on the circuit," he trailed off.

"What happened?"

"Did Sonny give you permission to talk to me?" Etlas inquired.

"He did," Ava assured him.

"Okay then. As you know, Sonny is strictly a fly fisherman. He won't touch a conventional spinning or baitcast rod. In fact, he is the only professional fly fisherman on the bass circuit."

"Is that a disadvantage compared to the usual fishing equipment you and your fellow fishermen use?" Ava asked.

"I think it is. Even with Sonny's considerable fly fishing skills, he can't place his lures -- or flies in his case -- in the same areas that the rest of us can. How technical would you like me to get?"

"Not too technical," Ava answered. "Just an overview will be fine."

"In short, with conventional equipment, anglers like me and my colleagues can get right up to a lake bank with trees and bushes behind us and still make casts out into the open water. Or we can flick our lures over grass mats into clear water. But a fly fisherman is restricted in doing this because he or she needs some open space behind them for their backcasts. Now a skilled fly fisherman like Sonny can do a roll cast as a method of avoiding obstructions behind him. But a roll cast is not as effective as a normal fly cast."

"You seem to know a lot about fly fishing," Ava mused.

"Not really. But in our early days on the circuit, Sonny and I would often go fishing together during some of our practice sessions. So, I had a chance to see his considerable fly fishing skills up close. And he is a gifted fly fisherman for sure, but he still couldn't place his flies in the same places that I could place my lures. And often, that is the difference in placing first or in the middle of the pack."

"Is that the main reason why Sonny doesn't win many bass tournaments?" Ava queried.

"Probably so. But he also has a history of bad luck," Etlas paused.

"For example?" Ava asked.

"He pushes the edge of the envelope a good bit. I can recall one tournament in which he was in the top three entering the last day. So, he was already in the money if he caught a similar weight of bass on the last day. He had a rough morning with only a few small keeper size bass but probably enough to still place in the money. But he wanted to win the tournament. So, he decided to fish right up to the 5 p.m. dock deadline. Well at around 4:30 p.m., he hooked and boated a monster bass that would have won the tournament. But when he tried to start his outboard motor, it wouldn't fire up. He waved down some other professional anglers but they flew right by him as they were also racing against the clock. Incidentally, I wasn't one of those guys as I had already returned to the dock. Anyway, Sonny figured out that his outboard motor battery died so he connected his trolling motor battery to the outboard motor and successfully fired it up. He hauled ass to the dock but missed the deadline by two minutes! In the end, none of the fish in his livewell counted. That dropped him out of the top ten and the money. So, the battery debacle cost him valuable points and $50,000 in winnings."

"I take it there are other similar bad luck stories about Sonny?" Ava asked reluctantly.

"There are, but I'd rather tell you about some good stuff relating to Sonny that you probably don't know about either," Etlas replied.

"Such as?" Ava asked hopefully.

"One story involved me so I can speak to that directly. Like the story I mentioned earlier about Sonny's boat breaking down, I found myself in a similar situation on the last day of a different tournament. In my case, the motor died but it wasn't a battery problem. I pulled the cowling off the motor..."

"What's a cowling?" Ava cut in.

"Oh, sorry. The cowl is the removable covering of an outboard motor. Anyway, Sonny was cruising by and saw the cowl off on my motor so he correctly assumed I had a motor issue. Even though we were both pressing up against the 5 p.m. dock deadline, he pulled up beside me and asked if he could help. He correctly diagnosed the problem as a frozen starter. He rapped the starter with a hammer while I cranked the motor and it turned over, meaning it started. I thanked him profusely and we both made it to the dock in time. Well, it turned out that I won the tournament because of his kindness. But unfortunately, my winning pushed him out of the money," Etlas shook his head sadly.

"Was Sonny angry at you?" Ava asked gently.

"On the contrary. He came up to me after the official results were posted and congratulated me on my victory. And he said this in all sincerity. I told him I felt terrible about how this played out, especially since my victory cost him a money spot. Do you know what he said?"

Ava shook her head.

"He said he couldn't just pass by a disabled boater, regardless of the financial consequences. That wasn't how he was raised. I suppose you know what happened to his father, right?"

Ava nodded.

"Even though Sonny was only twelve when his father died, he must have taught Sonny proper boat etiquette because Sonny's done this type of thing several times in the past with fellow fishermen."

Seizing the moment, Ava said, "Would you be interested in returning the favor?"

"Absolutely! What did you have in mind?"

Ava then explained the SSN Fund relating to the Big Rock Tournament.

"As a reporter, I cannot in good conscience ask you to make a donation to the SSN Fund, but after our conversation, I don't have a problem passing along the contact information for Sonny's business manager, Dan Jones, should you decide to participate," Ava said.

"I heard about Sonny's participation in that tournament. Unbelievable!"

"Unbelievable good or unbelievable bad?" Ava asked.

"Both meanings, I suppose," Etlas responded thoughtfully.

"Can you please elaborate, Etlas?"

"Can we keep this part off the record?" he pleaded.

Ava nodded.

Etlas continued, "Thanks. I have no doubt that Sonny is an expert fly fisherman. Heck, he could have won several more bass tournaments if he only had a bit more luck. But a big-game fish tournament like the Big Rock? I don't know. It seems a bit far-fetched to me. I mean those guys are a different breed than bass anglers. Now don't get me wrong, it takes a lot of skill, knowledge, and persistence to win in our league. But the fish we're catching are in the 4- to 12-pound range compared to offshore fishermen who are catching fish over 500 pounds in some cases. Plus, our environments are completely different. Bass anglers do their work in rivers and lakes so we can often find shelter from the wind and waves. But offshore anglers have no such shelter. They are often fishing 50 miles or more offshore so they get pounded with waves, wind, rain, lightning, and even waterspouts from time to time.

"You're a sportswriter so this would be comparable to an amateur boxer going straight to a heavyweight championship bout. So, my question to you, Ava, is do you think he is serious about winning The Big Rock or do you think this is some sort of publicity stunt?"

Ava's heart sank when she heard these discouraging words from a professional angler, especially someone who thinks so highly of Sonny. But she did her best to hide her disappointment and said, "I can assure you, Etlas, that Sonny is putting everything on the line to win that tournament."

Etlas was impressed with her confident demeanor particularly after his discouraging words about Sonny's chances. He closed the interview with just three words, "Then I'm in," even though he was convinced his investment was gone. After signing off with Ava, he contacted Dan and sent $5,000 to Sonny's SSN fund as promised. He felt he owed Sonny at least that.

Over the next couple of days, Ava interviewed several other professional bass anglers on Sonny's circuit and they echoed Etlas's thoughts about Sonny. Sonny was a hard-luck fisherman but a very decent man. Not one of them gave Sonny a remote chance of winning the Big Rock tournament, but almost all of them spoke respectfully about Sonny. The one exception was Brad West.

"Sonny Blue? Oh yeah, I know him," Brad smirked as they started the video interview. "What would you like to know about him?"

"Well, how about you start by telling me how you know him and your thoughts about his participation in the upcoming Big Rock Tournament," Ava started.

Brad then told Ava about the tournament in which he was paired with Sonny and how Sonny "stupidly" lost the winning fish by holding the line instead of the mouth of the fish. "What an idiot," Brad laughed. "Even though I was just an amateur at the time, I knew better than that."

"What an arrogant ass," Ava thought to herself. Maintaining a straight face, she continued, "So what do you think about Sonny's chances of winning the Big Rock Tournament?"

Brad started laughing so hard, tears came to his eyes. "I'm sorry. But when I read about Sonny taking part in that tournament, I thought it was a joke. I mean, come on. He can't win in our league. How the hell can he compete in that league, right?"

Ava was going to remind Brad that Sonny won the Kerr Lake Bass Tournament last fall but bit her tongue instead. She decided right then that Brad wasn't worth a word of print so she made an excuse about a deadline, thanked him for his time, and was about to sign off when he cut in.

"Don't you want to know more about me? Afterall, I'm a much more successful bass fisherman than Sonny. Also, you're pretty cute. How about we go to dinner the next time you cover one of our tournaments?" he leered.

"As tempting as that offer is Mr. West, I'm going to have to pass. Bye…" she cut off the video call before Brad could say anything else. *"Yeesh!"* Ava thought to herself, *"What a jerk!"*

On her drive to Beaufort from D.C., Ava asked herself if she should share with Sonny the skepticism from his fellow professional bass anglers about his long-shot chances in the Big Rock. He'd read about it anyway, so she figured she might as well tell him. Her editor had agreed to let Ava stay in Beaufort for the entire six-day tournament plus two days before to interview some of the Big Rock contestants. She still had other assignments to cover but those could be completed remotely.

She smiled when she thought of seeing Sonny again tonight. It had been about two weeks since they were last together. Over the past couple of months, they continued to see each other whenever they could but the distance between their homes made frequent visits challenging. And yet, she felt the bond between them was growing stronger. She still got butterflies every time she saw him. No words were ever exchanged about being exclusive. It was just correctly assumed they were.

She crossed the Turner Street Bridge leading to Beaufort just in time to catch the last rays of sun glittering off the water. Sailboat masts from nearby marinas pointed up to the orange-hued skies. As she meandered through side streets lined with historic homes leading to Alan's cottage, her mouth dropped open when she read the dates posted on the homes. Some were from the late 1700s!

The GPS directed her vehicle to a tiny bungalow nestled between two larger historic homes. A ruggedly handsome man sat on a rocker on the porch with a bottle of wine jutting out of an ice bucket. He smiled broadly when she stepped from her car. She ran into his open arms and kissed him long and passionately.

When they finally extracted their lips, he whispered, "We need to be quick. My girlfriend may arrive any minute now."

She laughed, "Same for my boyfriend. Let's hurry!"

An hour later, the sensuously satisfied couple snuggled on the bungalow's porch swing sipping chilled white wine, gently rocking back and forth.

"So how are you holding up, Sonny?" Ava asked softly.

"Better, now that you're here," he smiled and then kissed her lips. "But I'm not going to sugar coat this. It's been a tough couple of weeks. As I mentioned on the phone earlier this week, I finally got my first blue marlin on the fly but it was only about 250 pounds, which is small for a blue marlin. In fact, it didn't come close to the 400-pound minimum size requirement for Big Rock."

"But that's wonderful, Sonny!" Ava said encouragingly. "Even though it wasn't as big as you hoped, at least you know how to hook and play one now, right?"

Sonny nodded suddenly buoyed by her belief in him.

Ava continued, "Do you have confidence in your boat crew?"

"For sure. The captain is a bit unusual, but he put us in blue marlin waters almost every day and kept us safe even in some rough seas. And the first mate is terrific, as was Pipes. The angler is the weak link of this crew," Sonny laughed sardonically.

Brushing aside his self-deprecating words, Ava asked, "So how did you finally manage to hook a blue marlin?"

Sonny had been dreading this question ever since he hooked the big fish. The only other person who knew about *Percival* was Pipes. Sonny was reluctant to expand the list of people who knew about the magic fly but he didn't want to lie or hide anything from Ava. He was trying to build something with Ava and a lie was a weak foundation brick.

Gazing into her sea green eyes, he took a leap of faith, "I'm going to tell you something, Ava, but I'm going to ask you to keep this between you and me, okay?"

Ava nodded. Sonny then proceeded to tell Ava the entire story of how he acquired *Percival*, leaving out nothing including his victory at the Kerr Lake Bass Tournament and the blue marlin catch earlier this week. After he finished the *Percival* story, he asked, "Your thoughts?"

After a long thoughtful pause, she said, "I must confess, Sonny, it's a tad unbelievable that a magic fly, *Percival* as you call it, is the reason for your recent success. May I see this magic fly?" Ava asked.

Sonny nodded. "Yes but no photos, okay?"

"Agreed."

Sonny disappeared and came back with a large yellow fly box. He opened the box on his lap and plucked out the long shimmering fly. Even in the dark, the fly cast an iridescent glow.

Ava had to admit the fly looked different from any of the other flies she'd seen in Sonny's collection or at fly fishing shops she visited as part of her background story.

Sonny held the fly up and said with a smile, "Ava I'd like to formally introduce you to *Percival*. *Percival*, this is Ava."

Ava laughed, "It's a pleasure to meet you, *Percival*." She playfully tugged gently on the unusual strands of material behind the hook as if shaking its 'hand'. But when she touched the fly, she felt a pulse of energy course through her body. It wasn't an electric shock or anything unpleasant. Just energy of some type. The fly also seemed to glow brighter upon her touch.

"Wow! How do you explain this thing…*Percival*, right?"

"Yes, its name is *Percival*," Sonny answered. "And no, I can't explain it."

They sat in silence for several moments just gazing at *Percival*. Ava finally cut the silence and said firmly, "I agree with Pipes. We should not show *Percival* to anyone else. Speaking of Pipes, when am I going to finally meet him?"

"As I previously mentioned, he's very shy. Other than my crew, he doesn't want to meet with anyone else, especially reporters. In fact, if we get lucky enough to catch a qualified blue marlin, he asked me to first drop him off at a boat dock near the Morehead City weigh-in dock. It's nothing personal about you. He had a bad experience with the press several years ago and decided to never engage with them again."

"Care to elaborate?" Ava asked.

"Not really. I promised Pipes I would never disclose any details about that experience to anyone else."

Ava didn't push the matter.

Sonny continued, "But the good news is that the captain and first mate of '*Fly Knot?*' have agreed to meet us for dinner tonight at *Painkillers Pub* in downtown Beaufort."

"Excellent! I'm starving! When shall we leave?"

Sonny glanced at his watch, "Our reservation is in 15 minutes so we can leave in five minutes. It's only three blocks from here."

A few minutes later, they were holding hands and strolling down the backstreets of Beaufort. Many of the gas-lit porch lights and streetlamps cast a soft light on the multi-centuries-old homes. Ava tried to imagine life in the 1700s.

"These houses are incredible," Ava remarked. "I've never seen so many historic homes in a coastal city before. Given the number of hurricanes impacting North Carolina over the years, how did these homes stay intact for more than 200 years?"

On cue, they turned right on Front Street, the waterfront street of the town. "Do you see that island over there?" Sonny said pointing across the water.

Ava peered across the water and, with the aid of a full moon, she could make out the island just a couple of hundred yards across. "Yes," she replied.

"This body of water is called Taylor's Creek and it leads to the ocean via Beaufort Inlet just a few miles from here. That island straight ahead is called Carrot Island. There is another island a few miles on the other side of Carrot Island called Shackleford Banks. Well, those two islands provide effective barriers from hurricanes and Nor'easters that might otherwise destroy this town. With the increasing impact of human-caused climate change, I fear it's only a matter of time before storms beat those islands into submission, exposing Beaufort to the full force of future storms and hurricanes."

"So, you believe in climate change?"

"Of course. Only an idiot could deny the overwhelming data compiled by reputable scientists over the years," Sonny replied.

Ava nodded in agreement.

As they walked closer to the waterfront restaurants and shops, Front Street and the boardwalk were packed with tourists.

"Is it always this crowded?" Ava asked.

"The summer is the peak time here, but the Big Rock Tournament leads to near zero availability of hotels and vacation homes during the six-day period of the tournament. That's why Alan's offer to let us stay in his bungalow is especially generous." Ava nodded thoughtfully.

As they navigated through a sea of tourists on the boardwalk, Ava glanced at the impressive number and size of sailboats, yachts, and offshore vessels moored at the town docks. Many of the offshore vessels were packed with crew members drinking and laughing on their boat decks.

"Do you think many of these boats are entered in the Big Rock Tournament?"

"Most definitely. I recognize some of these vessels from past Big Rock Tournaments. Even though I never took part in the tournament before, Alan and I would sometimes go to the weigh-ins at the Morehead City dock. As you can see, it's a fun, festive environment leading up to Day 1 of the tournament. But don't fool yourself. Once the tournament begins, these fisher men and women put their game faces on and it's all business each day of the tournament. As you know, it's big money for the winner. Even more important, it's a lifetime of bragging rights."

"Is your captain's vessel moored here?" Ava asked as she scanned the vessels.

"Yup. There she is," Sonny pointed to *Fly Knot?* at the eastern-most end of the docks.

Sonny laughed aloud when he saw Ava's mouth drop open once she locked eyes on the vessel.

"No offense, Sonny. But it's tiny compared to these other vessels," Ava remarked.

"True. But don't be deceived by her size. It handled some rough seas over the past couple of weeks. And the captain and first mate are top-notch. Speaking of which, they're on deck right now. Let's head over."

They walked up the pier where *Fly Knot?* was moored and stopped at the port side. Sonny asked, "Permission to come onboard, Captain."

"Granted," responded Eli formerly but with a hint of a smile.

After boarding the vessel, Sonny shook hands with Eli and Mason and introduced them to Ava.

"Pleasure, ma'am," Eli and Mason said tipping the bills of their fishing hats.

During their walk toward the vessel, Ava had time to recover from her disappointment. "I love your boat, Captain!" Ava cheerfully said.

"Ha! I can see in your eyes that it's not what you expected or hoped for, Ava," Eli laughed.

"Guilty! I'd make a terrible poker player, wouldn't I?" Ava volunteered.

"Probably, but I appreciate your kind words, nonetheless. Shall we grab a bite?" Eli offered.

"Absolutely!" Ava and Sonny simultaneously responded.

A few minutes later, they entered *Painkillers Pub*. Like the other restaurants in Beaufort, it was packed with tourists and locals. But they had reservations at an outside table overlooking the water so they didn't have to wait.

A server approached their table and said, "Hey, Fellas. The usual?" The guys nodded.

"And you, ma'am?" she looked at Ava.

Ava asked Sonny, "What's 'the usual'?"

"Painkillers, of course," Sonny smiled.

"Of course. What is a Painkiller?" Ava continued.

"Try it. You'll love it. Especially here. They make the best in Beaufort."

Ava shrugged and said, "Okay, I'll have a painkiller, please."

"Double shots all around, Sonny?"

"Yes please, Amy," Sonny responded.

A few minutes later, they were all sipping double-shot painkillers. Ava had to admit that it was a delicious cocktail. It was a wonderful blend of rum, pineapple juice, cream of coconut, and nutmeg garnished with a maraschino cherry and pineapple wedge. The moon-lit water, star-laden sky, boats, and Carrot Island made a spectacular backdrop. A warm gentle sea breeze only enhanced the evening.

Over painkillers, grouper bites, and tuna tacos, the crew discussed their tournament strategy.

"Captain, can you please give me a brief summary of the tournament rules?" Ava inquired at one point.

"Of course. Basically, there are six days in the tournament. But each boat can only fish four of those six days. Weather can play a major factor, particularly for smaller boats like *Fly Knot?*. So, we rely heavily on weather apps, radar, and other boaters for wind, wave, and weather info to help us decide which days we'll fish. There are several other gamefish categories, in addition to blue marlin. But I won't bore you with those other gamefish rules since we are focused primarily on blue marlin."

Ava nodded.

Eli continued, "You can only fish between the hours of 9 a.m. and 3 p.m. The official scales typically close at 7 p.m. but can stay open later if a blue marlin is hooked before 3 p.m. the same day. No blue marlin under 400 pounds can be brought back to the Morehead City weigh-in station, with significant penalties assessed to the offending boat, including disqualification. There are also strict rules about nefarious activities but we have no intention of breaking or even bending the rules so I won't bother you with those details."

"How are the winners determined?" Ava asked.

"For the blue marlin category, the boat that brings a marlin over 500 pounds to the scales first wins the *Fabulous Fisherman Award*, which includes a significant cash payout. This award alone is estimated to exceed $700,000, based on the total prize money in this year's tournament. If this first fish ends up being the largest blue marlin of the tournament, the victor wins an added, even larger cash award estimated to exceed $1.5 million. For these reasons, almost all participating boats try to hit the ocean on Day 1 of the tournament."

"Thank you for the explanation, Captain. I also want to thank you and Mason for allowing me to be present on your boat during the tournament. A firsthand account of *Fly Knot?*'s quest for a blue marlin should enhance the series I'm writing about Sonny."

Both men nodded.

Ava then heard boisterous laughing at a nearby table. She glanced over and noticed a few guys pointing their fingers at their table.

"What do you think that's about?" Ava asked Sonny.

Eli turned and then frowned, "That's Bartholomew Winslow and his crew of *Devil Maker*." Eli pointed to a massive 60 foot offshore vessel just a few slips away from *Painkillers*.

"Wow! That is an impressive boat!" Ava said.

"Humph," grunted Eli. "Yeah, but Bart didn't earn that boat. His dad was a Dukie just like Bart and gave him *Devil Maker* as a graduation present several years ago."

"Dukie?" Ava cut in.

"Duke University alum. Bastard blue bloods just like Bart and his dad," Eli sneered. "Can you imagine a million-dollar graduation present? I certainly can't," Eli said. Sonny and Mason shook their heads as well.

"Is he entered in the Big Rock Tournament and, if so, has he won it in the past?" Ava asked.

"Sadly, yes to both questions. In fact, he's won it twice including last year's tournament," Eli lamented.

Just then, Bart stood and sauntered over to *Fly Knot?'s* table. His perfectly sculpted 6 foot 3 inch frame towered over the table.

When he spotted Ava, he smiled broadly revealing his bright white teeth and said, "Well hello, pretty woman. I think you're sitting at the wrong table. The winner's table is over there," Bart said pointing to his crew who were all smiling arrogantly.

"I think she's fine right where she is, thank you," Eli cut in. "She doesn't wish to cough up the delicious meal she just ate."

Still smiling, Bart slowly turned his head from Ava to Eli and said, "Well hello, Eli," then turning his head again to Sonny and Mason. "And who might you be, lovely lady?" Bart leered.

"Ava Tyson from the *D.C. Tribune,*" Ava responded cooly but politely.

Bart then paused as if searching for a memory. He then suddenly snapped his fingers, "Got it! You're the reporter who has been writing articles about this loser...I mean, Sonny, right?"

"Well first off, Sonny is certainly no loser," Ava responded defensively. "But yes, I'm the reporter who has been writing *The Sonny Blue Chronicles.*"

"So why are you wasting your time writing about this guy?" he said pointing to Sonny. "He's never entered the Big Rock Tournament, and from what I've heard, he's not even successful in that bush league bass circuit. If you want to write about a winner, then how about interviewing me?"

Sonny had enough. He stood up and moved inches from Bart. Even though Sonny was three inches shorter than Bart, he did not back down.

"I'm right here, you blue-blooded a-hole. If you have something to say, then say it to my face," Sonny seethed.

Bart's other crew members stood up and walked over to defend their captain. Eli and Mason stood up as well.

Ava sensed a fight so she cut in, "Now, boys. Let's take it easy. Bart, sure I'll be happy to interview you. How about tomorrow morning?"

Bart and Sonny continued donning their fight faces until Bart finally broke into a victory smile, "Sure, Ava. I would love to talk to you tomorrow. How about we meet at 8 a.m. on the deck of *Devil Maker*?"

"Done. Now gentlemen, I'm tired so I think I'll turn in. Sonny, I'm completely lost. Can you please show me the way back to our Bungalow?"

It suddenly dawned on Bart that Ava was with Sonny. For an instant, Bart dropped his cocky smile just a tad. But Sonny picked it up. It was now Sonny's turn to smile, "Sure, Ava. Gentlemen. It's been a pleasure," he said shaking hands with Eli and Mason. He then took Ava's hand and walked by Bart and his crew without a glance.

After they left the restaurant, Ava and Sonny took a stroll down Front Street to cool off from their encounter with Bart.

"Nicely done back there, Ava. If things don't work out at the *Tribune*, you can apply for a job as a diplomat," Sonny said half-jokingly.

"Thanks, Sonny. As a sportswriter, I've been in enough men's locker rooms to spot the early signs of a fight. And it sure looked like one was brewing between you and Bart. I've never seen you so angry before. What gives?"

"I don't know. It's something about that whole aura that Bart and his cronies give off. As you know by now, I'm not a violent person. I just wanted to smack that arrogant smile right off his face," Sonny admitted.

They arrived at the end of Front Street and took a seat on a wooden bench overlooking Gallant's channel, a body of water on the West side of Beaufort joining Taylor's Creek on the North side. Behind them sat a large historic home.

"See that house?" Sonny pointed behind their bench. "That's the Duncan House. The original house was built in 1728 but it has been restored over the years. A couple of years ago, it was lifted high above the ground and renovated yet again. Despite the protective islands I mentioned earlier, Mother Nature can still put a hurt on these coastal homes."

"It's magnificent!" Ava exclaimed. Turning her head back to the water, she pointed across the channel, "What kind of ships are those?"

"Oh, those are commercial shrimp trawlers. They plow the ocean waters a good bit in the fall."

"Are they a good or bad thing for the environment?" Ava asked.

"It depends on your point of view. On the positive side, they supply a necessary food source for a lot of people, including many of the restaurants in this area. On the negative side, shrimp yield is only about five to ten percent."

"Meaning what?" Ava cut in.

"It means for every 100 pounds of fish and shrimp these trawlers haul in with their nets, only about 5 to 10 pounds are shrimp. The rest are called 'bycatch' and include pinfish, croaker, and other smaller fish species."

"Can't they just release these bycatch fish?" Ava inquired.

"Unfortunately, most of those fish are dead by the time the nets are hauled back to the vessel. Fish get their oxygen from water through gills. Once they are swept into nets, they can't breathe, so they suffocate."

"Not to sound cold but are these bycatch fish species that important?" Ava asked.

"Bycatch is comprised of lower food chain organisms so, yes, they are very important to the ocean ecosystem, particularly for larger fish species including gamefish like speckled trout, red drum, and the like."

"So, what's the solution?" Ava asked.

"I don't know," Sonny admitted. "But maybe scientists from those groups of buildings can help find the answer," Sonny pointed across Gallant's Channel. "That first group of buildings belongs to NOAA and the second group is the Duke Marine Lab."

"Wait a minute. The same Duke where Mr. Yuppie back there went?"

Sonny laughed, "Well it's the same University but Bart went to school at the main Duke campus in Durham, North Carolina. The Duke Marine campus across that channel is a whole different animal. They are made up of serious marine scientists who seem more focused on helping the environment than partying."

Sonny stood up and offered his hand to Ava, "Shall we head back to the bungalow? Afterall, you have a big day tomorrow with Bart blue-blood, right?" Sonny chided. "I am curious what you plan to ask? Do you really plan to write an article on him?"

"You should know better than to ask those questions, Sonny. A good reporter does not reveal the content of her story before it's been written. I'll go to the interview tomorrow open minded and see what he has to say. Maybe you and your crew can learn something from the interview. Afterall, he did win the Big Rock Tournament…twice in fact," she winked.

Sonny could have been offended by that dig but he wasn't. Ava was right. He might indeed learn something from Bart. Sonny learned long ago to filter out the arrogance of some anglers and capture their knowledge in his quest to become a better angler. He had to admit that some anglers like Bart made it challenging to ignore their arrogance. For the sake of his team, however, he planned to give it his best effort.

Sonny's eyes then locked onto Ava's. His heart still fluttered even after several months of seeing her. In the moonlight, her sea-green eyes were soft yet magnetic. He drew closer. She closed the gap and kissed him softly on the lips. Their kiss lingered. Ava pulled back and said, "I'm curious about something."

"What's that?" Sonny replied.

"You didn't seem the least bit jealous when I accepted Bart's invitation for the interview on his boat tomorrow. Why is that?" Ava asked.

"Jealousy is a wasted emotion. I like what we're building together. Perhaps it's wishful thinking on my part, but I sense you feel the same. The last thing I wish to do is blow it up with petty jealousy. Besides, it's your job."

Ava smiled, "It's not wishful thinking, Sonny. I feel the same." She wrapped her arms around his neck and planted a longer passionate kiss on his lips to punctuate her thoughts. "Now, how about we continue this party back at the bungalow?" she asked playfully.

"I couldn't agree more!"

And that is exactly what they did.

XII. Tournament Day 1

'What a friggin zoo,' thought Sonny. He scanned the armada heading out of Beaufort Inlet at six a.m. on June 14. There were more than two hundred boats! The scene reminded him of the start of many of his bass tournaments when the boats tore out of the starting gate like a drag race. Except in his present situation, there were significantly more and larger boats, together generating mini tidal waves across the inlet. Given that *Fly Knot?* was the smallest boat in the fleet, Captain Eli wisely kept their vessel in the rear to avoid the wave turbulence from the fleet. He patiently waited until most of the fleet cleared the inlet. He then scanned his crew to ensure all were wearing life jackets and were secured in their seats.

"Is everyone ready for warp speed?" he asked. They all gave a thumbs up gesture.

"Engage!" Eli screamed. He then pushed the throttle down near the max, and *Fly Knot?* lurched forward like an Olympic sprinter leaving the starter block.

Ava was surprised at the acceleration of *Fly Knot?* and had to grab hold of a nearby railing to avoid being tossed from her seat. The boats in the armada ahead of them were starting to spread out in different directions. Wave turbulence was not as intense a few miles offshore as it was in the Inlet. Ava saw the wisdom in Eli's patience at the start as they now shot by several larger vessels on *Fly Knot?*'s 50-mile journey to the Gulf stream.

Ava was grateful that Eli let her join the *Fly Knot?* crew during the tournament. Perhaps the captain's decision was made easier when Pipes decided not to join the crew during the tournament…much to the chagrin of Sonny. The night before the tournament, Sonny informed Ava while sitting on the porch swing that Pipes decided not to take part in the tournament.

"Why?" she asked incredulously.

"He said his work was done because he helped me hook and boat my first blue marlin a couple of weeks ago. Personally, I think it's because the tournament field this year is the largest in history. The added media coverage probably kicked him over the edge," Sonny said sadly.

"Do you think I'm responsible for his decision to cancel?" Ava asked nervously.

"Not at all," Sonny said reassuringly. "I think he planned all along to help me hook and boat a blue marlin and then step away. As I mentioned before, he hates the limelight. But there is one silver lining."

"And what's that?" Ava asked hopefully.

"Captain Eli has agreed to let you join the crew for the entire tournament, if you like," Sonny smiled.

"I'd love to!" Ava smiled in delight as she squeezed Sonny's arm.

Ava stared in wonder at the ocean wildlife surrounding their boat. She had considerable experience fishing with her dad on small rental boats on the Chesapeake Bay during her childhood. But the Atlantic Ocean was a different beast altogether. On their journey to the Gulf Stream, or "Blue Water" as the locals refer to it, she saw dozens of dolphins playfully swimming near *Fly Knot?*. A few miles later, she caught sight of a large sea turtle on the ocean surface. As soon as it spotted their boat, the turtle darted below. Ten minutes later, Ava spotted some large fish propelling completely out of the water and spinning.

"What are those fish?" Ava asked loudly enough for First Mate Mason to hear above the roar of the engines.

"Oh, those are spinner sharks," he casually replied.

"Amazing! Why do they jump out of the water like that?"

"It's how they catch their prey. They charge through a school of baitfish, fly out of the water, spin 360 degrees, and crash back into the bait school with their mouths open. Meal. They're one of the fastest sharks in the ocean, too. They can swim over 40 mph."

"Incredible! You probably see this stuff all the time, Mason. Do you ever get tired of it?"

"Never," Mason responded with a smile. "That's the main reason I gave up my office job. Accounting. How can that job compete with this?" he said spreading his arms all around.

Ava nodded in agreement.

A couple of hours after leaving the inlet, Eli eased back on the throttle.

Ava noticed a significant change in the ocean water. "Wow, the water color really is different out here. I now see why they call it Blue Water," Ava remarked to Sonny who was sitting next to her on their journey. "So, what's the plan now, Sonny?"

"As you can see, the captain slowed the boat to a trolling speed that is optimal for blue marlin catching. He's using his fish finder to locate an area that holds baitfish and big gamefish like marlin. At exactly 9 a.m., Mason is going to peel out some line from those baitcast rods and then troll some hookless surface plugs called teasers to hopefully entice a blue marlin to the surface. Once a marlin surfaces, Mason will reel in those teasers and then throw baitfish in our wake to hold its attention. If we spot a large enough blue marlin to qualify, I'll start fly-casting *Percival* in that general area. If I somehow manage to hook one, then all hell will break loose. This is one time we want that to happen," Sonny laughed.

"How are you feeling?" Ava asked.

"I feel good. Win or lose, I have a lot to be grateful for. I couldn't be prouder of my team. I mean, look at all the people who have helped me to this point, with you at the top of the list. There is no way I would be here without you, Ava. So, I'm playing on house money from this point forward."

Ava modestly waved off the compliment, "Well, I hope you still feel that way on Day 6 of the tournament!" she joked.

"Ha! Me too! Now if you'll excuse me, I've got some work to do."

Sonny then assembled his two-piece sixteen weight fly rod with *Percival* firmly attached to the 100-pound test monofilament leader. At precisely 9 a.m., Mason started flinging bait fish in their wake. The game was on!

Back in Beaufort, Dan was sipping hot coffee at an outdoor table at *Beaufort Brew,* a local café. It was a beautiful sunny morning with just a hint of a breeze. For the sake of the crew of *Fly Knot?,* Dan hoped the weather was as pleasant offshore as it was here. Sonny offered the second bedroom of Alan's bungalow for him to stay at during the tournament. Given that there was zero vacancy anywhere in a 30-mile radius during the tournament, he gratefully accepted Sonny's invitation and arrived last night. Dan reflected on the past two months. Ava's *Tribune* chronicles on Sonny's journey to this point generated enough interest to help fund Sonny's expenses in the Big Rock Tournament. Dan had hoped to garner even more sponsors -- his long-term goal was to capitalize on Sonny's Big Rock participation to help forge some sustainable sponsor contracts.

Sadly, no such long-term contracts had materialized. If anything, interest from major publications seemed to be dwindling. Ava's paper kept up its coverage of Team Sonny and a few fly fishing magazines such as *Fly Fisherman, Fly Fishing in Saltwater,* and *Tail Fly Fishing Magazine* ran stories. Even though reporters from those magazines were skeptical of Sonny's chances of even boating a blue marlin of any size, let alone a qualifying blue marlin, the David-and-Goliath story was too compelling to ignore. And yet, the story was pushed to the back pages of these magazines and only covered a few short sentences. The general vibe Dan got from these magazines was Sonny's participation in the Big Rock Tournament was merely a gimmick, a publicity stunt to gain sponsors.

And Dan admitted to himself, there was some truth to this line of thinking. At least as far as sponsors go. Where Dan departed from the reporters' logic was the "gimmick" part. He knew Sonny well enough to understand that he took this tournament seriously. Given the effort Sonny put into preparing for this tournament, his entire team believed this as well, particularly after Sonny boated his first blue marlin a few days ago. Much to Dan's chagrin, Sonny insisted that Dan not share the successful blue marlin catch with anyone else due to disclosure concerns about *Fly Knot?*'s location, which could be discerned via satellite imagery. Dan argued this catch could help validate Sonny's participation in the tournament as a serious contender which could generate more publicity and future sponsorships. He solemnly added that Sonny's bank account would run dry shortly after the tournament unless they secured some more sponsors.

But Sonny would not back down. He promised his captain and first mate to be discreet about the catch and he planned to honor that promise. Although frustrated that he couldn't leverage Sonny's blue marlin catch into some much-needed publicity, Dan couldn't argue with Sonny's promise to his crew. So, he stopped pressuring Sonny and decided to play with the cards dealt to him at this point. In a few minutes, he was scheduled to meet with a sports reporter from the *Raleigh Times*. Ava knew the reporter, Chris Staples, and arranged the interview with Dan to help stimulate interest from nearby Raleigh, Durham, and Chapel Hill, the area often referred to as the Triangle. With a population base of over a million people, the Triangle had considerably more people than the entire Crystal Coast cities combined.

A shadow crossed Dan's table. He looked up and saw a medium built, mid-thirties man in shorts and a Big Rock T-shirt. "Dan Jones?" he asked.

"Guilty. You must be Chris Staples from the *Times*." Chris nodded. Dan continued, "Can I order you some coffee?"

"I'm fine, thanks. I've only got a few minutes because I've got some other interviews scheduled this morning. Shall we get started?"

Dan sensed this interview was a mere professional courtesy to Ava rather than anything particular about Sonny's journey here. But beggars can't be choosers, so Dan decided to make the best of it.

"Of course. What would you like to know?" Dan asked.

"I've read Ava's chronicles on Sonny to this point, so I won't ask questions about his background and such. I'll get right to the point. Sonny has raised, what, $50,000 to fund his participation in the Big Rock Tournament?"

Dan nodded, sensing where this was going.

"My first question is, is Sonny's participation in the Big Rock a mere publicity stunt or does he truly think he can win this tournament?"

Dan's blood was starting to boil but he kept a cool exterior. "Let me ask you a question, Mr. Staples. What makes you think Sonny has no chance to win this tournament?"

Chris flipped open a small journal and said, "Well, I've conducted interviews with about ten other captains participating in this tournament, as well as some local fly fishing guides."

"And what do they say about Sonny's chances?" Dan asked, knowing the answer before he even asked the question.

"I won't sugar coat this, Dan. The consensus is that Sonny has almost no chance of catching a qualified blue marlin and even less chance of winning the tournament. You must admit the odds are daunting. Look at his record. Except for that small bass tournament at Kerr Lake last fall, he hasn't won a single bass tournament in his entire seven-year career, right?"

Dan offered no response.

Chris continued, "So, if Sonny can only win one bass tournament in seven years, how can he possibly win a tournament in which he needs to catch a world record blue marlin on the fly rod just to qualify?"

Dan paused before coolly responding, "Let me tell you something about Sonny, Mr. Staples. He's beaten long odds in the past. He lost his dad when he was just 12-years-old. He worked at odd jobs while pursuing his undergraduate and graduate degrees. His dad had no money when he died, so Sonny carried out these impressive feats without the benefit of an inheritance or trust fund. And while it's accurate that he hasn't been financially successful to date, he's working in a field he's passionate about. How many people do you know who can honestly say 'yes' to that question regarding their jobs?" Not waiting for an answer, Dan continued, "So yes, I think Sonny can win this tournament."

Just then, Chris's cellphone chirped. "Excuse me, Dan."

As Chris spoke on the phone, Dan noticed his eyes grew wide with excitement. A minute later, Chris signed off and said,

"You're not going to believe this, Dan. One of the charter boat captains in the tournament just contacted the media room via a satellite phone. He said another boat just hooked a big blue marlin."

"Okay, so why is that interesting to me?" Dan asked.

"Because that angler is Sonny!" Chris said with a smile.

It had been two hours since Mason first started hurling baitfish off *Fly Knot?*'s stern. No sign of marlin to this point.

Looking down at his fish finder, Eli barked, "Something big is coming to the surface."

"I don't see it yet, Captain," Mason said.

"Wait for it," Eli responded calmly.

"There it is!" Mason yelled excitedly as he pointed at a spot 50 yards behind the boat.

Ava's eyes grew wide, "Holy cow, that is huge!" and beautiful, too she thought.

"Is it a qualifying marlin, Mason?" asked Sonny.

"I think so. What do you think, captain?" Mason asked.

"I believe it just might be," Eli responded.

"Shall I start casting?" Sonny asked excitedly.

"Not yet. I'll let you know when," Eli said.

Ava could not believe how clear this water was and how close this gorgeous beast was to the boat! She pulled her cellphone out and clicked on the video function key. Behind the stern, the marlin was thrashing at the bait near the surface. The water was so clear she could see the marlin feeding twenty or more feet below the surface.

Sonny was standing at the stern with his fly rod in his right hand while pinching fly line in his left forefinger and thumb. He started peeling off several feet of fly line which now lay in a loose pile to his left on the boat deck. The marlin was swimming nearer and nearer to the boat as Mason continued to throw baitfish as close to the boat as possible.

Sonny glanced back and forth from the marlin to the captain until finally Eli screamed, "Now!"

Sonny at once started working the stout fly rod in a ten o'clock to two o'clock configuration while simultaneously playing out the fly line from the deck. After just two false casts, Sonny placed *Percival* about 70 feet behind the boat.

"Nice cast, Sonny, but you're too far left of the bait. Bring it in and try again," Eli said encouragingly.

Sonny quickly retrieved the fly line and was about to start casting again when Eli added, "Now the marlin is only about 50 feet from our stern. This time cast your fly past the marlin but in the same general line. Then retrieve the fly past the marlin to hopefully get its attention."

Sonny did exactly as Eli suggested and placed *Percival* about 15 to 20 feet past the marlin. He then waited a few seconds for the fly to inch down from the surface. The intermediate fly line combined with the slow trolling speed of the boat, allowed the fly to sink a couple of feet below the ocean surface.

Even as the fly was sinking, Ava observed that it still radiated a multi-color shimmer. Perhaps the bright sun enhanced the effect. Whatever the reason, the marlin seemed interested as well. As soon as the fly shot passed the giant fish, the marlin bolted for it.

Mason shouted, "Get ready, Sonny."

But Sonny was more than ready. In fact, he'd waited his whole life for this moment. '*Patience',* he kept telling himself.

"Tease it, Sonny," Eli yelled.

As directed, Sonny started twitching the fly line ever so gently. Ava correctly surmised this action was designed to imitate a wounded baitfish. Evidently, the marlin bought this as well and it crashed onto the fly with its mouth wide open.

"Wait for the tug, Sonny," Eli shouted.

Just then, Sonny's fly rod bent over like a willow branch in a hurricane.

"Set the hook!" Eli screamed.

Even before Eli could spit out the words, Sonny grabbed hold of the fly rod with both hands and pulled back hard, setting *Percival* deep into the marlin's hard mouth.

"Game on!" Mason laughed.

Ava continued video recording the event.

The marlin seemed to finally sense that it was hooked and began a series of acrobatic surges out of the water. Ava, her heart pounding, alternated pointing the camera at Sonny and the marlin with occasional shots of Eli and Mason. She could then hear the fly line and backing peel off the fly reel as the marlin was now charging into the depths. Ava wondered if Sonny had enough line to capture this massive creature before it was exhausted from the reel. She kept that thought to herself.

Sonny had the same thought and screamed, "Captain, I'm losing a lot of line! I might get spooled soon!"

Eli at once pulled the throttle back to neutral. "Roger that. Walk around to the bow of the boat when I turn us about."

"Aye, Captain" Sonny answered.

Ava walked up to Mason and quietly asked, "What's going on?"

"Sonny's fly reel is dangerously close to getting spooled, meaning empty," Mason responded. "If the Captain puts the boat in reverse to chase the fish, ocean water would flood the deck. So, he's pivoting the boat so he can chase the fish in a forward rather than backward direction. Do you see that white line peeling off his fly reel?"

Ava nodded.

"That's called backing. It's a lot thinner in diameter than the intermediate fly line attached in front of it but it's quite strong. The thin diameter of backing allows you to put several hundred yards of line on larger arbor reels like the one Sonny's using. But a big fish like he's fighting can still spool that reel if we don't chase it."

As soon as Mason finished those words, Eli successfully turned the boat 180 degrees while Sonny maneuvered his way to the bow. As Mason described, Eli was now chasing the marlin in a forward direction.

"Good job, Sonny! Now take up the slack!" Eli yelled.

"Believe me, I'm trying!" Sonny shot back as he furiously began reeling in some backing. He gained back 50 yards before the marlin peeled even more line out. Just then, the line went slack and the fly rod went from a bent bow to a straight arrow.

"Damn it! I lost it!" Sonny yelled in frustration.

"I don't think so, Sonny. I believe it's charging the boat. Keep reeling!" Eli instructed.

Renewed hope supplied the fuel for Sonny's frantic reeling. He finally retrieved the slack until he felt the weight of the fish again.

"You're right, Captain. It's still on!" Sonny screamed in delight.

Ava captured Sonny's face on video at the moment he realized the marlin was still hooked. When she viewed the video later that evening, she tried to discern all the emotions that flashed across his face in that instant: Surprise, relief, joy, hope, happiness, confidence, and passion, all at once. Whatever the next moments held, it was clear from Sonny's face that, win or lose, he was meant to be here. He belonged.

"Come on!" Chris yelled at Dan. "Let's head back to the media tent in Morehead City. We've got work to do!"

Dan leapt out of his chair and chased after the reporter. "Hey Chris, what were you saying about Sonny's chances of catching a blue marlin?" Dan smiled.

"He hasn't boated the fish yet so don't look so smug," Chris shot back.

"Good point," Dan conceded. "So, what's the plan?" Dan asked.

"You can do what you want but it might be worth following me to Morehead City so we can start reaching out to fly fishing groups and the like. I'll get you a media pass. So, does Sonny know any fly fishing groups in the area?"

"Yes, he does. Two in fact. When he went to UNC-Chapel Hill and NC State, he joined Raleigh Fly Fishers, or RFF as it was abbreviated. He said he learned a lot from those members including refinements in fly tying and fly casting. He also recently joined the Crystal Coast Flyfishers group or CCFF here in Morehead City".

"I know about RFF. In fact, I wrote an article on the RFF group a couple of years ago. Several of the RFF members meet weekly or biweekly at a bar in Durham and tie flies and tell lies. They call themselves "Beer Tyers." Chris laughed at the memory. "One member in particular, Markham, loved to tell stories. He usually prefaced each story with the line, 'what could go wrong?'. And, of course, everything went wrong! He was usually the butt of his stories, so the other members love him for his self-deprecating humor. Anyway, it might be worth reaching out to him to see if he can get some members to attend the weigh-in tonight to support Sonny, assuming of course, he boats the marlin."

"From Raleigh, it's a three-hour drive to Morehead City," Dan said. Glancing at his watch, he added, "It's 11:30 now so I guess it's possible for a few RFF members to arrive by the weigh-in time tonight, assuming they're available, of course."

"How about the other fly fishing group you mentioned?" Chris asked.

"Oh, the Crystal Coast Fly Fishers Group or CCFF for short. That's an easier call. They are based in this area so many members live here. I'll reach out to the president and give him the news. So, I have a question for you, Chris. Why are you helping Sonny?" queried Dan.

Chris paused before answering, "It's David and Goliath, baby. Here's my car." He reached inside and pulled out two items. "Parking is a mess in Morehead City so here's an extra parking pass as well as a press badge. I'll see you there." He then drove off.

Dan hoofed over to his car and peeled off toward Morehead City, a 15-minute-drive from Beaufort.

Over an hour had passed since Sonny first hooked the marlin. Ava could not tell who was winning the war at this point- Sonny or the marlin. Whenever Sonny gained some line back on the reel, the marlin would take off again. The arial acrobatics lessened a bit but the marlin was still peeling line off the fly reel. Eli did several stop-and-go maneuvers with the boat to keep the fish off the bow while still allowing Sonny to gain some line onto his reel.

From time to time, Sonny would shift the fly rod to his left hand and then shake his right hand back and forth to avoid cramping. A minute later, he shifted the rod back to his right hand and continued the battle.

"You look exhausted, Sonny," Ava remarked. "How about you give the rod to Mason for a few minutes so you can take a quick break?" Ava suggested.

Both Sonny and Mason burst out laughing at Ava's suggestion.

"What's so funny?" Ava asked, not getting the joke.

Mason answered, "If that marlin is indeed big enough to qualify for the tournament, it would be a world record blue marlin caught on a fly rod. If anyone else touches Sonny's fly rod before he touches the leader, the catch wouldn't count. It would still qualify for the tournament, mind you, but it wouldn't count toward a world record."

"Gotcha. After he touches the leader, can anyone else help him boat the fish?" Ava asked.

"Absolutely! In fact, we'll all need to assist Sonny at that point, including you!" Mason responded with a broad smile.

"Me? What can I do?" Ava asked incredulously.

"Whatever the captain tells you to do," Mason laughed.

"Mates! We've got a lot of work to do to boat that fish," Eli pointed out. "So, let's not jinx ourselves, okay?" The other three nodded.

After a long pause, Ava said, "Not to sound devious, Mason, but how would anyone in the tournament know if someone other than Sonny touched his fly rod during the fight?"

"Because each crew member, including you, will be subject to a polygraph test before the tournament concludes if a fish is a potential winning and/or world record catch," Mason answered solemnly.

"Are you serious?" Ava asked wide-eyed.

"As a heart attack," Mason answered. "And it's not just our vessel that would be polygraph tested. It's any vessel that brings a Top 3 gamefish to the scales. The tournament officials are very strict about the rules here. With millions of dollars in prize money at stake, you can understand why. I can recall one case several years ago when a boat caught what the crew believed was the winning blue marlin. As they headed back to Morehead City for the weigh-in, the captain went through the formality of checking each crew member's fishing license to ensure they were current, a tournament requirement. They were indeed current. Unfortunately, the captain forgot to check his first mate's fishing license before they headed out to the Gulf Stream that morning. Sadly, this turned out to be a million-dollar mistake because the first mate didn't even have a North Carolina fishing license. The captain later claimed the blanket fishing license for his boat covered the entire crew, including his first mate. As a precaution the first mate applied for a fishing license online while still at sea. But it was a couple of hours after the marlin catch so the tournament official disqualified the catch."

"So, what happened?" Ava asked.

"It was a total cluster fuck. The crew from the disqualified boat sued the tournament, then the tournament countersued. It went back and forth through the court system for several years until the case was finally settled out of court for an undisclosed amount. As you might guess, the only victors in that fiasco were the lawyers…as usual. The lesson learned? Don't bend or break the rules. And I guarantee Captain Eli will do no such thing" Mason nodded proudly at his captain. "That was the reason Captain requested a copy of your fishing license before you set foot on *Fly Knot?* this morning," he added.

"I'm gaining some line, Captain. I think he's tiring," Sonny yelled. Just then, another 100 yards of backing screamed off Sonny's reel. "Damn it!" Sonny cried out in frustration.

"You didn't think this would be easy, did you?" Mason laughed.

"Evidently not," Sonny acknowledged.

The fight continued for another 45 minutes before the crew finally spotted the marlin near the surface about 75 feet off the bow.

"Do you see him, Captain?" Sonny yelled behind him.

"I do. We can't boat it off the bow. So, I'm going to pivot the boat so he's on our stern. When I turn the boat, you'll need to walk back to the stern. Are you ready?" Eli asked.

"Aye, Captain."

Eli then slowly turned the boat 180 degrees. As directed, Sonny walked back to the stern while keeping steady pressure on his line.

"Good job, Sonny. Mason, are you ready?"

"Aye, Captain," Mason replied while putting on some fishing gloves.

Mason turned to Sonny and said, "Alright, Sonny. He really is tiring now."

"Yeah, well, me too!" Sonny laughed while Ava wiped sweat off his brow with a nearby rag.

"Here's where it gets tricky. I need you to tighten your drag just a bit and then reel in enough line so you can touch the leader to make it a valid catch. Once you do that, I'll take over," Mason replied confidently.

"What can I do?" Ava asked helpfully.

"You can keep video recording this, but please stay out of the way for your own safety's sake. Those pointy bills have been known to impale a person during a boating. And make sure you get a shot of Sonny touching the leader after he reels most of it through the tip guides to validate the catch," Mason replied.

"I'm on it!" Ava replied. She was grateful that she remembered to bring a cellphone battery pack on the journey today. Otherwise, the battery on her cellphone would have surely been exhausted given the amount of video she was recording.

As directed by Mason, Sonny tightened the drag, then reeled the fish close to the boat. He then reached over and touched the leader. Ava's video recording captured Sonny's leader touch. Mason then grabbed the leader with both hands and pulled the line along the port side of the boat to get a better look at the fish. He then turned to Eli and yelled, "I think it's a legal-size fish, Captain."

"I agree. Now, let's boat it!"

Eli put the engine in neutral and walked beside Mason.

"What can I do to help?" Sonny asked.

"Hang on to your rod in case we lose our grip on the leader. We don't want to hold the leader too tightly, otherwise it could break," Eli said.

Then turning to Mason, Eli said "Ready?" Mason nodded.

Mason then grabbed the marlin's bill with his left hand while keeping his grip on the leader with his right hand. The marlin started thrashing wildly at that point probably realizing it was its last chance at escape. But Mason's grip on the marlin's bill held strong as he navigated the fish toward the large winch hook held in Eli's hand. Eli then jammed the winch hook into the marlin's mouth and started cranking the fish up using the winch. Once it was high enough to clear the gunnel, he and Mason pushed it over and into the boat.

The crew simultaneously erupted into a raucous cheer. High fives and hugs ensued all around. Despite the number of gamefish that Eli and Mason had successfully boated over the years, they never tired of this type of celebration.

Mason then grabbed a tape measure and measured the marlin from the V-notch in the tail to the tip of the lower jaw. He smiled broadly, "115 inches! That's five inches more than the minimum!"

Eli turned to Sonny and Ava and said with a grin, "Congratulations, Sonny. You not only caught a marlin that qualifies for this tournament but it's also a world record marlin on a fly rod."

Despite his exhaustion, Sonny beamed in jubilation. As did Ava.

Just then, the radio crackled, "Hey guys. *Devil Maker* is hauling ass to Morehead City. I think they caught a legal-size marlin."

"Damn it to hell," Eli barked. Then turning to Mason, he said "Let's put that fish on ice ASAP. We need to head back to port like right now if we want to win the *Fabulous Fisherman Award*."

Mason nodded and said, "Don't wait for me, Captain. I'll pack it up while you drive."

"Good man, Mason," Eli said turning toward the console. He then fired up both engines and *Fly Knot?* took off like a bat out of hell toward Morehead City.

"What's happening, Sonny?" Ava asked with concern in her voice.

"Unfortunately, our 'friends' from *Devil Maker* appear to have caught a legal-size marlin as well. Do you see that vessel about a mile behind us?" The vessel was heading North under full throttle.

Ava nodded.

"That's *Devil Maker*."

"Aren't we closer to the weigh-in dock than *them* and isn't *Fly Knot?* a faster boat?" Ava asked hopefully.

"Right on both counts, Ava. Under calm seas, we'd have a significant edge. But as you can see, the winds have kicked up as well as the waves. *Devil Maker* is a much bigger boat and can cut through rough seas much more so than *Fly Knot?*. But Eli is an excellent captain, so you never know. It's going to be tight."

Ava glanced down and watched Mason expertly packing ice all around the marlin inside the tuna blanket before fastening it tight.

"Now what?" Ava asked Mason.

"Hang on. It's going to be a rough ride back to port," Mason replied.

"Oh my God!" Chris exclaimed to Dan in the press tent as he clicked off his cellphone.

"What?" Dan asked anxiously.

"I just heard from one of the other captains. *Fly Knot?* just boated the marlin that Sonny was fighting. And they think it's a legal catch!" Chris said excitedly. "There is one fly in the ointment though, no pun intended," he added.

"I'm afraid to ask," Dan said tentatively.

"One of the other boats also caught a legal-size marlin and they're not far behind *Fly Knot?*," Chris said.

"What's the name of the other boat?" asked Dan bracing for the inevitable.

"*Devil Maker,*" Chris answered.

Dan swore under his breath. "So, what do you suggest we do now?"

"Did you reach out to Sonny's fly fishing friends yet?" Chris asked.

"Yes. Two hours ago. Several RFF members have already left Raleigh and are heading this way as we speak. Others are expected to arrive later tonight. Several members from the local Crystal Coast Flyfishers group are on their way here now as well. They should arrive at the weigh-in station well before *Fly Knot?* does."

"Very good. How about you reach out to your fly fishing magazine contacts? The local newspapers and TV stations are already here so we don't need to reach out to them. But I have some contacts with national media players like ESPN, Fox Sports, CBS, NBC, ABC, and CNN. I'll reach out to them. You never know."

Dumbfounded by this sudden turn of events, Dan merely said, "Okay, thanks." And for the next two hours, they grabbed their cellphones and got to work.

In the 50 miles the two boats had traveled since the race back to Morehead City began in the Gulf Stream an hour and a half ago, *Devil Maker* significantly closed the gap between the two boats. The *Fly Knot?* crew kept checking their stern every few minutes. It was like watching a train wreck. They simply could not keep their eyes off *Devil Maker* as it motored agonizingly closer and closer to *Fly Knot?*. As Mason predicted, the weather and wind conditions worked against *Fly Knot?*. The waves had increased from two to three feet in the Gulf stream to four to six feet in the waters approaching Beaufort Inlet. Despite Eli's expertise at the helm, he was losing the battle to a larger, superior vessel. *Devil Maker* was now only a few hundred yards behind *Fly Knot?* and gaining.

It was like an invisible hand keeping *Fly Knot?* in check. Despite the stakes, Eli was not about to jeopardize the safety of his crew. As the ocean conditions worsened, he moved the throttle back and forth to find a happy medium between speed and safety. Eli thought to himself that if he could stay ahead of *Devil Maker* until they reached the No Wake Zone of the Morehead City Port, both boats were required by U.S. Coast Guard law to slow down to a speed that does not generate a wake. This can vary from boat to boat but is generally less than seven mph. He looked down at his GPS and noted they were only three miles from the No Wake Zone. He glanced behind him. *Devil Maker* was less than 100 yards behind them now…and closing.

Fly Knot? was almost through the Inlet and was passing by Fort Macon State Park. They were less than two miles from the No Wake Zone and leading *Devil Maker* by less than 50 yards. Miraculously, the water laid down as soon as they passed the Fort Macon jetty. The waves went from five feet in height to less than two feet almost instantly! The advantage now shifted to *Fly Knot?* as Eli could go full throttle without the impediment of waves slowing his boat down. Eli smiled for the first time since the race began. "*We got this!*" he thought to himself.

When they were less than a mile from the No Wake Zone, Eli observed a small bass boat ahead of them on their starboard side heading directly into the path of *Fly Knot?*. Despite repeated blasts from Eli's air horn, the bass boat was undeterred as it continued its path across *Fly Knot?*'s bow. Eli had no choice but to cut back on the throttle to avoid crashing into the bozo ahead of him. As soon as the bass boat passed them, Eli slammed the throttle down. *Devil Maker* never slowed down during the near collision episode ahead of them. Despite trailing *Fly Knot?* by 50 yards when the bass boat crossed *Fly Knot?*'s bow, *Devil Maker's* steady speed allowed it to catch up and shoot past *Fly Knot?*.

The drama that just unfolded was not lost on the other *Fly Knot?* crew members. To make matters worse, Bart and his *Devil*

Maker crew members were grinning from ear-to-ear as they shot past *Fly Knot?'s* starboard side. Captain Bartholomew Winslow then held up both hands, palms up mouthing the word, "Sorry," which of course he wasn't. The *Fly Knot?* crew members were livid. Middle fingers shot up like a jack-in-the box and much cursing ensued. The *Devil Maker* crew clicked beer bottles and continued laughing while Captain Bart plowed ahead at full throttle.

Sonny shifted his gaze from the *Devil Maker* crew to its captain. It was subtle, but Sonny detected a quick thumbs up gesture from Captain Bart to the bass boat driver. The driver just nodded and then sped off. Sonny thought it odd that a freshwater bass boat would be fishing in this saltwater environment. But then again, he'd seen all kinds of vessels in these backwaters including similar freshwater boats as well as even smaller vessels like kayaks, canoes, and even paddle boards. Still, there was something vaguely familiar about that bass boat driver...

By the time, *Fly Knot?* had achieved maximum speed again, *Devil Maker* just crossed the invisible No Wake Line a mere 25 yards ahead of *Fly Knot?*.

"Look how slow they're going now. Can't we just shoot by them?" Ava pleaded.

"Nah, once we hit the No Wake Zone, you can't change your boat position. That would be poor form," Mason resignedly stated. "No way our captain would do anything like that."

Sonny walked to Eli and quietly said, "Something doesn't smell right about how that played out back there."

"I agree, but there's nothing we can do about it. Let's see what unfolds at the weigh-in, okay?" Eli said.

Sonny nodded.

"So, what happens when we get to the weigh-in station, Mason?" Ava asked.

"Well, from the radio squawking we all heard on the way back, it appears that *Devil Maker* and *Fly Knot?* are the first boats back to port with qualifying blue marlins. As Captain mentioned during dinner the other night, the boat that first brings a marlin to the scales that exceeds 500 pounds wins the *Fabulous Fisherman Award*. And given the large purse this year, the buzz I'm hearing is that award will be close to $700,000."

Ava's eyes opened wide, "Wow! So, in short, we need to hope that *Devil Maker's* blue marlin is less than 500 pounds and ours is more than 500 pounds, right?"

"Precisely."

Both vessels arrived at the weigh-in station 15 minutes later with *Devil Maker* leading the way. It was only 6 p.m. so there was plenty of daylight remaining. After securing *Fly Knot?* to the dock, Eli told the crew not to mention the events that happened back in the Inlet when *Devil Maker* shot past them. He said it would look like sour grapes if they mentioned it to the press. "I know you're all pissed. I'm pissed too. We can vent to each other over drinks tonight, but not here. Understood?" They reluctantly nodded but understood the wisdom of Eli's words.

Sonny was stunned to see the number of people standing in wait at the weigh-in station. They were raucous too. Front and center were Dan Jones and a shorter bearded man standing next to him. Dan was sporting a Cheshire cat grin. They were standing in front of a rope strung around the weigh-in station to keep the masses from crowding the contestants. Several other boats had previously arrived back to port to weigh their non-marlin gamefish. *Caught 6* was at the top of the leader board for biggest dolphin caught so far, an impressive 39.6-

pound fish. Sonny smiled when he saw that result as he knew the owner/angler of that vessel. In fact, he was sitting on the deck of his boat with a cigar in his hand and a big smile. Sonny nodded to him and the owner nodded back.

As soon as Sonny stepped off *Fly Knot?*, the crowd let out a roar! Sonny assumed the roar was for Bart as he Stepped off *Devil Maker* at about the same time that Sonny stepped onto the dock. Bart waved to the crowd, then strutted to the scale like a professional golfer walking to the eighteenth green of Day 4 of the Master's Tournament. The Big Rock staff hoisted *Devil Maker*'s blue marlin to the scale. It read 526 pounds. It was a legal catch that easily met the 500-pound criterion for the *Fabulous Fisherman Award*. It was a $700,00 winning fish. A round of polite applause from the crowd ensued. Bart was hoping the crowd would be a bit more enthusiastic. He wouldn't have to wait very long.

The blue marlin from *Fly Knot?* was then hoisted onto the scale: 515 pounds. Sonny's shoulders slunk. But then the crowd let loose a thundering roar, much to the surprise of Sonny and Bart as well as their crew members. The crowd then yelled, "Sonny! Sonny! Sonny!"

"I don't get it," Sonny remarked to Dan who had just walked up to him. "Why are we getting this insane reaction from the crowd? We didn't win the *Fabulous Fisherman Award*. In fact, we just lost $700,000 in prize money by arriving second behind *Devil Maker*."

"Clearly you don't have clue, do you? You just caught a world record blue marlin on a fly rod! Not only that, but you also destroyed the previous record by more than 200 pounds!"

"True, but that doesn't pay the bills does it, my friend?" Sonny said wistfully.

"You're missing the big picture here, Sonny. We'll talk more about this later."

Ava walked beside Sonny and smiled.

"Hey, Ava. This is…" Dan started.

Ava cut in, "Hey, Chris. It's good to see you again. Chris Staples, this is Sonny Blue, the star of this show."

"I'm hardly a star, but it's pleasure to meet you, Chris," Sonny said offering up his hand, which Chris firmly returned.

"So, what's next?" asked Sonny.

"Chris has arranged a press conference for you and the *Fly Knot?* crew in about 30 minutes," Dan replied.

Just then, the fifty-ish owner of *Caught 6* stepped off his boat and confidently walked toward Sonny. A second roar erupted from the crowd. As he approached, Ava, Dan, and Chris stood motionless and speechless. His handsome, lean six foot six inch ebony frame was impossible to ignore.

He then extended a hand to Sonny and said with a perfect smile, "Nice fish, Sonny."

"Thanks, Michael," Sonny said firmly accepting his hand. "And you as well. That's a big dolphin," Sonny replied calmly.

"Thanks, Sonny. Good luck for the rest of this tournament. Let's beat that cocky Dukie, okay?" he said nodding to Bart who was staring open-mouthed at the icon standing next to Sonny.

"Agreed. Good luck to you as well, Michael."

Michael nodded and then walked to his limo while politely waving to the adoring crowd.

Once the limo door slammed shut, Ava shot a glance back at Michael's boat and the meaning hit her. *"Caught 6. Of course!"* she thought. *"Championships, not fish!"*

She then punched Sonny in the arm, "Why didn't you tell me you knew him!"

"Ouch!" Sonny yelped rubbing his arm. "You never asked! Besides, I've been sworn to secrecy," Sonny laughed.

"I've got to ask you how you know him," Ava pressed.

"Okay, I'll tell you but you all have to promise to keep this to yourselves, okay?" Sonny asked seriously.

Ava, Chris, and Dan all nodded.

"As you know, we're both UNC alums," Sonny started. "A lot of people don't know this, but he is passionate about fishing. Not just saltwater like this tournament, but brackish water and freshwater fishing as well. He treasures his privacy and doesn't want a throng of people surrounding him every time he goes fishing. He doesn't have a choice at this tournament, of course. Anyway, about 10 years ago, his business manager reached out to our UNC fishing club and asked if there was a club member who could discreetly take Michael fishing in some remote waters where he wouldn't be swarmed with fans or the press. The president of our fishing club recommended me because I live in a remote area of Eastern North Carlina where it's unlikely that he'd be spotted by the press or anyone else for that matter. Ava you've seen those waters firsthand. You might only see a handful of boats all day."

Ava nodded.

"Each of the past 10 years, I've taken Michael Big Drum fishing on the *Whisker*. Until now, I've never disclosed our friendship to anyone else. But he obviously revealed that by walking over to me tonight in front of this insane crowd so I guess the secret is out now," he said reluctantly.

Finally recovering from this shocking disclosure, Dan said, "I forgive you for not telling me this sooner. But do you realize the opportunity you missed by not leveraging your connection with Michael? Can you imagine how many sponsors we could have secured for you by just mentioning your friendship with him?"

Sonny shook his head before responding, "Look, Dan, I'm not going to sell out a friendship just to make a few bucks. I promised Michael I would never reveal our friendship to anyone else, or our annual fishing trips for that matter. And I've honored that promise."

Both Chris and Ava just stared dumbfounded at Sonny. Ava smiled. *"Who is this guy?"* she thought to herself, not for the first time.

Chris broke the silence, "I get that, Sonny. Very noble. But now that Michael took the first step in revealing his friendship with you, how about we run a story of how you two met and the friendship you forged with him over the past 10 years?"

Sonny shook his head again, "That story was revealed to you all in confidence. The people seeing Michael shaking hands with me a few minutes ago could interpret our handshake as one competitor congratulating another. And that is exactly what we'll tell everyone who asks, agreed?"

Confounded by Sonny's stubbornness, Dan, Ava, and Chris nevertheless nodded.

Dan sighed, "You sure make things difficult for me at times, Sonny."

"That's why I pay you the big bucks, right?" Sonny laughed as did the others. Dan and Chris then peeled off to the press tent.

Just then, a group of guys and one woman pushed to the front of the rope and screamed, "Hey, Sonny!"

"Hey, Fellas and Sarah!" Sonny yelled in surprise. "Come on in!" he nodded to one of the tournament officials who obliged and lifted the rope to let Sonny's friends through.

"Ava, these are some of my fly fishing friends. Markham, Gordo, James, Kevin, Preston, Joe, Jake, and Sarah, this is Ava."

Ava smiled at the group, which they eagerly returned.

Markham then turned to Sonny and said, "Congrats, Sonny. You make us all proud. Now let's see this record-breaking fly of yours." Turning to Ava now, Markham remarked, "I mean no disrespect to Sonny, but he is one of the worst fly tyers of our group," Markham paused, waiting for Sonny's response.

"It's true, Ava," Sonny agreed.

Markham continued, "So you can imagine my surprise when Dan called me earlier today and said Sonny hooked a blue marlin that might qualify as a legal catch. It reminded me of a story…" The other RFF and CCFF members rolled their eyes at yet another Markham story.

Sonny cut in, "Here's the thing, Markham. I didn't tie that fly."

"That's okay," Markham reassured him. "A lot of us use flies that other people tie. It's whatever works, right? I'd still like to see it if you don't mind."

"You know how superstitious I am, right?" Sonny said. "Well, I promised our crew that we wouldn't reveal that fly until the tournament was over. But you all will be the first group outside our boat that I'll show it to, okay?"

This seemed to satisfy the RFF and CCFF flyfishers so they dropped it.

Gordo then said, "How about we meet for drinks tonight?"

"Most definitely! How about we meet at *Painkillers* at, say 9 o'clock?" Sonny responded with a smile.

Thirty minutes later, Sonny, Eli, and Mason were sitting at a table fielding questions from the media.

Reporter One: "Sonny, I noticed that Michael from *Catch 6* greeted you today. Are you two friends?"

Sonny was prepared for that question. He didn't want to lie but he didn't want to reveal too much either. "I think it was just one competitor congratulating another. I congratulated him on catching the largest dolphin so far."

Reporter One: "Just a quick follow-up question for Captain Eli. We heard that *Fly Knot?* was in a race with *Devil Maker* back to port to weigh the first qualified blue marlin on the scale. We also heard that *Devil Maker* made a controversial maneuver in the Inlet to shoot past your boat. Given this maneuver cost you and your crew about $700,000 in prize money, are there any words you wish to express to the captain and crew of *Devil Maker?*"

"Just three. Karma's a bitch" Eli said without a trace of a smile. Most of the crowd laughed.

Reporter Two: "Sonny, how about you tell us details about the marlin fight?"

Sonny breathed a sigh of relief that the question shifted to a topic more suited to his comfort level. He then described in broad strokes the hookup, fight, and boating of the blue marlin. He gave most of the credit to Eli and Mason for their successful catch. Both Eli and Mason looked stunned as they listened to Sonny deflecting credit for the catch.

Reporter Three: "Captain, do you agree with Sonny's accounting of the marlin catch?"

Eli replied, "I agree with everything Sonny said except for one important thing." He then paused for effect.

The reporters suddenly leaned forward in anticipation of a conflict brewing among the *Fly Knot?* crew members.

Reporter Three: "And what might that be?"

Eli smiled and replied, "Sonny is being far too modest. It's true that you need a good captain and first mate to locate and boat a fish the size of the blue marlin we caught today. I've taken a lot of very good flyfishers out in the Gulf Stream. But I've never seen anyone play a fish on a fly rod the size that Sonny fought and boated today. He was patient, persistent, and relentless. More importantly, he was smart enough to listen to his captain and first mate!"

Everyone laughed.

Reporter Four: "Sonny, it appears that your blue marlin is a world record catch on a fly rod. But it likely won't even finish in the money at the end of this tournament. How do you feel about that?"

Sonny: "I'm not going to lie. I'll be disappointed if that fish finishes out of the money. But there are five more days of the tournament, so anything can happen."

Reporter Four: "Wait a minute. Do you think you can catch an even larger blue marlin?"

Sonny replied stone-faced, "Yes. Just one more question please."

Reporter Five: "We noticed that Ava Tyson from the *DC Tribune* was on *Fly Knot?* today. Is she part of your crew?" he asked with a hint of smarminess.

Sonny replied, "If it weren't for Ava, I wouldn't even be here talking to all of you. It was her idea for me to compete in the Big Rock Tournament in the first place. So yes, she is very much part of our team." Both Eli and Mason nodded in agreement.

"Thank you everybody," Sonny said as he, Eli and Mason stood and left the media tent.

Ava had been sitting quietly among the other reporters in the media tent during the press conference. She figured there was no point in asking Sonny any questions during the conference because she would have more intimate access to Sonny than anyone else. Besides, she had time on the boat today to verbalize the raw content of her latest chapter of *The Sonny Blue Chronicles* to her cellphone. She would clean it up and get it to her editor later that night for web publication. The print version will be in tomorrow's edition of the *Tribune*.

She approached Sonny, Dan, Chris, Eli, and Mason as they were heading to the parking lot. She sidled up to Sonny, cupped her hands around his left ear, and whispered, "Thank you, Sonny," and then darted the tip of her tongue inside his ear for a brief but potent instant.

Sonny smiled, "For what? Not that I'm complaining, mind you."

Ava said, "For making me part of the crew, of course."

Eli cut in, "Ava, you ARE a part of the crew. Now, do I get that same kind of thanks?" he joked.

"No, but it was nice try," Ava laughed. "What's the plan, Captain?"

Looking back toward the water, Eli said, "As you can see, the winds have kicked up even more since we made it back to port. There is a small craft advisory for the next two days, so it's highly unlikely any of the contestants, including the larger boats like *Devil Maker,* will be able to safely navigate the ocean waters leading to the Gulf Stream. Looks like we'll be grounded for at least the next two days. On the plus side, no other boats brought another 500-plus pound blue marlin to the scales, so we are still in second place. If that position holds, we'd win some prize money."

"Given your knowledge of this tournament, do you think it's realistic to think our fish will hold onto second place?" Ava asked.

"Not really, especially since there are a record number of boats entered in the tournament this year. Plus, the marine forecast indicates the final days of the tournament will be boatable and therefore fishable. So, it's quite likely that one or more boats will eclipse the size of our blue marlin as well as *Devil Maker's* marlin," replied Eli.

"I'm curious about something. What happens to the blue marlin after they are weighed on the scales?" Ave inquired.

"I'm pleased to report the NC State University Marine Lab right down the road here in Morehead City will be taking these blue marlins back to their labs for research," Sonny said.

"You went to school there, didn't you?" Eli asked.

"Yes, I earned my master's degree in marine sciences there a few years ago," Sonny replied.

"College basketball is huge down here, right? Since you attended both UNC-Chapel Hill and NC State, who do you root for when they play each other?" Ava asked.

"That's easy," Mason cut in. "Sadly, he probably roots for UNC, right Sonny?" Sonny nodded.

"Why 'sadly', Mason?" Ava asked.

"Because I earned my bachelor's degree in accounting at NC State University and you're always loyal to your undergraduate school," Mason said. "But the good news for both of us is that we universally hate Duke, so I'll root for UNC whenever they play Duke and I'm guessing Sonny roots for NC State when they play Duke."

"Well, I don't really hate Duke, but I have to admit that everything else you said is true," Sonny said.

"After what transpired today with Mr. Bartholomew Winslow back there," Eli said nodding to the press tent where Bart was conducting his own interview with the press, "You might feel differently about Duke toward the end of this week."

"Perhaps, but I don't hold Duke responsible for what Bart did today. Besides, I'm friends with several researchers at the Duke Marine Lab here in Beaufort, so I've nothing against the university," Sonny added.

"Perhaps you're right, Sonny. But I'm guessing the local press here will somehow make the battle between the two boats a Duke-UNC rivalry thing, particularly now that Michael publicly congratulated you," Ava accurately predicted.

Changing topics, Sonny then asked Eli, "Since we won't be fishing over the next two days, do you have any suggestions on any prep steps?"

"It's been a long day. I suggest we take the day off tomorrow and meet for breakfast at the *Beaufort Brew* the day after tomorrow to discuss our strategy. Sound good?" Eli asked the group. Everyone nodded.

"May I join you as well?" Chris asked hopefully. "I feel like I'm a part of this this now. At least I hope I am."

Eli glanced at the others who all nodded. "Okay, you're in. I'll see you all then." Everyone then left.

Bart was seething after he left the press conference. He caught the first and, so far, the biggest blue marlin of the tournament. And yet, the number of reporters at his press conference was about half the number who were at Sonny's. Bart was dumbfounded that Sonny was getting that much attention for a fish that would likely finish completely out of the money. What really irked Bart was the easy banter and rapport Sonny had with the reporters. To Bart's credit, he kept his emotions in check. The other *Devil Maker* crew members seemed oblivious to his envy of Sonny, as they continued to grin and fist-bump each other after leaving the press conference. They all came from wealthy families, so the prize money wasn't as important to them as the bragging rights for winning the *Fabulous Fisherman Award* and, quite possibly, the biggest blue marlin of the tournament.

Back at the Beaufort bungalow, Sonny and Ava showered and made passionate love. Despite their exhaustion, their primal desire for each other coupled with the excitement on the ocean today trumped the tired factor. Afterwards, they lay naked in each other's arms. Several quiet moments passed before Ava finally broke the silence. She held up an invisible microphone to Sonny's lips, smiled and said, "So Mr. Blue, how does it feel to catch a world record blue marlin on a fly rod?"

Laughing softly, Sonny said, "Well Ms. Tyson, I give all the credit to my captain, crew, and gorgeous girlfriend. Speaking of which, you'll need to leave soon because she is due to arrive any minute now."

For the second time that day, she punched his arm.

"Ouch!" he cried out. "You deserve a good tongue lashing for that, me lady." And that is exactly what he did. Before things got too heated again, Ava pulled her lips from his and said, "Whoa cowboy, it's almost 9 o'clock and you promised to meet your fly fishing buddies at *Painkillers*, remember?"

"Yes, but we have time for a quick roll-around, right?" he asked hopefully.

"When you come back, yes. But right now, I've got an 11 p.m. deadline to submit the latest chapter of *The Sonny Blue*

Chronicles to my editor. I've got just two hours to finish. So, scat!" Ava said playfully pushing him out of bed.

Sonny reluctantly donned his clothes and headed out the door for the short walk to the pub. When he arrived at *Painkillers*, it was jammed with tourists, locals, the press, and tournament contestants. He scanned the bar and saw his fly fishing buddies sitting at a long rectangular table at the back of the bar. Several of them waved him over.

"Well, if it isn't the giant slayer himself. We saved a seat for the guest of honor," quipped Markham.

"Where's your lady friend?" Gordo asked. He was clearly disappointed at her absence.

"She's writing her story that's due tonight. So, guys, I want to thank each of you for making the hike to Beaufort to support me," Sonny said sincerely.

"What are you talking about? We heard that some sap agreed to pay for our beers and dinner if we drove to Beaufort today so it was an easy call," Markham joked.

Sonny laughed, "Okay, okay. But you all realize that I haven't won a nickel at this tournament yet, right?"

"What's your point?" Preston asked smiling.

"No point. Just stating facts."

"Regardless, you're still paying for dinner," Preston stated his own fact.

Sonny sighed, "Okay."

After Sonny took his first sip of a cold Yuengling draft, James asked, "We're on pins and needles here, Sonny. Tell us about the fight."

After a second, longer sip of beer, Sonny told them details about the hookup, fight, and boating of the blue marlin. The only detail he left out was *Percival*. And, of course, that was the detail most sought after by this group of avid fly tyers.

"Come on, Sonny," James pleaded. "Can you tell us anything about the fly?"

"As I mentioned earlier, I didn't tie that fly. It was given to me as a gift."

"By whom? Where did you get it? What's it made of?" James pressed.

Sonny said, "I'll be happy to answer those questions in the unlikely event that the fly hooks the winning fish."

There was a collective sigh among the RFF members but they dropped the topic. The rest of the evening was a chaotic blend of simultaneous animated conversations, few of which featured Sonny as the main topic. Sonny loved it.

XIII. Tournament Days 2 & 3

The next two days played out as the marine weather apps predicted. High winds and seas grounded the Big Rock Tournament boats. Dan decided to use the break to arrange interviews for Sonny with several fly fishing magazine reporters. Sonny was reluctant to spend his down time with reporters, but Ava encouraged him to go forward with the interviews. Besides, she already had the inside scoop with her latest *Sonny Blues Chronicles* chapter published on Day 2 of the tournament. Editor Ed Gray had let Ava know that the readership of her *Chronicles* tripled in just one night after Sonny's marlin catch.

"Stay put, Ava," Ed directed.

"If you insist, Boss," Ava laughed. *"I love my job…"* Ava thought to herself. *"and…"* she shook her head and said quietly, *"Don't go there, Ava."*

As Ava suggested, Sonny followed through with the fly fishing magazine interviews. During the interviews, Sonny directed most of the credit to his captain and first mate. The questions from each reporter were similar. All wanted to know what fly was used to hook the marlin. Sonny deflected this question saying that he would reveal the fly if he was fortunate enough to win the tournament. This drew laughter from the reporters, each of whom understood the low chance of this occurring.

Despite a strong buzz from the fly fishing community, Dan was surprised that few of the major media outlets showed any interest in Sonny's blue marlin catch. As far as they were concerned, Sonny's marlin was in second place and likely to be pushed out of the money when the other boats bring in their catches after the weather breaks on Days 4, 5, and 6. The fact that Sonny caught a world record marlin on the fly had no real appeal to such reporters. It was all about the size of the fish, not how it was captured. Aside from the fervor over Sonny's handshake with Michael on Day 1 of the tournament, Bart was now getting most of the media attention. Afterall, he and his crew were guaranteed $700,000 in prize money for winning the *Fabulous Fisherman Award*. With the reduced number of fishable days remaining in the tournament, the odds improved for *Devil Maker* winning the grand prize for the largest blue marlin as well.

On Day 3, the *Fly Knot?* crew was sipping coffee at an outside table at *Beaufort Brew*. A look of concern cast across Eli's face.

"We've got a problem," Eli began. "As you know, we've been landlocked for the past two days, due to the weather. The forecast for tomorrow is an improvement but the marine forecast is predicting waves over six feet in height with a three-to-four second frequency."

"In layman's terms, what does that mean?" Ava asked.

"It means the waves are too high and too close together for *Fly Knot?* to safely navigate the ocean," Mason answered. Eli nodded.

"Will the other boats go out?" Sonny asked.

"The bigger boats probably will," Eli conceded. "As you know, *Fly Knot?* is one of the smallest boats in the tournament. Unless the forecast dramatically improves, I cannot risk the safety of our crew by going out tomorrow. I'm sorry, Sonny."

"I understand," Sonny replied thoughtfully. And he did. Despite the high stakes, Sonny did not fault Eli for his decision to ground *Fly Knot?* on Day 4 of the tournament. Sonny had three rules whenever he took guests on his boat: be safe, have fun, and catch fish…in that order. He'd be a hypocrite if he faulted Eli for grounding *Fly Knot?* tomorrow.

"What's the plan then?" Dan asked.

"Mason and I are going to thoroughly clean the boat and do some light maintenance on *Fly Knot?* tomorrow to ensure everything is tip-top before our next trip to the blue water. Sonny, I suggest you check your fly fishing equipment and flies to make sure everything is in good working order.

Sonny nodded, "Aye, Captain."

"Incidentally, Mason noticed that you left your fly rod and reel in the rod rack onboard *Fly Knot?*."

"Shit! I completely forgot. With all the excitement two days ago, it completely slipped my mind. Thanks for letting me know. I'll head over to the boat right now and bring it back to the bungalow to clean the rod and lube the reel." Eli nodded in agreement.

Sonny never had a theft issue in Belhaven so he didn't lock anything around his property, including his fly rods and reels onboard *Whisker*. But he didn't know Beaufort as well as Belhaven. *Fly Knot?* was moored around several other boats at the marina so security was not that tight. He suddenly panicked at the unspeakable thought that someone could steal his fly rod, reel, and *Percival*!

He practically galloped toward the marina. When he arrived, he noticed a man with a blue ballcap walking along a pier where several boats were moored including *Fly Knot?*. By the time Sonny stepped onto the pier, the blue cap man had already exited the pier. Sonny said, "Hey" as a friendly greeting but the blue cap man just grunted and kept walking with his head down. He looked vaguely familiar but Sonny couldn't place him.

Sonny then stepped onboard *Fly Knot?* and was immensely relieved to discover his fly rod, reel, and *Percival* were safely secured along the rod rack on the starboard gunnel. After his relief subsided, he noticed the rod was secured in a different position on the rod rack than the position he'd placed it in. At least he thought it was. With all the excitement after the blue marlin catch, he couldn't be sure of how he left his rod. He shook it off as a memory lapse. In hindsight, he wished he trusted his gut.

XIV. Tournament Day 4

As Eli predicted, on Day 4, most of the Big Rock boats motored to the blue water while *Fly Knot?* remained at the Beaufort marina. The five-to-six-foot seas in the Gulf Stream were confirmed by the marine apps and the captains who radioed back to the tournament officials. Despite knowing this was the right decision, it still frustrated *Fly Knot?*'s captain and crew to be landlocked while the bulk of the contestants were actively fishing.

"Damn! I just received a report that three other boats hooked and boated blue marlin that are all likely bigger than the one we brought to the scales. If that plays out, your marlin is out of the money. I'm sorry, Sonny. I bet you're wishing you picked another captain with a bigger boat now," Eli lamented over lunch at *Painkillers*.

"Not on your life," Sonny reassured him. "I never would have hooked and boated that marlin if it weren't for you, Mason, and the rest of my team." Sonny spread his arms around the outside table acknowledging Mason, Ava, Dan, and Eli. "Besides, we've got two more days left. How does the forecast look?" Sonny asked hopefully.

"Tomorrow looks good but the forecast for the next day, the final day, is calling for a good chance of afternoon thunderstorms and stiff winds. So, if we go out that day, we'll probably need to head back by noon to avoid the storm." Everyone nodded.

Ava turned to Dan and asked, "Is Sonny getting any more interest from the media?"

Dan shook his head, "Sadly, the only media outlets still showing interest after Day 2 are the fly fishing magazines and the like. As you know, the readership of these journals pales in comparison to those of conventional fishing journals and online newsletters. How's the traction on *The Sonny Blue Chronicles* in the *Tribune*?"

"My editor says the readership continues to grow each day of the tournament," Ava responded.

"Excellent! Maybe we can leverage that interest into some new sponsorships once the tournament ends," Dan replied.

"Perhaps but…" Ava didn't finish her sentence because everyone at the table knew significant sponsorships were unlikely to happen if Sonny finished out of the money. And with the news from Captain Eli about the marlin catches earlier today, they were staring straight into the face of that reality.

Sonny scanned the table and smiled, "Don't look so glum, everyone! From my perspective, we are playing on house money. We caught a world record blue marlin on the fly. I've got the best captain and first mate on the East Coast. I've got the most loyal manager I could hope for. And to top it off, I've got the most beautiful girlfriend in the world. No matter how you cut it, we're winners."

"You're also broke," Dan cut in.

"Such a killjoy, Dan," Sonny laughed.

Ava smiled too because that was the first time Sonny referred to her as his girlfriend out loud.

Their food arrived and they dined on scrumptious tuna tacos, black beans, and fried plantains. Ava gazed across Taylor's Creek and spotted some wild horses sauntering along the shoreline of Carrot Island. *"I could get used to this…"* she thought wistfully.

As the crew was getting ready to leave, a tall lean forty-ish man walked up to Sonny and said, "Excuse me. Are you Sonny Blue?"

"Yes Sir. May I help you?" Sonny politely responded.

"My name is Stewart Grainger," he extended a hand which Sonny shook. "Do you have a few minutes we can talk in private?" Sonny nodded.

After the team left, Sonny waved to the now open seat next to him.

"How can I help you?" Sonny asked.

"Actually, I might be able to help you."

This piqued Sonny's interest. He raised an eyebrow and asked, "How so?"

"A mutual friend of ours asked me to keep an eye out for anyone or anything that might have a negative impact on you and your crew."

Sonny cut in, "Who is this mutual friend?"

Stewart waved him off, "He'd prefer to remain anonymous. The point is that, for whatever reason, the *Devil Maker* crew seems to have it in for you. Have you noticed anything suspicious about this crew?"

Sonny thought to himself, *"Do you mean other than flying by us near the No Wake Zone for the Day 1 weigh-in?"* but he bit his tongue. "Not really," he responded.

"Hmmm…interesting," Stewart responded a bit skeptically. He then added, "Well, I just wanted you to know that our mutual friend has your back."

"Okay, then. Thanks for the support, Stewart," Sonny stood up, shook the stranger's hand, and headed back to the Bungalow.

When Sonny arrived back at the bungalow, Ava was furiously typing on her laptop.

"Wow, you are a lady on fire with that thing. What gives?" Sonny laughed.

"Hang on. I'm finishing the next chapter of *The Sonny Blue Chronicles*. Now let me send this to Ed…done! I'm all yours now," she smiled.

"Careful what you say, me lady. I might just take your words literally," Sonny smiled hopefully.

Ava then stood up, wrapped her arms around Sonny's neck and drew his lips toward hers. "I'm counting on it." She then kissed him softly on the lips. As usual, Sonny's knees grew weak at her kiss. Ava then took Sonny's hand and guided him to the bedroom. They spent the entire afternoon making desperate love, both unclear of their paths after the tournament. Once their passions were fulfilled, they collapsed beside each other, arms still entwined.

Several minutes passed before Ava broke the silence. "What do you think is going to happen to us after the tournament, Sonny?"

"What do you want to happen?" Sonny replied.

"That's not fair. I'd like your thoughts first."

"My answer is unequivocal. I'd love to continue seeing you. No matter how this tournament plays out, you are the best thing that has ever happened to me, Ava."

Now it was Ava's heart that skipped a beat. "I feel the same, Sonny," she squeezed his hand. "But what about the distance between us? We're five hours apart. I can't see you living in the rat race of D.C., can you?"

Sonny somberly shook his head, "No I can't. Can you envision living down here?"

After a long pause, she said, "Not 100 percent of the time, but maybe part time."

"Perhaps that's something we can start with and figure out the rest later?" Sonny offered.

After a long, thoughtful pause, Ava said, "That works for me." Ava then kissed Sonny on the lips and snuggled back into his arms, her head nestled on his chest.

"Hey, who was that guy that came up to you after lunch today?" Ava queried.

Sonny recapped the conversation.

"Interesting," Ava mused. "Any thoughts on who this mystery friend might be?"

"None. But Stewart didn't seem like a kook. And given what we saw first-hand with the *Devil Maker* crew on Monday, I believe him."

Ava nodded, "Good point. Still, it's rather strange that he would approach you at this stage, don't you think?"

"Always the reporter, aren't you?" Sonny laughed. Ava did too.

XV. Tournament Day 5

"Damnit to Hell!" Eli spat. "Two more blue marlins were caught last night that kicked us out of the money. But *Devil Maker's* marlin got bumped to the third position."

"Well, that's something, anyway," Sonny laughed sarcastically.

"True," Eli conceded. "So, we are back at square one. Everybody ready to shove off?" Eli asked the *Fly Knot?* crew.

Sonny, Mason, and Ava shouted in unison, "Aye, Captain!" Mason untied the last line and pushed the boat away from the dock as Eli slowly motored away from the pier. It was 6 a.m. and the sun was just easing over the horizon. As they left Beaufort Inlet, a similar type of chaos ensued today as on Day 1 of the tournament when more than two hundred boats roared out the channel toward the Gulf Stream.

Sonny and Ava sat next to each other sipping coffee from a thermos as Mason prepped the boat for the two and a half hour journey to the Gulf Stream. About 10 miles into their journey, Ava jumped up excitedly.

"What is that?" she asked pointing off the portside bow. Eli slowed the boat so everyone could get a better look. On the ocean surface was a large ovular looking fish basking in the early morning sun.

"Oh, that's an ocean sunfish, also known as mola mola," Mason answered. "Pretty cool, eh?"

"My God, it's huge! It sure doesn't look the type of sunfish my dad and I used to catch in my youth."

Mason laughed, "Different species of sunfish. Believe it or not, that one is a small ocean sunfish. It's probably only about 500 pounds."

Ava's eyes grew wide, "How big can they get?"

"Over 3,000 pounds and up to nine feet in length."

Ava whistled, "Wow! I know I asked you this before, but do you ever get tired of all this, Mason?" Ava spread her arms out.

"Not for a minute," Mason smiled. "I kind of like my office view too, don't you?"

Ava smiled and nodded.

Mason got back to work. The night before, he and Eli captured some live bait using a cast net. He was currently tending the bait to ensure it was alive and well.

An hour and a half later, Eli slowed the boat to about 8 to 10 mph. He turned his head to face his crew and said, "Okay, I'm marking some big fish on the finder. There's a good chance they're marlin. Mason, start scattering some bait. Let's draw 'em up. Sonny, get your fly rod ready."

"Aye, Captain," Sonny said.

Ava scanned the horizon and noted a few boats scattered about. She pulled out her cellphone and hit 'video' mode on the camera setting.

Sonny pieced together his fly rod and peeled about 70 to 80 feet of fly line off his reel and onto the deck. Sonny inspected *Percival* to ensure it was properly tied to the leader. It was. The fly radiated an iridescent emerald glow. Sonny shook his head and smiled to himself: *How can this fly look so different every time I see it?*

Mason started hurling bait in their wake. A few minutes later, Eli peered into the fish finder and barked, "A big one is coming up. Get ready, Sonny."

"Ready, Captain," Sonny replied.

"There!" Mason exclaimed, pointing 50 yards off the stern.

"That's a big one, probably 600 pounds!" Eli yelled.

Sonny's eyes opened wide when he spotted the behemoth devouring the bait.

"Keep throwing bait but closer to the stern this time, Mason," Eli said calmly.

Mason nodded and, per Eli's instructions, dropped some more bait over the stern but closer to the boat this time. Eli slowed *Fly Knot?* to around four to five mph to draw the marlin closer to the boat. It worked.

"Okay, Sonny. It's 60 feet off our stern. Start casting!" Eli instructed.

Sonny started working his fly rod, playing out about 20 feet of fly line for each false cast until he let loose about 70 feet of fly line across the ocean surface.

"Great cast!" Mason and Eli said simultaneously. And it was. *Percival* landed 10 feet past the marlin which is exactly what Eli wanted.

"Now count down five seconds and start stripping your line fast," Eli said.

Sonny followed Eli's instructions to a tee and, a few seconds later, could see the fly shooting past the marlin's mouth.

"He doesn't like it!" Sonny yelled aloud.

"Wait for it," Mason said patiently.

On cue, the marlin seemed to be annoyed at this strange thing shooting through the water and thrust its open mouth at it most likely in anger rather than hunger. Whatever its reason for lunging at the lure, the effect was the same. Sonny's fly rod slammed down from the impact.

"I'm on!" Sonny screamed in surprise, elation, and shock.

"Really? It's so hard to tell," Mason laughed.

Everyone was smiling now. Ava captured it all on video, including the bait tossing, casting, and hookup. She hoped the camera caught the passion each crew member radiated after the initial hookup. It was certainly etched in her mind.

Eli then put his game face on. "Okay, everyone. We've got a lot of work to do to get that beast in the boat. I think it's north of 600 pounds." If that were indeed true, that would put *Fly Knot?* in the lead for the tournament, assuming, of course, that they successfully boated the fish.

Sonny was into his backing now, and line was screaming off his reel.

"I'm getting spooled, Captain!" Sonny screamed.

"Roger that, Sonny. You know the drill. As I turn the boat about, walk up to the bow so I don't cut the line with the prop. Once I turn us 180 degrees, we're going to chase it," Eli directed. Mason cleared the deck so Sonny had a clear path to the bow.

"Copy that, Captain," Sonny replied as he walked toward the bow, rod in hand. Line was still peeling out of his reel and Sonny was dangerously close to running out of line. Fortunately, the seas were relatively calm today so his footing on the deck was secure. "*At least that's something I don't have to contend with,*" thought Sonny.

Once the boat was in position, Eli slowly pushed the throttle forward to chase the fish. Sonny started furiously reeling in the slack with his fly reel. He started gaining back some line.

"Well done, Sonny! Keep on reeling. Keep some tension on the line as you're reeling it in. We don't need any knots in the line."

Sonny nodded, understanding exactly what Eli meant. The scenario Eli described happened one time when Sonny was fighting a big drum in the Pamlico Sound a few years earlier. After the first hookup, the big drum charged the boat. Sonny furiously reeled in the line to keep tension on the hook so it didn't pop loose from the fish's mouth. Unfortunately for Sonny, he didn't put enough tension on the line while taking up the slack. This created a loop in his fly line. As soon as the fish made another run, the loop kinked up in the reel and… ping…the leader broke. Although disappointed that he lost the big drum, he vowed he'd never make that same mistake.

Sonny gained about half the line back on the reel.

"How's your drag setting?" Eli asked.

"About 30 to 40 pounds," Sonny answered.

"Good. Let's keep it that way for now."

"Roger, Captain," Sonny acknowledged.

The battle went back and forth for another two hours before Ava noticed the waves were increasing in frequency and height. *Fly Knot?* was pitching up and down while Sonny was trying to match the wave frequency with his fly rod. When the boat went up, he raised the rod. When the boat went down, he lowered the rod. *"So much for calm seas,"* Sonny thought as he now tried desperately to keep his footing.

"Why is he doing that with the rod?" Ava asked Mason.

"He's trying to keep tension on the line but not so much that it breaks the leader. If he didn't lower the rod when the boat dropped, the sudden impact might break the line. He's doing a great job of matching the waves with his rod. In fact, I've never seen a fly fisherman so instinctively aware of his surroundings. Even though he's still on the bow, he's going to have to move back here with us on the stern because the wave height might throw him off the boat. Besides, the fish is finally tiring. As you can see, Sonny has a lot more line on his reel than an hour ago," Mason explained. A look of concern then crossed his face, "Hey, you don't look so good, Ava. Are you okay?"

Ava was trying to ignore what she was feeling, but degrading sea conditions were having an undeniable sea sickness effect on her. With no land in sight, she had no horizon to steady herself. The nausea suddenly hit her like a tsunami and she lost her breakfast and lunch over the gunwale. Rather than make light of this, Mason gently put his hand on her shoulder and spoke in a soothing manner, "There, there. I know the feeling, Ava. You feel miserable. But all of us have experienced sea sickness at one time or another. You'll get over this. But I won't lie to you. You won't feel better until we get back to port."

Sonny glanced over his shoulder and asked aloud, "Ava, are you alright?"

Mason answered on her behalf. "Just a touch of seasickness, Sonny. She'll be fine."

Ava raised her head up for a moment and shot him a brave smile before hanging her head back over the gunwale and resumed retching.

"Get back in the game, Sonny," Eli ordered.

With her head still hanging over the gunwale, Ava shot her thumb up as a gesture of assurance for Sonny to continue the fight.

That was all he needed. Sonny turned his head back to the rod and started reeling in some line.

"Okay, Sonny. It's tiring. We can't boat the fish with you on the bow. I'll turn the boat 180 degrees and you walk back to the stern as I turn the boat. On three, okay?"

"Got it, Captain."

"One, two, three!" Eli said loudly. Eli then turned the wheel hard and rode a wave that crested just under the boat. While the boat was turning, Sonny quickly walked back to the stern while keeping tension on the line. Once the maneuver was completed, Eli yelled, "Great job, Sonny! It's still on and it's a big one -- probably over 600 pounds!" Even through her seasick misery, Ava glanced back at the marlin and was astounded at its size.

He then added, "Mason, are you ready?"

"Aye, Captain," Mason yelled back while putting on his fish-handling gloves.

"Here's the plan, Sonny. Just like last time, I'd like you to reel in enough line so Mason can grab the leader. You should touch the leader first in case the marlin is another world record. Mason will then pull the leader in and grab the bill of the marlin. Once he grabs the bill, he'll pull the fish along the port side of the boat. You'll stay slightly ahead of him in case he loses his hold on the fish…"

Mason yelled back, "I won't lose hold of it, Captain!"

"Probably not but, just in case, I want Sonny to hang onto the rod as you walk the fish toward the bow. This is likely a $2 million fish. I don't want to take any chances." Mason and Sonny nodded.

Eli continued, "Once Mason grabs the bill, I'll cut the motor and stand behind both of you. We'll then boat the marlin with the rope and pulley rig," he said glancing at the device hanging over the port gunwale. "Ava, do you feel up to filming this?"

Ava pulled her head up, "Aye, Captain. Just give me the word."

All three men admired her gumption given how miserable she looked.

"Okay everyone, let's go. Sonny, start reeling in some line. Ava, start filming. Mason, get ready."

Sonny complied. Ava pulled out her cellphone and pointed the camera at the marlin thrashing on the surface. *"My Gawd, it's huge!"* she thought.

"How much leader do you have attached to the fly line, Sonny?" Eli asked.

"Twelve feet, Captain. You can see the knot connecting the leader to the fly line just above the surface," Sonny nodded toward the connection since both hands were firmly on the rod.

"Yup," Mason said. "If you reel in another 20 feet of fly line, I'll be able to grab the leader," Mason added.

By this time, Sonny's arms were weary with the two-plus hour fight, but no way was he going to give up now. *"Twenty more feet, twenty more feet…"* he told himself. He cranked the reel with a sudden burst of energy. Mason leaned over the gunwale and grabbed the leader.

"Got it!" Mason screamed.

Eli then cut the engine and walked behind Mason with the hook and rope in his hand. Mason wrapped the leader around one hand and pulled the marlin closer to the port side of the boat. Just as Mason was about to grab the marlin's bill, the fish thrust its mighty head sideways and snapped the leader. Time seemed to stop as everyone froze…even the marlin. A few seconds later, the marlin seemed to sense its newfound freedom and swam back into the depths of the ocean.

The *Fly Knot?* crew didn't recover as quickly as the marlin. Each was devastated for different reasons. Eli saw his share of the $2 million fish evaporate. Mason felt tremendous guilt for believing he was responsible for the line break. Ava was heartbroken for Sonny. But Sonny's despair was mainly due to the loss of *Percival*. His mind meandered down a deep rabbit hole of anxiety. A slew of questions shot through his mind, first and foremost were *"What just happened and why?"*

Almost reading Sonny's thoughts, Mason hung his head and said quietly, "I'm sorry everyone, this is on me."

In a supporting tone, Eli said "I'm not sure about that, mate. Let me look at that leader."

Mason handed over the two-foot fragment of broken monofilament leader that was still attached to the fly line.

After a close inspection, Eli said to the crew, "Do you see this nick?" Everyone bent forward and then nodded.

"That is not a normal break. Do you see how smooth the first part of this cut is? That was done with a very sharp knife. The next portion is splayed out like normal line break from a fish."

"I don't get it, Captain," Ava started. "Sonny fought that fish for over two hours. How come it didn't break off during the fight but broke off when Mason grabbed the leader?"

Sonny answered for the Captain, "I set the drag of my fly reel at around 30 to 40 pounds tension which means I didn't come close to the maximum tension rating of the monofilament leader which is 100 pounds. Even though the marlin is considerably larger than 40 pounds, our Captain chased the fish with the boat, so I didn't run out of fly line backing. This allowed me to keep most of the backing on the reel without applying too much tension on the fish. But with this small cut," Sonny said pointing to the broken leader, "the tension rating on this leader dropped to around..." Sonny glanced toward Eli for an answer.

"Probably 60 pounds or so," Eli responded. "But the tension of grabbing a leader by hand versus a fish on a reel is significantly more. Mason has boated hundreds of big fish in the past and he knows how much tension to apply when grabbing a leader. It was not excessive in this case."

In that moment, the guilt shifted from Mason to Sonny.

"Mason, this wasn't your fault. This is squarely on me," Sonny said looking into Mason's somber eyes. "It was my job to inspect every aspect of my fly fishing equipment including the leader. Obviously, I failed to do this. This was a monumental, $2 million mistake. I apologize to you, Captain, and Ava."

Ava put a reassuring hand on Sonny's shoulder.

After a moment of silence, Eli said, "Sonny, do you have any idea who could have done this?"

Sonny reflected a bit and then shared the incident two days earlier about the suspicious looking man with the blue ballcap exiting the pier where *Fly Knot?* was moored. "I'm not sure if he was on your boat or not but he was coming from that direction. He didn't look me in the eyes either. He kept his head down. He just seemed a bit off. The hairs on my neck stood up so I practically ran to *Fly Knot?* to check on the fly rod and *Percival.* I checked the knot between the fly and the leader and it seemed fine. But I did not strip off all 12 feet of the leader to check the connection between the leader and the fly line because I put new monofilament leader on the day before."

"And no one else would think to do that since you replaced the leader the day before with a brand new one," Eli added reassuringly. Mason nodded in support.

The *Fly Knot?* crew was so immersed in this discussion that they didn't notice the large sportfishing vessel pull up on their starboard side.

"Ahoy, Maties!"

The *Fly Knot?* crew glanced over and noticed Bartholomew Winslow and his *Devil Maker* crew grinning like Cheshire cats.

"We couldn't help but notice that you lost a very big marlin right at the boat. Tsk, tsk. I'm so sorry," Bart said still grinning. "But take heart. We just caught one that will likely be the winning marlin," he said nodding to the crew. One of his crew members then hoisted up a large blue marlin on a rope-and-pulley. It was indeed a big marlin but Eli thought it wasn't quite as big as the one they had just lost.

"Ava, you look kind of green. Would you like a ride back to port with the winners in a bigger boat? It's getting rather sporty out here right now. I'll even give you an exclusive interview."

Ava leaned her head over the starboard gunwale and threw up in the direction of *Devil Maker*. She then shot up her middle finger in the direction of Bart.

Bart laughed, "I guess I have my answer. Okay, boys, let's head back to port."

Just before Bart put his boat in gear, Sonny spotted a man with a blue ballcap slither out of the *Devil Maker* cabin. He glanced briefly at Sonny and then turned away.

"Captain," Sonny said quietly to Eli. "I think that's him," he said pointing to the blue cap man.

"Are you sure?" Eli asked.

"I'm not 100 percent certain, but I'm pretty sure that was the man I spotted near your boat the other day," Sonny replied.

"It's sort of a moot point anyway," Eli sighed, "because I don't keep cameras onboard *Fly Knot?*. But it would be nice to know for sure if it were him so we could mention the issue with the tournament committee. But without proof, it's your word against his."

"I understand," Sonny said resignedly.

"That said," Eli continued, "we will not go quietly into the night. I'd like to confront him in person to get a sense if he nicked the line or not. My brother used to say that I have a built-in lie detector inside my brain."

"Remind me not to lie to you," Sonny said sardonically.

"That's the least of my worries with you, Sonny." Then to the rest of the crew, Eli said, "It's 2 o'clock and the waves are kicking up so I'm calling it for the day. Let's put our gear away and head back to port."

While Sonny and Mason started packing up, Ava walked up to Eli and, out of earshot of Sonny and Mason, asked, "So what's the marine forecast and plan for tomorrow, Captain?"

"You're not going to like this, Ava, but the forecast is calling for stiff winds and high waves with a good chance of thunderstorms in the afternoon."

"Will you cancel the trip?" Ava asked somewhat hopefully given her current nauseous state.

"It's a borderline call, but I think we can fish in the morning and head back to port in the afternoon to avoid any thunderstorms."

"So, what do you think the odds are that Sonny can hook another big marlin tomorrow?" Ava asked quietly.

"To be honest with you, I'm stunned that we could hook two big blue marlins on the fly rod in less than a week. With the loss of his magic fly…what did he call it again?"

"*Percival*," Ava answered softly.

"Right. Anyway, Sonny's confidence is probably at an all-time low right now. And this may sound strange, but if you don't have confidence in your lure, or fly in this case, you are generally not as good a fisherperson as when you believe in your lures and equipment."

"I want to support Sonny, but I want to do what's right. Do you think I should go fishing with you all tomorrow?"

Eli gave a long pause before answering, "In the short time that we've known each other, it's clear to me how much you both care for each other."

"There's a 'but' here isn't there?" Ava asked.

"Not really. When you first got seasick, Sonny looked very concerned about you and maybe was a bit distracted. I don't think that had anything to do with the marlin we lost today but tomorrow is our last shot at a marlin and…"

"You want Sonny 100 percent focused on fishing tomorrow," Ava finished for him.

"Something like that," Eli admitted. "I suggest you ask him tonight. Personally, I love having you on the boat. You know when to get involved and when to step aside. I'm sure Mason feels the same."

Ava read nothing but sincerity across Eli's face so she didn't pursue this line of questioning any further and decided to follow Eli's advice.

"I've got a few calls to make. May I borrow your satellite phone?" Ava asked.

"Of course," Eli said pointing to its location.

About a mile away, a tall lean man onboard the vessel *Caught 6* observed, using high powered binoculars, the exchange taking place between *Fly Knot?* and *Devil Maker*. When he saw Ava thrust her middle finger at the *Devil Maker* crew, he shook his head and laughed quietly to himself. The wheels started turning inside his head…

At 5:30 p.m., the crew members of *Fly Knot?* were sipping beers at an outdoor table at a watering hole within eyesight of the Big Rock weigh-in station. Sonny was playing back the past few hours in his head. *Fly Knot?* arrived at the Morehead City dock at 5 p.m. with little or no fanfare. Word of the crew's lost blue marlin spread quickly as the only people who greeted them at the dock were Chris Staples from the *Raleigh Times* and Dan Jones. After Mason secured the boat to the dock, Chris walked up to Sonny and asked, "Other than that, Mrs. Lincoln, how was the play?"

Sonny laughed, "Yeah I guess we do look like we've come from a funeral, don't we?"

Chris then added empathetically, "Yeah, Ava called me from the boat with the news. She supplied no details other than the fish was lost during the landing. I'm sorry, Sonny."

"Thanks, Chris. Yes, it was most unfortunate. I'm not sure if you're writing a story on this debacle or not but, if you are, please mention in your article that I was the sole reason the fish broke off. The captain and crew were amazing."

Chris shook his head, "Nah, I'm not that kind of reporter. This is off the record but can you supply more details on how the fish broke off at the boat?"

"It was a failure on my part not to check every piece of my equipment and leader at the outset of our journey this morning."

"Care to elaborate?" Chris probed.

"Not really," Sonny replied.

A few boat slips away, a deafening roar erupted. Sonny glanced over and saw the *Devil Maker* crew hoisting a blue marlin on the scale. It read 605 pounds, making it the largest blue marlin caught during the tournament.

"Our fish was bigger," Eli said quietly to Chris.

Chris's eyes opened wide, "Really? Their fish is a monster!"

Eli nodded.

Color was finally coming back to Ava's face as she joined Chris, Dan, Eli, Mason and Sonny at their table.

"Thanks for the call, Ava. Hey, you don't look so good," Chris said sympathetically.

"You should have seen me earlier," Ava groaned.

Their eyes drifted back to *Devil Maker*. It was like a train wreck. No one from Team Sonny wanted to look, but they couldn't help themselves as they witnessed all the crew members stroking the big marlin and grinning at the cameras with their perfect white teeth and chiseled jaws. Eli closely studied the faces of each *Devil Maker* crew member, including the squirrelly blue-cap man. *"Sonny is right,"* Eli thought. *"Something is off about that guy."*

"Damn blue bloods," cussed Eli. "Probably not one of 'em earned an honest day's wages in their lives. Now they will likely win the whole shooting match--the first big marlin and the biggest."

Chris did the math in his head and whistled, "So that ends up being, what, $2 million?"

"Closer to $2.7 million," Eli said shaking his head.

Eli then glanced over at Sonny and, noting his crestfallen face, quickly added, "Look it's not over, Sonny. We've still got tomorrow, right?"

Sonny nodded slowly, but he understood the reality of the situation.

Quiet to this point, Dan pulled Eli aside and asked, "So what are Sonny's chances tomorrow?"

"I'm not going to lie to you, Dan. We already beat the odds by landing a world record marlin on the fly on the first day of the tournament. Today's marlin would have shattered that record. But that is not what concerns me the most. Sonny lost his magic fly, *Percival*. Look at his face. His confidence is shattered. You seem to be a numbers guy so I'd put our odds at about a million to one."

Dan looked closely at Sonny and agreed with Eli's assessment. Sonny looked defeated.

"So, what do you suggest we do?" Dan asked hopefully.

Loud enough so the rest of the team could hear, Eli said, "I suggest we clean up, then meet at *Painkillers* and drink copiously."

"Hear, hear! That's the best idea I've heard today!" Mason chimed in.

A few hours later, Team Sonny was sitting around an outside table at *Painkillers* finishing off the first round of the double signature drink. Despite the compassionate presence of his friends, Sonny couldn't shake the guilt he felt for the events that played out on *Fly Knot?* earlier today. He was in a deep hole he couldn't seem to climb out of. Shortly after Eli ordered a second round, Sonny felt something licking his hand. He looked down, smiled, and shouted, "Milly!"

The golden retriever was excitedly wagging her tail while simultaneously licking Sonny's hands and nuzzling his lap. Close on Milly's heels were Alan, Holly, and Colt sporting broad grins.

"Surprise!" they simultaneously yelled.

Alan had graciously agreed to look after Milly throughout the tournament. He loved Milly almost as much as Sonny did and he often cared for her during Sonny's fishing tournaments. Until this moment, Sonny didn't realize how much he missed her. He lowered his face and was instantly rewarded with a slobbery kiss. His somber mood instantly lifted.

"A little bird," Alan nodded toward Ava, "told us that you needed a boost tonight. So here we are."

Sonny looked toward Ava and silently mouthed, "Thank you." She just smiled and nodded.

They grabbed three stray chairs and squeezed around the table. Milly plopped down with a contented sigh between Sonny and Ava. She rested her head on Sonny's foot with a paw on Ava's.

"I think she missed you two," Holly laughed.

Sonny introduced the new arrivals to the *Fly Knot?* crew and Chris. When the drinks arrived, Alan held his drink up in Sonny's direction and said, "No matter how tomorrow plays out, Sonny, you've made us all proud. Cheers!" They all raised and clinked their glasses.

Sonny said quietly to Alan, "You heard what happened today, right?"

"Yeah, I heard that you fought the biggest blue marlin ever hooked on a fly rod and played it for more than two hours before the equipment failed. And on Day 1 of the tournament, you boated the biggest blue marlin ever hooked on a fly rod. How can you consider this week anything but a success?"

"Other than the fact that we have zero winnings?" Sonny added dryly.

"Apple crap, Sonny. Money comes and goes. You forged a legacy this week. Now the rest of the world knows what only a handful of us already knew, and that is you have a remarkable gift."

"It's true, Sonny," Eli cut in. "I've chartered hundreds of nearshore and offshore fly fishing trips and I've never seen anyone handle a fly rod the way you do. It's as if the fly rod is an extension of your arm. Very little wasted energy. Just two or three false casts and you lay your fly in the precise target area, with great distance and even into a stiff wind."

Mason nodded in agreement.

"But I lost a $2 million fish today! How can either of you forgive me for that?" Sonny asked in despair while looking at both Eli and Mason.

Mason said, "Am I disappointed that we lost that fish. Hell yes! But none of us considered sabotage would play into this…"

"Wait a minute," Chris cut in. "Sabotage?"

"Damn! I'm sorry, Captain," Mason said.

Eli brushed his apology aside, "No worries, mate. Look everyone. We can't prove any of this so I'm going to ask all of you to keep this to yourselves, okay?" Everyone nodded. Eli then shared what happened on the boat earlier today.

"Holy shit," Colt spat. "We can't let them get away with this!" he said gritting his teeth.

"Unfortunately, we have no way of proving our suspicion that one of *Devil Maker's* crew members nicked Sonny's leader. So, yes, that is precisely what we must do."

Holly shook her head, "This is just not right."

"No, it's not. But those are the cards we've been dealt and we must somehow push this travesty aside and focus on tomorrow," Eli said.

Alan, who had been like a second father to Sonny glanced at him and said, "Why the heck are you smiling right now, Sonny?"

Ava followed Sonny's gaze and noticed an attractive sixty-ish woman approaching their table.

Sonny at once stood up and wrapped his arms around the woman. "Mom! You're here!"

"Of course, son. I wouldn't miss this for the world!"

"Mom, I'd like to introduce you to my team. Of course, you know most of these people. As for the others, this is Captain Eli, First Mate Mason, reporter Chris, and finally, this is…"

Sonny's mom cut in, and donning a warm smile said, "And you must be Ava. Hi, Ava. I'm Noreen."

Ava stood and offered a hand.

"I'm sorry but a handshake won't do," Noreen said, wrapping her arms around Ava.

"I've heard so much about you that I feel like I've known you for years," she whispered in Ava's ear.

Ava felt nothing but warmth and acceptance from Noreen. She liked her at once. Ava offered her seat to Noreen while Sonny grabbed an empty chair from a nearby table. Ava and Noreen started conversing like long lost friends while the others discussed fishing strategy for the next day.

Thirty minutes later, Ava glanced at Sonny and saw a broad smile for the first time since the day before.

Dan noticed this too and said, "Why are you smiling, Sonny?"

"I honestly don't know." But Sonny did know. Here he'd lost a $2 million prize today and his friends and family were still firmly behind him. He smiled at Ava and she smiled right back. She got it.

"Okay, what's the plan for tomorrow, Captain?" Holly asked, jolting everybody back to reality.

"Pray for a miracle," Eli responded.

"That's it?" Holly laughed.

"Pretty much," Eli laughed back.

After their passions were spent later that evening, Ava and Sonny remained entwined on the bed. Air from a ceiling fan was slowly evaporating beads of sweat from the surface of their naked bodies.

Ava kissed Sonny softly on the lips, "Penny for your thoughts?"

"I don't know. I'm still trying to shake off the loss of *Percival*. Strangely, that bothers me more than the lost marlin today. Can you believe that?"

Ava said, "Actually, I can. I've seen firsthand the effect that magic fly had on you over the past several months. You probably felt like you lost a good friend."

Sonny nodded slowly.

Just then, Sam Hunt crooned from a bed-side blue tooth speaker:

...so say I'm someone that you wish you never met
Your best mistake, your worst regret
Say everything, say anything but nothing
'Cause nothing lasts forever
Nothing lasts forever...

They both laughed aloud at the timing of the song.

"But seriously, Sonny, you are an excellent fly fisherman. I've seen you catch big fish without *Percival*. Can you somehow push aside the loss of *Percival* and take an alternate approach?"

"Such as?"

Ava hesitated a long while before answering, "You may have noticed that I got a tad seasick today. Eli said the weather conditions will be at least as bad tomorrow -- maybe worse if a storm kicks in. I'd love to be with you tomorrow but..."

Sonny cut in, "Say no more, Ava. It's miserable being seasick. I completely understand if you'd like to sit tomorrow out."

Ava breathed a sigh of relief, "Thanks, Sonny. But I was wondering if you could ask Pipes to go in my stead? He knows a lot more about fly fishing than I do!"

"True. But you are a lot prettier than he is. Besides, you are my lucky charm," Sonny smiled.

"Thanks for your understanding. Rest assured that I'll be at the dock when you arrive tomorrow afternoon. I'll keep tabs with Chris throughout the day to check on *Fly Knot?'s* progress. I plan to write the last chapter of *The Sonny Blue Chronicles* sometime tomorrow night."

"I hope it's a happy ending," Sonny said hopefully. But neither was thinking of the tournament at that moment.

XVI. Tournament Final Day

Fly Knot? departed the Beaufort dock with no fanfare this morning. Most of the reporters were hovering around *Devil Maker* a few boat slips away. Bart was grinning ear-to-ear as he spoke to some members of the press while his crew readied the boat for departure. Sonny shook his head, *"The rich get richer."* But then he glanced at his friends and family standing on the dock in front of the *Fly Knot?* boat slip: Dan, Alan, Holly, Colt, his mom and, of course, Ava. Despite -- maybe because of -- the lack of media attention at the *Fly Knot?* slip, Sonny suddenly felt buoyed with optimism. In his heart, he knew he had almost no chance of catching a winning marlin today, or any marlin at all, for that matter, given the poor weather forecast and loss of *Percival.* But he also knew the people at the boat slip would stand behind him, no matter how today played out.

Before *Fly Knot?* shoved off, Ava waved Sonny over to her. He hopped off the boat and walked over to her. She took his hand and walked a few steps from the small group.

Ava said sheepishly, "Um, Sonny. There's something I've been meaning to tell you for a while…"

"Yes?" Sonny smiled.

Ava cupped her hands over Sonny's ear and whispered something the others could not hear.

Sonny pulled back with a look of surprise. Then a slow, broad smile crept across his face. They locked eyes for a long while before they kissed for an even longer period.

Eli yelled, "Get a room, you two! But right now, we've got work to do!"

"Aye, Captain!" Sonny yelled back with a grin. He then hopped onboard *Fly Knot?* while Mason kicked the boat off the pier. Sonny waved to Ava and the others as *Fly Knot?* motored out to sea.

Two hours later, Eli was navigating *Fly Knot?* through stiff winds and big rollers. The sky was gray and misty but so far had held back the rain. Above the roar of wind, he turned to his crew and said, "We've only got about three hours of fishing before the weather turns for the worse. So, let's make the most of this time, okay?" The crew nodded.

While Mason was tending the bait for casting, Sonny pulled out his fly box and asked quietly, "Okay, Pipes, what fly shall we use?"

Pipes looked carefully over each fly in Sonny's fly box. "How about that one?" Pipes asked pointing to a large chartreuse and white Clouser fly.

For the second time that day, a look of surprise cast across Sonny's face. "Really? Why that fly?" Sonny asked.

"Two reasons. First, it's the largest fly in your box. Second, you recall the words of the late great Lefty Kreh, right?"

"Of course. 'If it ain't chartreuse, it ain't no use!'"

"Precisely," Pipes answered. "But there's something else isn't there, Sonny?"

After a long pause, Sonny nodded but remained silent. He thought to himself, *"This is the last fly my father tied for me."*

Sonny tied the fly to the new leader on his fly rod. Pipes smiled. Within 10 minutes, Sonny hooked and boated a large dolphin that Mason put on ice in the fish storage bin. Although it wasn't their target species, it provided a confidence boost to Sonny that he could hook a saltwater fish with the fly. If it didn't place in the money, the crew would at least have some nice mahi mahi dinners with the dolphin fillets.

Thirty minutes later, Eli slowed the boat and yelled, "I'm marking some big fish. Mason, get the bait ready. Sonny, get your fly rod ready."

"Aye, Captain!" Mason and Sonny yelled simultaneously.

Mason started cutting up some fresh bonito into chunks and proceeded to scatter the chunks off the stern. Sonny stripped about 60 to 70 feet of fly line on the boat deck. He normally could cast 80 feet or more of intermediate fly line but the strong winds would cut this distance a good bit today.

Still looking at his fish finder, Eli yelled, "A big one is coming up. Keep throwing bait, Mason."

Mason hurled a dozen more chunks of bonito off the stern.

Eli kept up the play-by-play, "It's getting closer to the surface...there!" he screamed pointing behind the boat.

Sure enough, a large blue marlin was thrashing at the bait.

"Keep throwing the bait, Mason. Sonny, I'm going to slow the boat a bit. As soon as I do, try to cast your fly so it lands in the middle of that bait." Sonny nodded.

As soon as Eli slowed the boat, Sonny made three false casts and landed the fly about 10 feet off target.

"Damn it!" Sonny lamented.

"That's okay, Sonny," Pipes said reassuringly. "Pull in your line and cast again. But this time adjust for this strong wind."

Sonny quickly stripped in the line and began casting again. This time, he cast the fly smack in the middle of the bait.

"Great cast, Sonny!" Eli said. "Let it sink for a few seconds. That's right. Now strip hard and fast!" Eli screamed.

But Sonny was in a different mind-set. He didn't exactly ignore Eli's instructions. Rather, he was trying to get a feel for this fish. Several questions flashed through Sonny's mind just then. *Why did this fish come to the surface? How can I grab its attention? How fast should I move the fly to trigger a strike?*

Sonny suddenly turned to Eli and yelled, "Stop the boat and turn off the engine, Captain!" He said this with such conviction that Eli instantly stopped the boat and cut off the motor.

Sonny retrieved the fly line and cast again but this time past the marlin. The marlin slipped below the surface.

"Sonny, what are you doing?" Eli asked in frustration. "It's losing interest."

"Maybe," Sonny said coolly as he started slowly stripping his fly line. A few seconds later, the fly line went taut and the rod bent over like an archer's bow. Sonny jammed the hook in the mighty beast's hard mouth.

"Or maybe not," he laughed.

"Fish on!" Mason yelled in delight. Line began screaming off Sonny's reel.

Eli then fired up the twin outboards. By this time, the crew knew the drill. Sonny walked toward the bow of the boat keeping tension on the fly rod while Eli slowly moved the boat in the direction of the fish. Line continued to scream off Sonny's reel until Eli finally matched the speed of the fish. Line suddenly went slack on the reel.

"Did we lose it?" Mason asked.

"I don't think so," Sonny replied. "I think the fish turned and is now charging the boat."

Sonny began reeling in line as fast as possible to catch up to the fish. Finally, the line went taut and, once again, the rod bent over. Everyone breathed a sigh of relief.

"The fish is still on!" Sonny announced unnecessarily.

"This battle is far from over," screamed Eli from the wheel. Almost on cue, Eli heard a rumble of thunder off their stern. He then glanced at his radar screen and cussed, "Dammit to hell! The forecast didn't call for any weather until later this afternoon. But there is a storm brewing about 10 miles south," he said to Mason as he pointed to the screen. Adding emphasis to his words, the winds kicked up as did the waves.

"What do you want to do, Captain? Should we cut the line and head in?" Mason asked.

After a thoughtful pause, Eli said, "Not yet. Let's see if this storm tracks any closer before exploring that option."

"Roger, Captain," Mason replied.

Eli then turned the boat 180 degrees so that Sonny could fight the marlin off the stern, rather than the bow, to allow sturdier footing. The boat pitches are less severe on the stern than the bow, particularly in high wave conditions like the ones they were now facing. Even so, the waves were increasing in height and frequency, making footing challenging for Sonny. The light mist turned to a hard rain, reducing visibility to less than a mile. Now the deck was slippery, making it even tougher to find a steady footing. On top of that, the boat was making large up-and-down pitches due to the high waves. These pitches created extra tension and slack on the fly line that could either break the line or dislodge the fly. To compensate for these pitches, Sonny would continually raise and lower his fly rod with each wave, trying to keep steady pressure on the fish without breaking the line.

Sonny flashed back 21 years ago when a storm, like the one they were now facing, took his father's life. Fear was coursing through Sonny's body as he relived that tragic event. He started plunging deeper and deeper in despair when, suddenly, he felt a hand rest lightly on his shoulder.

"You're going to be okay, Sonny," Pipes said in a soothing tone.

"How can you be sure?" Sonny asked.

"I just know," Pipes answered reassuringly.

At that moment, Sonny took a leap of faith and decided to let go of his fears, anxiety, and insecurity. He reflected on his team including this crew, plus his friends and family back at the dock. To his core, he trusted them all. Win or lose, this group of friends and family would stand behind him. He was 100 percent confident of this. This sudden epiphany gave him a level of confidence he'd never experienced before. It was a shot of adrenaline he sorely needed at this juncture.

The crew watched in quiet admiration as Sonny battled the marlin without complaint. In fact, he seemed oblivious to the mounting obstacles he now faced. On the contrary, he seemed energized by the events playing out.

Mason stepped beside Eli and discretely asked, "How's the storm tracking, Captain?"

Pointing at the radar screen, Eli said, "The good news is the lightning is still about 10 or 15 miles offshore. But, as you can see, the sea conditions are degrading. Wait a minute. Look at that!" Eli said pointing to a new object on the screen.

Mason said, "I think that's a boat coming up on our stern."

Eli pulled out his binoculars and, sure enough, a large sportfishing boat was heading in a perpendicular path toward their stern.

"God damn it! That's *Devil Maker* heading right in the path of our fish!"

"Fuckers!" Mason yelled.

Sonny saw it too.

Eli then picked up the radio mic and yelled, "*Devil Maker, Devil Maker!* Be advised that we are hooked up and you are heading right toward our line. Veer off, veer off! Do you copy?"

Silence.

Eli repeated the same message.

Silence.

To make matters worse, the blue marlin was now surfacing about 200 yards behind *Fly Knot?* thus exposing the fly line to an easy break-off should a vessel cross its line. The prop would cut the line like a hot knife through butter.

The crew felt helpless. It was like a nightmare playing out in slow motion as they watched in horror as *Devil Maker* plowed relentlessly toward their stern.

Back at the Beaufort bungalow, Ava was pounding out the last chapter of *The Sonny Blue Chronicles.* Milly lay at her feet providing occasional groans of contentment which made Ava smile. Although Sonny and Ava insisted that Noreen, Alan, Holly, and Colt stay at the bungalow the previous night, they had made prior arrangements to stay at a nearby historic home in Beaufort owned by friends Charlie and Debbie Lewenthal. However, Alan acquiesced about Milly.

After scratching Milly's neck, Ava returned to writing her article. She left the end open until *Fly Knot?* returned to port later today. Although she was overall pleased with the *Chronicles* project, she was apprehensive about her future with Sonny. The two were so focused on the months leading up to the tournament that they didn't really have a plan afterwards. Financially, the *Tribune* paid for her travel expenses leading up to the tournament, but that would end after today. The paper also supplied the time which helped nurture their relationship. Given the distance between the two, however, a long-distance relationship didn't seem sustainable. But she could not deny the strong feelings she had for Sonny, that she believed were reciprocated. Was that enough to keep them together? She hoped so.

Her cellphone buzzed, jolting her back to reality.

"Hi, Chris. What's up?"

"Sonny hooked another blue marlin!" Chris Staples said breathlessly.

"What? How do you know this? Where are you?" Ava replied excitedly. She glanced at the phone for the time: 11:45 a.m.

"I'm in the press tent at the Morehead City weigh-in area. Another captain called in from the Gulf Stream a few minutes ago to report that *Fly Knot?* was hooked up. But here's the thing, Ava. The weather is getting nasty out there. The winds and waves have kicked up and there have been reports of lightening as well."

Ava's emotions plummeted from joy to concern in a flash.

"What else can you tell me? Is it safe for them to be out there?" Ava pressed.

"Ava, you know what I know at this point. If you come here now, you can listen firsthand to any future call-in reports."

His suggestion was not necessary as Ava was already packing up her laptop, leash, and Milly. "I'll be there in 15 minutes," she said just before hanging up.

Once she arrived at the press tent, Ava spotted Dan, Alan, Holly, and Colt standing anxiously around Chris who was talking on his cellphone. Leash-tethered Milly greeted the group with licks and a whirling tail.

Cupping his hand over his cellphone, Chris looked up at Ava and glancing at the group, said, "I called the others immediately after calling you. I hope you don't mind."

"Of course not. I'm glad to see everyone," she said, smiling nervously at the group. "Where's Noreen?" she added.

"She'll be here later. She's a bit on edge about the weather situation *Fly Knot?* is facing right now," Dan answered solemnly. Ava nodded.

Chris then disconnected his call and said to the group, "Okay here's the latest report from the captain who originally called in *Fly Knot?'s* hookup. He's not sure when Sonny originally hooked the marlin but the captain estimates it's been at least an hour. The good news is that Sonny is still hooked up. The bad news is the weather is continuing to degrade offshore and visibility is now greatly reduced. In fact, this captain can barely see *Fly Knot?* now. He didn't want to move his boat any closer to *Fly Knot?* than necessary for fear of breaking off Sonny's fly line." Everyone nodded in understanding.

"Are there any other vessels within eyesight of *Fly Knot?*?" Ava inquired.

"Yes. Just one other. Any guesses?" Chris inquired.

"*Devil Maker?*" Colt accurately guessed.

"Yup."

"Shit!" the group said collectively.

They instinctively glanced at the huge electronic screen near the weigh-in station where the display read:

Hookups

Fly Knot?
Hooked up at 11:17 a.m.

Ava said, "So *Fly Knot?* is the only boat with a blue marlin hookup right now. That's a good thing, right?"

Chris said, "Normally this would be a great thing. But most of the boats are heading back to port now due to the poor weather and sea conditions. So, there are very few boats, if any, out there to report what is happening right now. To make matters worse, no one can reach *Fly Knot?* via satellite phone. This could be a weather or technical issue with their phone, so I wouldn't get too concerned at this point."

But, of course, they were all concerned. Their worry shifted from losing a contest to survival.

Holly asked, "Do all of the participating boats check in here after they return to port?"

"Unfortunately, the only boats that return to this weigh-in station are the ones who caught fish that may be eligible for prize money. Before you ask, *Fly Knot?* did not need to pull up to a nearby slip on the day they had their marlin break-off. But Captain Eli informed me later that night that he wanted to see the looks on the *Devil Maker's* crews' faces when they hoisted their blue marlin. He mentioned something about being a human lie detector- whatever that means. Given that Sonny is the only boat hooked up with a blue marlin right now, the other boats will return to their respective marinas scattered up and down the North Carolina coast."

Holly pressed, "Can the Big Rock officials reach out to the other boats to find out what is going on?"

"Sure, but there are over two hundred boats returning to port right now so reaching out to all of them will take time. Plus, they are dealing with the same sea conditions that *Fly Knot?* is experiencing, so they will have their hands full trying to get safely back to port."

Ava asked, "Is there anything we can do at this point?"

"Just be patient and see how this plays out," Chris answered quietly. After a pause he continued, "But I'll check in periodically with the tournament officials to see if they are able to reach *Fly Knot?* by satellite."

"Thanks, Chris. How about we take turns checking in with them?" Ava suggested. Chris nodded.

At 3:13 p.m., 60-foot *Excalibur* pulled into the weigh-in slip with a dolphin measured at 38.5 pounds. The electronic display board only showed blue marlin hookups, so boats hooking up other gamefish weren't known until their boats pulled into the weigh-in slip. Ava took a keen interest in the crew of *Excalibur*, hoping to glean information on *Fly Knot?*. After the official weigh-in was completed, the captain pulled the boat out of the weigh-in slip and moored it to a nearby slip so his crew could wash down the boat.

Ava walked over to the slip and called out to one of the crew members washing down the rods and reels, "Excuse me, may I please have a word with your first mate or captain?" Before glancing up, the mate was about to reject this request. He then locked eyes on the beautiful woman standing on the pier and changed course, "Absolutely!" He then handed the hose to another crew member and hopped off the boat. The crew member took the hose and smirked as he's seen this movie before.

"Hi. My name is Scottie. I'm the first mate on this vessel," he said while extending his hand.

Ava briefly shook his hand and said, "Hi Scottie. My name is Ava Tyson. I'm a reporter with the *DC Tribune*. First off, congratulations on your dolphin! That is a prize-winning fish, isn't it?"

"It is indeed," Scottie answered with pride. "It won $2,000 for the largest dolphin caught today and is the second largest dolphin caught thus far in the tournament. If that weight holds, there will be another $25,000 in prize money. Given the conditions out there, I doubt any other boats will bring in a larger dolphin."

"Speaking of sea conditions, you are probably aware that *Fly Knot?* hooked a blue marlin, right?" Ava asked.

Scottie nodded his head solemnly, "Yes, I heard he hooked up. But I can't imagine that boat holding up under those sea conditions. I mean look at the size of our boat. It's 60 feet long with an 18-foot beam. We were tossed around like a cork in those waters. *Fly Knot?* is what, 40 or 42 feet in length?"

Ava nodded, "Something like that."

"I mean, Eli is a great captain, but the conditions out there would test the skills of any captain especially on a boat that small."

After seeing Ava's sudden crestfallen face, Scottie quickly added, "But if anyone can pull this off, it's Captain Eli."

These add-on words did little to assuage Ava's feelings of despair. She then asked, "When your boat headed back, did you see any other boats still fishing in your vicinity?"

Scottie paused before answering, "No. For safety reasons, the boats in our area decided to head back to port at about the same time in case there were any issues."

Ava thanked him and headed back to Team Sonny to update the group about her conversation with Scottie.

"Anything new from the tournament officials?" she asked Chris.

He shook his head, "Unfortunately not. They have reached out to several participating vessels but most of those vessels are either heading back now or have already returned to their marinas."

Alan asked, "Should we ask them to contact the Coast Guard?"

Chris said, "I asked them that as well and the officials said, unless there is a mayday distress call from *Fly Knot?* or a nearby vessel, they are reluctant to contact the Coast Guard."

"So, we just sit here and do nothing?" Holly asked in exasperation.

"For the time being, yes. I'm afraid so," Chris replied.

"So, what are the rules about when a marlin catch has to be brought to the scales?" Colt asked.

Holly punched Colt's shoulder, "Is that all you can think about right now? Our friend may be in dire trouble, and you're worried about catch eligibility?"

"Ouch! I'm just trying to be practical, Sis!" Colt replied rubbing his shoulder.

Chris interrupted, "No, it's quite all right, Holly. It's a fair question your brother asked. Colt, if the blue marlin hookup occurs before 3 p.m., there is no time limit on when the marlin can be brought back to the weigh-in slip. For safety reasons, most boaters prefer to return to port before sundown which is usually around 8:30 this time of year." Glancing at his watch, he added, "It's 4:30 now, so there are about four hours of daylight left."

Seconds crept to minutes which crawled to hours. Word spread quickly about *Fly Knot?*'s predicament. The last day of the tournament is normally one of the most crowded days of the event. But the turnout of fans and onlookers tonight was even larger than normal due to the dire situation playing out in the Gulf Stream right now. Several thousand spectators crowded around the large digital screen at the weigh-in slip for an update of *Fly Knot?'s* status. The number of media personnel grew as well. The last night of the tournament is usually a festive occasion, but the mood tonight was somber, almost wake-like. Many of the spectators previously read about Sonny's plight either through local media outlets or Ava's *The Sonny Blue Chronicles*. Thus, most of the attendees were emotionally invested in the events playing out today.

At 8 p.m., the director of the tournament decided to contact the U.S. Coast Guard and start a search for *Fly Knot?*.

Despite the lack of a mayday call from *Fly Knot?* or any other vessel in its vicinity, she didn't want to take any chances. Less than 10 minutes after receiving the call, the Fort Macon Coast Guard branch sent a helicopter in the direction of the last reported coordinates of *Fly Knot?*. They also sent a cutter toward the same coordinates.

A torrent of emotions flooded Ava's body. She had kept them in check to this point but when Sonny's mom, Noreen, arrived shortly after the director placed the call to the Coast Guard, they poured out. Noreen locked eyes with Ava and opened her arms. Ava ran to Noreen and the two embraced. Tears poured out from both women. After a few minutes, they separated. Ava then updated Noreen on *Fly Knot?'s* status.

"We don't know anything yet, Noreen. For all we know, *Fly Knot?* could be working its way back to port right now. Even though it doesn't look too windy here at port, the marine weather reports indicate the seas are rough in the Gulf Stream right now. I spoke with some of the boat captains here and they said a boat the size of *Fly Knot?* would take a while to navigate those seas. A Coast Guard helicopter left a short while ago, so hopefully they'll spot them and report back to the tournament officials."

While Ava's report tilted toward the optimistic, Noreen could read the concern in Ava's eyes. The gut feeling Noreen initially felt when meeting Ava yesterday were now solidified: "*She truly cares for my son,*" she thought to herself.

"What can we do to help?" Noreen asked.

"There's really nothing else that any of us can do at this point other than wait. How about some coffee?"

"I'd love some. Thank you, Ava. Oh, hey, Dan." Dan had quietly approached the two women.

Dan didn't say a word. Rather, he opened his arms and gave Noreen a warm hug. As much as he tried to hide his tears, he couldn't hold back the waterworks.

"It's okay, Dan" Noreen said while patting his back. "This is Sonny we're talking about here. As we both know, he's a resourceful young man. He's escaped a lot of dicey situations in the past. And, from what I hear, the captain and mate of *Fly Knot?* are top notch at running that boat. I choose to be optimistic and I hope you do too."

Wiping tears away, Dan just nodded. Ava did too.

Two more agonizing hours passed with no news on *Fly Knot?*.

At 10:30 p.m., Noreen asked Ava, "I'd like to meet the tournament director, Ava. Can you make that happen?"

"Of course. Chris knows her. I'll ask him to join us."

The three walked to the second floor of the Big Rock Tournament building and found the executive director talking excitedly on her cellphone. After she disconnected, she glanced up and spotted Chris.

Chris made quick introductions. "Hi, Melinda. I'd like you to meet Sonny Blue's mother, Noreen Blue and Sonny's girlfriend, Ava Tyson. Noreen and Ava, this is Melinda Stetson, the tournament director."

The three exchanged brief handshakes.

"Any new developments?" Noreen asked hopefully.

"As a matter of fact, there are. I've got excellent news. I just got off the phone with the Coast Guard and they spotted a vessel that matches the description of *Fly Knot?*!"

"Oh, my goodness!" Noreen exclaimed. "How far away is the boat?"

"They just entered Beaufort Inlet so they should arrive here in the next 20 or 30 minutes."

"Thank you so much!" Noreen said smiling. She walked around the desk and hugged Melinda who was smiling as well.

Noreen and Ava were giddy with the news. As they left the building arm-in-arm, a tournament official on the loudspeaker announced the news that *Fly Knot?* was safe and would be arriving soon at the weigh-in station.

A roar erupted from the crowd like none heard that week. By the time Ava, Noreen, and Chris reached the rest of Sonny's team, the party was in full swing. Dan, Alan, Holly, and Colt greeted the three with happy shouts, broad smiles, and huge hugs. The group was standing on the water side of the roped off area in front of the weigh-in station. The tournament officials allowed this as a courtesy to the team.

At 11:28 p.m., *Fly Knot?* backed into the weigh-in slip. The boat was carrying a flag with an upside-down blue marlin which shows a release. Perhaps that was why the *Fly Knot?* crew members were sporting grim faces. Despite the upside-down flag, the crowd roared again as the crew secured the lines to the dock cleats. When Sonny spotted Ava, his mom, and his friends, he smiled for the first time since they arrived at the slip.

Ava was itching to leap into Sonny's arms, but the *Fly Knot?* crew had to check in with the officials first. Eli mentioned to the official on the dock they caught a dolphin that needed to be weighed. Mason then handed the dolphin over to the official for weighing on the scale.

Thousands of spectators surrounded the weigh-in station but many could not see the fish being weighed. For this reason, a tournament official with a microphone and speaker gave a play-by-play of the weigh-in process.

"Okay, everybody. First off, let's give the crew of *Fly Knot?* a big round of applause for safely navigating home and for catching such an impressive dolphin. And with a fly rod, no less! So, let's see the measurement. Okay, it weighs 38.7 pounds which puts it in second place for the tournament!"

Polite clapping along with a few shouts of encouragement ensued.

Dan whispered to Chris, "How much do you think that fish will earn the crew?"

Chris said, "That's a big dolphin." Glancing at his smart phone, he added, "Probably around $25,000."

Dan nodded approvingly, "Well that's something anyway."

After icing down the dolphin, the tournament official called out to Eli, "Any more fish to weigh, Captain?"

Eli shook his head. He then paused before answering, "Wait a minute. We do have one more fish to weigh come to think of it." He then nodded to Mason.

Mason then bent down and, with one fell swoop, yanked off an insulating blanket covering a very large blue marlin. For the first time that evening, each crew member sported huge grins.

The crowd let out a collective gasp! They were so stunned, they didn't know how to react at first. It didn't take them long to recover and they simultaneously let out hoops, hollers, clapping, and laughter. Even the announcer looked shocked. He quickly recovered and said, "Wait a minute, folks. It appears the *Fly Knot?* crew is playing with us a bit," he said laughing. He continued, "Okay, then. Let's put it on the scale."

As they were hoisting the blue marlin up by the tail, the announcer said, "As most of you all know, the boat currently in first place is *Devil Maker* with a blue marlin weight of 605 pounds."

Bart and the rest of the *Devil Maker* crew were present at the weigh-in and pushed their way to the front of the roped off area. For the first time this week, Bart seemed nervous. Beads of sweat and a clinched jaw betrayed his calm exterior.

With each pull off the rope, the crowd noise continued to build. It seemed to take forever to finally position the marlin high enough above the pavement for an accurate measurement.

The announcer continued, "Ladies and gentlemen, we can finally get a measurement on *Fly Knot?*'s marlin. The scale reads…609 pounds! That beats *Devil Maker*'s catch by 4 pounds!"

The crowd went berserk. Ava couldn't stand back any longer and rushed to the boat. Sonny caught her as she jumped onto the boat. They embraced like they never had in the past. Ava didn't care if Sonny won or lost the tournament. Rather, her joy was his safe return to port.

Recognizing Ava from earlier that week, the announcer quipped, "Well, I hope a reporter gives me THAT kind of interview someday!" Everyone laughed, including Ava and Sonny.

"Back to business," the announcer continued. "Our officials are currently inspecting the marlin for any signs of mutilation but, from this angle, it appears undamaged by sharks."

Many spectators were aware of the heart-breaking story of a past Big Rock participant that appeared to win the top biggest blue marlin prize of over $2 million only to have the fish disqualified due to a shark attack during the fight. The tournament rules state that a blue marlin may not be mutilated in any way for it to qualify as a legally caught fish.

After a long pause, the tournament officials inspecting *Fly Knot?'s* marlin gave the announcer a thumbs up sign.

"Okay, ladies and gentlemen. The officials have confirmed that the *Fly Knot?* blue marlin has not been mutilated in any way.

Therefore, *Fly Knot?* wins the prize money for the biggest blue marlin in the tournament and will take home $2 million!"

If possible, an even louder roar exploded from the spectators than before. Eli waved the other team members onto *Fly Knot?*. After Dan, Alan, Holly, Colt, Chris, and Noreen stepped onboard the boat, Eli pulled out a bottle of champagne from a nearby cooler, popped the cork, and sprayed everyone. Noreen then wrapped her arms around her son and whispered, "Your dad would be so proud of you, Sonny. I know I am!"

He couldn't stop the tears, nor did he want to.

On the second floor of a nearby restaurant, a tall lean man took in the scene with a pair of binoculars. He had reserved this floor for himself, his crew, and some close friends to see the final weigh-in. After hearing the announcement of *Fly Knot?'s* victory, he shook his head, smiled, and quietly said, "With a friggin' fly rod! Way to go, Sonny. Way to go."

XVII. Day After Tournament

After the polygraph tests and press interviews were completed, the team went to *Painkillers* in Beaufort to celebrate their victory. The bar normally closes at midnight, but the owner decided to keep it open until 2 a.m. as a celebratory gesture to the *Fly Knot?* crew. He even reserved a large outside table that overlooked Taylor's Creek for the team. As soon as Team Sonny walked through the door at 12:30 a.m., the bar crowd let out a yelp followed by applause.

Many in the audience were other Big Rock participants including captains, mates, and anglers from competing boats. Although disappointed they didn't win the top prize, they were gracious in defeat toward the *Fly Knot?* crew, many taking the time to stop by the team's table and congratulate them on their impressive victory. Conspicuously absent was the *Devil Maker* crew.

Also present were Sonny's friends from the two fly fishing groups from Raleigh and Morehead City- Gordo, Kevin, James, Markham, Preston, Sarah, Jake, and Joe. Naturally, Sonny insisted on them joining their table.

Markham started the conversation, "So did anything go wrong out there, Sonny?" This elicited laughter from everyone present.

"I think the better question is, what didn't go wrong out there?" Eli answered.

James Roni was a fisheries biologist at NC State University who was keen on getting the facts. "So, what **did** happen out there, Sonny?"

"I think I'll let Eli and Mason answer that question, James," Sonny replied.

Eli said, "Okay, I'll go first and then turn it over to Mason, if that's okay with you, mate?" Mason nodded.

"First off, I'm going to ask every one of you to keep what I'm going to say next quiet. Do I have your word on that?" Intrigued, everyone nodded and leaned forward.

Eli then recounted the details of their final-day adventure onboard *Fly Knot?*. "The tournament rules state that each boat needs to report in with the tournament officials via VHF or satellite phone whenever they hook a blue marlin. It was only then I realized my satellite phone was missing. I charged it the day before and placed it in the glovebox of the console. But I didn't check its presence the next day until Sonny hooked the marlin. The phone had vanished."

Holly cut in, "How about your regular cellphone? Would that work?"

Eli shook his head, "A normal cellphone will work a few miles offshore, but not 50 miles. The only effective forms of communication offshore are satellite phones and VHF radios. And the VHF radio signal from my vessel only has a range of seven miles or so. But it can be used to communicate with other vessels. So, my hope was to contact a captain from another vessel via our VHF radio and request they call in our marlin hookup to the tournament officials. But when I turned on the VHF radio, there was no power. Upon closer examination, I noticed the power cord to the back of the radio had been severed."

"Sabotage?" Ava asked incredulously.

"Evidently," Eli answered soberly.

"By whom?" Chris asked.

"We don't know for sure at this point but we have our suspicions," Eli answered.

"Care to elaborate?" Chris pressed.

"Not at this time, Chris," Eli replied.

Reluctant to slow the momentum of Eli's story, Chris let it go. For now, anyway.

Eli continued, "Fortunately, I brought a portable VHF two-way radio as a backup. But the range on that radio is only about one to two miles at best. I could only see three other sportfishing vessels within two miles of *Fly Knot?*. Care to guess the name of one of those vessels?"

In unison, the group said, "*Devil Maker!*"

"Bingo!" Eli replied with a scowl. "Of course, we were bound by the tournament rule that any blue marlin hookup needs to be reported as soon as possible. So, I hailed the other three boats, explained our communication issues, and asked them to report our hookup to Big Rock officials in Morehead City. One of the boats replied right away and said they would be happy to do this on our behalf."

"Which boat was that?" Ava asked.

"More on that later," Eli said. He continued, "Standard protocol dictates that if a vessel hooks up a large gamefish, any other vessels in the vicinity should move far enough away to avoid any potential line cut-offs. Two of the three vessels followed this protocol. However, one vessel actually motored closer to us! Any guesses who that was?"

In unison from the group, "*Devil Maker!*" Eli nodded.

"Yup. At first, they kept an uncomfortable, but safe distance from our boat. But an hour into Sonny's fight with the marlin, the fish rose to the surface thereby exposing the fly line. Care to take it from here, Mason?"

Mason nodded and continued with the story. "As the Captain said, the fly line was perilously close to the surface. During the first hour of the fight, I caught a few glimpses of a *Devil Maker* crew member training his binoculars on the marlin and *Fly Knot?*. So, they knew we were hooked up. They also had a pretty good idea of the size of the marlin because of the number of leaps the fish made from the surface. And, as you all know, they were in first place at that point in the tournament."

A look of anger flashed across Mason's face at the memory of their boats' race to the weigh-in slip on Day 1 of the tournament. He bit his tongue and continued.

"On one of the marlin jumps, it somehow wrapped the fly line around its tail. This caused the fish to remain on the surface. And, of course, so was the fly line. *Devil Maker* must have seen this as well because a few seconds later, they started charging toward the exposed fly line with an obvious attempt to cut it off with its prop. Captain Eli pulled out the portable VHF and hailed *Devil Maker* and pleaded with them to turn around. It was torture for us because we knew we had a big marlin that would likely end up in the money. But *Devil Maker* kept coming. Five hundred yards, 400 hundred yards, 300 hundred yards." For effect, Mason then paused for a long while.

"So, what happened?" pleaded Holly. "I can't stand the suspense!"

Mason smiled, "Patience, young lady. Okay, out of nowhere a different sportfishing vessel came charging in our direction but on an intercept course with *Devil Maker!* This boat eventually positioned itself between *Devil Maker* and our fish. Both vessels then stopped within yelling distance of each other. Shouting then ensued between crew members of both vessels. After about five or ten minutes, *Devil Maker* turned about and headed away from our fly line and marlin. The other boat motored away in a different direction but also away from our marlin."

Ava jumped in, "Who was this mystery sportfishing boat?" Everyone around the table was on the edge of their seats aching for an answer.

Mason glanced at Sonny for approval. Sonny shrugged and slowly nodded his head.

"It was *Caught 6,*" Mason said coolly.

"No way!" Colt exclaimed. A UNC alum himself, he added, "Go Tar Heels!"

Holly rolled her eyes having graduated from a different North Carolina university.

"Yup," Mason replied. "Even though we couldn't hear what they were saying, the two boats were close enough that we could see who was doing the yelling. It was Michael and Bart. It was also clear who won the argument."

Everyone laughed.

Chris cut in, "What happened next?"

Mason said, "Captain, would you like to take it from here?"

Eli nodded and turned to the others and continued the story, "After *Caught 6* motored a safe distance away from *Fly Knot?*, I was hailed by the captain of *Caught 6* on the portable VHF radio. He said, 'You are all clear now. *Devil Maker* will not bother you anymore today. We've got to head back to port now but we wanted to know if you needed our assistance for anything else before we head back?' I thanked him profusely and said we're fine. 'Michael asked me to pass along a two-word message to Sonny: 'Win this!'

"I told him I'd certainly pass along the message. I looked over at their vessel and all the crew members waved goodbye. Michael gave a thumbs up gesture. And then they motored off. From that point on, we were alone at sea."

Holly said, "So about what time did *Caught 6* depart?"

"That was about 3:30 p.m. or so, right Mason?" Mason nodded.

James asked, "How many hours did it take you to boat the fish?"

"Once the other boats left our area, the weather continued to degrade. We were dealing with rain, high seas, and stiff winds. Fortunately, the lightning stayed south of us so I wasn't too concerned about a strike. Even so, fighting a big fish under those conditions in a small boat with a fly rod presented a unique set of challenges. To this point in our story, we haven't mentioned Sonny's skill at fighting that fish."

Sonny brushed aside the compliment, "And we don't need to, either."

"I beg to differ," Eli said. Facing the others, he continued, "I can't emphasize enough the skill it takes to cast, hook, and play a blue marlin with a fly rod, particularly under those sea conditions. Sonny was able to keep his footing on a very slippery deck and somehow match the frequency of each big wave that passed under our boat. Sonny kept just the right amount of pressure on the fish to keep slack out of his line without a line break. In all the years I've been chartering fly fishermen, I've never seen anyone like Sonny. He fought that fish for another five hours before it finally tired enough for us to boat it." He then smiled. The others applauded after Eli finished the story.

Sonny cut in, "Captain, you and Mason are far too modest. There is no way I could have boated that fish if you weren't such a terrific captain and Mason wasn't a fantastic first mate. I can't tell you the number of times that Mason helped keep me on my feet. And Eli had to adjust the engine throttle for each wave that passed under the boat—that takes skill, stamina, and an unmatched feel for the water."

Before they had the chance to continue their mutual admiration dialog, they heard a large commotion at the entrance of the bar. Sonny and the others glanced up to see the people standing around the bar parting like the Red Sea as a tall, lean man approached Sonny's table.

Sonny stood as the man approached. The man donned his patented million-watt smile and extended his catcher-mitt size hand. Sonny accepted his handshake but, once the two shook hands, the man pulled Sonny into him and briefly embraced him. He then pulled back and laughed, "Nice fish, Sonny."

"Thanks, Michael. I can't tell you how much we appreciate what you did out there."

Michael waved him off, "It was nothing. That guy was a lunatic. Obviously, we can't talk about that here, but I'd like to call you tomorrow with more details. Does that work for you?"

"Of course. By the way, the people around this table are my close friends and family. Everyone, this is Michael J…"

"As if we didn't know!" Colt cut in. Everyone around the table laughed, including Michael.

"Please join us, Michael," Sonny offered. The others enthusiastically nodded their heads.

Michael's security detail kept the other bar spectators at bay, but it was clear this would only be temporary as word spread of his presence at *Painkillers*. For this reason, Michael said, "Thank you, but I've got to run. I just wanted to stop by and congratulate you personally on your win. Incidentally, I'm glad you took my advice." Both men laughed, as did Eli and Mason. The others around the table looked puzzled but said nothing. The two embraced and then Michael and his security detail headed toward the exit.

After Michael left, Sonny said to his table mates, many with their mouths agape, "Look, I'm sure you have a hundred questions about my friendship with Michael but it's after 2 a.m. and, as you can see, the lights are flickering, so the bar is about to close. Plus, I'm beat."

Although no one was pleased with Sonny's statement, they understood. As the group was walking out the exit, Ava said to Sonny "Would you excuse me for a moment, Sonny? I need to talk briefly to Eli and Dan." Sonny nodded, "Of course."

After discretely pulling Eli and Dan aside on Front Street, Ava said quietly, "Eli, I couldn't help but notice that Sonny made no mention of Pipes to the press or anyone else at *Painkillers* tonight. Sonny previously told me that Pipes was shy, but I'm surprised that Sonny didn't even acknowledge him."

Eli raised an eyebrow in surprise. "Who is Pipes?"

Surprised at this response, Ava replied, "Sonny's fly fishing mentor. Sonny told me Pipes went on some practice offshore fishing trips onboard *Fly Knot?* just before the Big Rock Tournament. Sonny also said he was going to join you on the last day of the tournament."

After a long pause, Eli said solemnly, "I'm sorry, Ava, but I have no idea who Pipes is. Yesterday, it was just Sonny, Mason, and me onboard *Fly Knot?*. And it was just the three of us on those practice fishing trips ahead of the tournament as well."

Stunned, Ava stood motionless on the street before thanking Eli.

After he left, Dan stayed with Ava. She then turned to Dan and asked, "Do you know a guy named Pipes, Dan?"

Silent to this point, he finally said, "Yes, I do. Pipes was the nickname for Sonny's dad."

Epilogue

The week following the Big Rock Tournament, Sonny was flooded with interview requests which Dan vetted. In addition to interviews with many of the major newspapers and fly fishing magazines, Sonny also conducted interviews with ESPN, CNN, and 60 Minutes. Ava's *The Sonny Blues Chronicles* became such a big hit that a well-known publisher expressed interest in making a book out of the chronicles. Ava asked Dan to represent her in contract negotiations with the publisher, which he happily agreed to do. Prior to receiving interest from the publisher, Sonny, Eli, and Mason tried desperately to give her a share of their prize money. They argued that she was an integral part of their team. But she would have none of that, saying it could compromise the content of her chronicles. To this point, she was upfront with her readers about her relationship with Sonny. She thought the presence of prize money might further jeopardize the objectivity of the chronicles. This turned out to be a good move on her part, as the book eventually became a best seller.

A month after the Big Rock Tournament, Sonny, Ava, Alan, Holly, Colt, Noreen, and Dan were dining at an elegant restaurant in Belhaven called *Belhaven Bistro*. The owner of the restaurant, Tatiana, was a local legend herself as she started a Farm-to-Table restaurant 10 years earlier based on a vision she had for the small coastal town. Her husband owned a farm that supplied fresh greens, flowers, and herbs for the restaurant. Since she was a Belhaven native, she had lifetime connections with commercial fishermen and cattle farmers. An artist by trade, Tatiana decorated the restaurant with her own paintings as well as those of other local artists. She attracted a top chef by sharing her vision for the town. The net effect for diners was an unforgettable eclectic culinary experience. The formula worked, as patrons from all over the state frequented the restaurant, providing much needed financial and cultural benefits to the small coastal town.

As they sipped wine, dined, and laughed around the table, Sonny reflected on the past year and smiled at the dramatic changes in his life. His recent financial windfall was life changing, but that was secondary compared to the people sitting around this table. Money would come and go but the people around this table were his foundation.

Ava gazed into Sonny's eyes, "Why are you smiling?"

"No reason. I'm just grateful," he said quietly.

Alan overheard this and said, "I bet you are grateful, Sonny! So, tell us how the money was split?"

Holly and Colt groaned. "Filters, Dad. How about some filters?" Holly pleaded.

Sonny laughed and said, "It's okay, Holly. Here's how it played out. Do you remember Michael saying he would call me later that day after we met at *Painkillers*?" Everyone nodded.

Sonny continued, "Well, it turns out that the captain of *Caught 6*, Michael's boat, filed a complaint on *Fly Knot?*'s behalf about the events that played out on the last day of the tournament to the Big Rock tournament officials. He also supplied video evidence of one of *Devil Maker's* crew members boarding *Fly Knot?* on two separate days. The first time was the evening before our marlin break-off on Day 5 of the tournament. The second time was the evening before Day 6 of the tournament. The video showed a man walking onto the deck of *Fly Knot?* without a satellite phone. But when he left *Fly Knot?*, he had a satellite phone in his left hand."

"How did Michael obtain this video?" Ava asked.

"When Michael got wind of the events that played out during our race back to port with *Devil Maker* on Day 1, he had one of his security guys, a Mr. Stewart Grainger, request permission to install a camera on a vessel moored near *Fly Knot?*. This vessel was not taking part in the Big Rock tournament and its owner happily agreed when he found out who made the request. After the tournament officials viewed the videos, they insisted the *Devil Maker* crew members take another polygraph test, but this time the questions centered around the Day 6 events and the theft and sabotage that took place on *Fly Knot?*. The truth finally came to light and *Devil Maker* was eventually disqualified from the tournament. This will become official next week so, until it does, I would appreciate all of you keeping this quiet." Everyone nodded.

A math whiz, Colt jumped in, "Wait a minute. If *Devil Maker* was disqualified for the *Fabulous Fisherman Award*, does that mean *Fly Knot?* gets that $700,000 award for your first marlin plus the $2 million award for the heaviest blue marlin for your second marlin?"

Sonny smiled modestly.

"Wow! So, the question becomes more interesting! How did you split the $2.7 million?" Alan pressed.

"You won't let this go, will you, Dad?" Holly smirked.

Dan answered on behalf of Sonny, "I negotiated the contract so, with Sonny's permission, I'll give you the highlights." Sonny nodded.

"The original prize money split was 50:30:20 for Sonny: Eli: Mason, respectively. I get a small commission from Sonny's prize money as well."

"Not enough, in my opinion," Sonny cut in.

Dan waved him off and continued, "Remember, Sonny paid for the entrance fee, fuel, ice, food, and drinks, plus a daily labor rate for both Eli and Mason. Thanks to Holly's fundraising efforts, our sponsors, as well as some of you at this table, Sonny was able to cover most of those expenses. After their win, neither Eli nor Mason complained about the split. On the contrary, they were ecstatic about their share. No, it was Sonny boy here who decided to change the split. He insisted that all three split the prize money equally," Dan shook his head.

Noreen smiled with pride at her son, "I think that's wonderful, Sonny." He smiled sheepishly back at her.

"Oh, it gets better…or worse depending on how you look at this," Dan continued. "Not only did Sonny split the prize money equally but he insisted on repaying all of the *Sports Support Now* donors 100 percent of their money plus interest!" Dan exclaimed.

Holly said, "Sonny, you know you don't have to do that, right? That fund is not meant to be a loan. It's a grant. You don't have to pay those people back."

"I know. But if it weren't for them, I never would have been able to even participate in the Big Rock in the first place."

Always the practical one, Alan said, "Well, dinner is definitely on you, Sonny!" Everyone laughed and Sonny just nodded.

From the opposite end of the table, Noreen asked Sonny, "Given the events that played out this year, Son, are you glad you chose fishing over golf as a career?"

"Golf?" Ava interrupted. She turned to Sonny, "I didn't know you played golf."

"Yes, I played some," Sonny replied modestly.

"Played some?" Dan said incredulously. "As usual, Ava, Sonny is far too modest about his accomplishments. Sonny won the state high school golf championship in his senior year.

He also won a full scholarship to play on the UNC golf team. I've never seen a young man drive a golf ball as long and straight as Sonny did back then. In fact, the few times we manage to squeeze in a round or two, he still hits them long and straight. His iron game is terrific, too."

"So, what happened?" Ava asked.

Dan paused and Sonny finished for him, "I can't putt worth a lick. You know the old saying, 'Drive for show, putt for dough?', right?"

Ava nodded.

"Well, that's me to a tee, no pun intended," Sonny laughed.

An hour later, Sonny and Ava were driving on a single lane country road in Sonny's pickup truck. It was a moonless night and Ava wanted one last view of the stars before she headed back to D.C. the next morning. With no city lights, the stars popped brilliantly against the black backdrop of the universe.

Once they arrived back in town, Sonny glanced to his right and noticed some lights were still on at a nearby tackle shop.

"Hmmm, that's interesting. It's midnight and the lights are still on at Benny's. That's the shop where I got *Percival*. I've been meaning to stop by and thank Benny for the fly. Would you mind if we stopped by real quick?"

Ava said, "I don't mind at all. In fact, I would love to interview the man who sold you *Percival*."

"Actually, Benny didn't sell it to me," he waved his hand. "I'll tell you more later. Let's pop inside."

When they walked in the door, the old-fashioned bell chimed, but they didn't see anyone in the store. Sonny started perusing the fishing tackle on the counter. At the end of counter, he saw a golf putter standing with the blade on the floor and the handle against the counter. He picked it up and the handle melded perfectly into his hands. He looked down and noticed the blade seemed to radiate a soft iridescent pink light. There was a lone golf ball resting on the counter.

Sonny placed the ball in front of the putter and lined up a putt on a strip of artificial green that he'd never seen before. About 25 feet away, there was a golf ball putting machines that, if you putt the ball inside the cup, will kick it back to you. As Sonny lined up the putt, he noticed a ray of light that shot from the putter blade to a point slightly off-line from the cup. It seemed the putter was in control from that point on. When the blade met the ball, the ball traveled to the point and then slowly turned right until it landed smack in the middle of the cup. Benny's floor was obviously not level.

"Beginner's luck," Sonny laughed. He putted the ball several more times with the identical result. Each time, the ball hit the center of the cup.

"Maybe not," Ava mused.

Sonny felt a new presence in the room and suddenly turned around. Staring back at him was a 5 foot 2 inch bearded man with jet black eyes. With a half-smile he said, "Welcome back, Sonny."

ABOUT THE AUTHOR

Jason Caplan is a marine biologist, fly fisherman, teacher, entrepreneur, and inventor whose love of saltwater was sparked by his graduate research on the Chesapeake Bay. Fly fishing excursions on the Pamlico Sound and Atlantic Ocean fueled his passion, as did 30-plus years of fall fishing trips with his 'Boys of Summer' buddies on North Carolina's Outer Banks. Jason splits his time between Belhaven and Beaufort, North Carolina. He can be found fly fishing in nearby waters onboard his ancient 20-foot fishing boat, the *Retriever*, named after his beloved golden retriever. *Belhaven Blue* is Jason's first novel.

jasonacaplan.com

JASON A CAPLAN

Made in USA - Kendallville, IN
14065_9798876383969
04.13.2024 1104